Irresistible

Cloverleigh Farms
Series

D1704756

Melanie Harlow

For my daughters and my dad,
although none of them
has my permission
to read this book.
Ever.

Love has nothing to do with what you are expecting to get—
only what you are expecting to give—which is everything.
—Katharine Hepburn

One

Mack

ONE MORNING. THAT'S ALL I WANTED.

One morning to myself.

To sleep in. To sleep naked. To sleep with my bedroom door closed.

To wake up when I felt like it. To wake up and hear nothing. To wake up and do whatever the hell I felt like doing that morning—take a run or jerk off or go the fuck back to sleep.

"Daddy! Get up!"

This was not that morning.

Groaning, I rolled over onto my stomach and held my pillow over the back of my head. "Daddy's not here," I said, my voice muffled.

I heard giggling, then felt the mattress shift as one or more of my three daughters jumped onto my bed. Frankly, it was kind of surprising none of them had been here already. For months after their mother left, I hadn't had my bed to myself. Sometimes it was eleven-year-old Millie with a stomachache. Sometimes eight-year-old Felicity with nightmares. Often it was four-year-old Winifred hiding from the monster beneath her bed.

Occasionally it was all three.

One of them jumped onto my back like I was a pony and tugged at my T-shirt. "We're hungry." Sounded like Felicity.

"Again? I just fed you."

"It's morning. You didn't feed us since dinner last night."

"It can't be morning. It's still dark."

"That's because you have a pillow over your head." She giggled. "You were snoring too."

"Can't Millie get you guys cereal?"

"We don't want cereal. We want pancakes."

I sighed. "Can't she make pancakes?"

"She doesn't know how to use the stove. We need a grownup."

A grownup. *I* was the sole grownup in the house. How the fuck had that happened? "How do you know I'm a grownup?"

More giggling. "Because you're tall with big feet. And you have whiskers. And your name is Daddy."

"I told you. Daddy's not here."

"Then who are you?"

I flipped over, tossing her onto her back. "The tickle monster!"

She squealed and squirmed while I tickle-tortured her, prompting Winifred to come running in and hop on the bed. "Me too!"

Winnie was the rare kid who actually wanted to be tickled, or at least she wanted the physical affection, and she scooted close to Felicity on her back, presenting her tummy like a dog who wanted to be petted.

I tickled them both for a second, then sat back on my

heels and scratched my head. "You're still in your pajamas. Is it Saturday?"

"Yes," said Felicity.

"Good."

"Your hair looks funny," she told me.

"So does yours," I told her. Recently she'd given herself a "trim," hacking off the front of her hair in an attempt to create bangs like Mavis's from Hotel Transylvania. She even wanted to be called Mavis for a while. The girls' therapist assured me it was nothing to worry about and simply meant she identified with the character of Mavis, who also lived with her father without a mother in the house.

"You're sure it doesn't mean that she's a vampire?" I'd asked. Felicity hadn't bitten anyone yet, but she *had* taken to wearing black and asking if I could make her bed into a coffin shape. Talk about nightmares.

But the therapist had only smiled. "I'm sure."

Millie appeared in my bedroom doorway in her nightgown. "Dad, I need a black leotard for ballet today and none of them are clean."

"Damn. Are you sure?"

"Yes. I checked my drawer and my hamper. And that's a quarter in the swear jar."

I grimaced. That fucking swear jar was going to break me. "Did you check the dryer?"

"Yep. Not in there either."

"Shit."

"That's fifty cents," said Felicity.

I poked her in the ribs. "At least my swearing is contributing to your math skills. Millie, did you check the washer? I know I put a load of darks in yesterday." Which meant that I'd probably forgotten to put them in the dryer last night, and they'd have to be rewashed today.

"I didn't look in the washer."

"What time is ballet again?"

Millie rolled her eyes, an adolescent gesture I was already growing weary of. "Same time as always. Ten."

"Right." I looked at the digital clock on my nightstand. It was seven-thirty. "Okay, I'll have it done by then."

"And I need something for the bake sale this afternoon," she added.

"What bake sale?"

Another eye roll, accompanied by a foot stomp. "Daddy! The fundraiser for the eighth grade trip to Washington, DC! I've told you about it a hundred times."

I jumped off the bed and hitched up my flannel pajama pants. "Eighth grade! What the fuck, Millie, you're only in sixth. That trip is two years away—no wonder I filed that under Forget This Immediately." I went over to my dresser and grabbed a USMC sweatshirt, pulling it on over my T-shirt.

That earned me a heavy sigh. "That's a dollar in the jar, Dad."

"No, it's not! I was only at fifty cents."

"The F word is a whole dollar, Daddy," Felicity informed me.

"Oh, right." I paused. "You know what? It's worth it."

"So what am I going to bring for the bake sale?" Millie pressed.

"I don't know. We'll figure it out." *Somewhere between doing the laundry and getting your hair in a bun and feeding you all something that won't rot your teeth or kill your brain cells and getting you to ballet on time and checking in at work and filling the swear jar and grocery shopping for the week and making sure each of you is getting enough time and attention to feel secure and loved and*—I went over to the window and looked out—*shoveling the snow that fell overnight.*

Goddamn, it was only the beginning of February—Groundhog Day. And it was cloudy, which meant spring was supposed to come early (according to the lore), but right now it felt like spring was *never* going to get here. Winter in northern Michigan was always long and cold, with perpetually gray skies and knee-deep snow, but this one had felt particularly grueling. Was it because it was my first as a single parent?

The girls and I trooped from my first-floor bedroom to the kitchen, where I put on some coffee for myself, pulled frozen pancakes from the freezer for Felicity and Winifred, and scrambled an egg for Millie. They sat in a row at the breakfast counter that separated the kitchen from the dining room. There used to be a wall between the two rooms, but my friend Ryan Woods, who'd lived in this house before us, had remodeled the kitchen, making it more modern and open. In fact, we hardly ever ate at the dining room table. Mostly I used it to fold laundry.

"These taste like the freezer," said Felicity, making a face at her pancake. "Don't we have any muffins left over from Mrs. Gardner?"

"We ate them," I told her, pouring orange juice into three glasses. Mrs. Gardner was the ninety-four-year-old lady who lived next door, a widow who'd become sort of a surrogate grandmother to all of us since we'd moved into this house last summer. She loved to bake and often brought over delicious homemade muffins or cookies, which never lasted long. In return, I made sure her yardwork was taken care of in good weather and her driveway and front walk shoveled in the winter. The girls weeded her garden, brought in her mail, and drew pictures for her, which she proudly displayed on her refrigerator door.

"Do you want a banana or apple?" I asked the girls. The fruit, at least, was fresh.

"Banana," answered the younger two.

"Apple," said Millie.

"Anybody want bacon?"

All three nodded enthusiastically. Bacon was one of those rare things we all agreed on.

I sipped my coffee and tossed some strips into a pan, then ran down to the basement to rewash the load of darks I'd forgotten about last night. While I was down there, I scooped a load of whites from the dryer into a basket and noticed there was a decidedly rosy hue to everything. That's when I saw Winifred's red sock in the basket along with everyone else's white socks and underwear.

Great. Just what I needed—pink socks.

Cursing under my breath—at least no one heard me this time—I left the basket there and went back to the kitchen, where I flipped over the sizzling strips of bacon, gulped more coffee, and watched Winifred smear maple syrup all over her mouth. "It's lipstick," she said proudly.

"You're getting it in your hair," said Millie, moving her counter stool away from Winnie's.

Someone dropped a fork, and it clattered noisily onto the floor. A couple minutes later, someone's elbow knocked over a glass of juice and it spilled over the edge of the counter down the front of a cupboard. After cleaning that up (and adding fifty more cents to the swear jar total), I was supervising Felicity slicing up her banana at our tiny kitchen island when the kitchen began to fill with smoke. I turned off the gas under the bacon, pulled the pan from the burner, and opened the window.

"Ew, it's burnt," said Millie.

I closed my eyes and took a breath.

"That's okay, Daddy," said Felicity. "I like my bacon black."

Winifred coughed, and I opened one eye and looked at her. "Are you choking?"

She shook her head and picked up her juice.

"Good. No choking allowed." I put the overdone bacon strips on some paper towels. "Guess we're eating it extra crispy this morning, girls. Sorry."

"Oh Daddy, I forgot to tell you. Millie broke my glasses," Felicity announced as she returned to her spot at the counter with her sliced banana.

"I did not!"

"You did too. You sat on them."

Millie scowled at her. "Maybe you shouldn't leave them on the couch."

"Maybe you should look where you put your big butt."

"I don't have a big butt! Daddy, Felicity said I have a big butt!"

"No one in this house has a big butt," I told them, setting the extra crispy bacon in front of them. "Now finish your breakfast. Felicity, I'll look at your glasses in a minute."

I managed to get everyone fed, repair Felicity's glasses, clean up the kitchen, fold some laundry, get dressed, shovel my drive and Mrs. Gardner's, and start my SUV in time to drive Millie to ballet—barely.

"Okay, let's go!" I shouted from the front door.

"But my hair's not done," Millie cried, hurrying down the stairs in her black leotard and pink tights, her blond hair still a tangled mess.

"And Winnie never got dressed," said Felicity from the couch in the living room, where she was playing on her iPad.

I looked at Winifred, who was lying on the floor in her Hufflepuff pajamas watching cartoons. "There's no time now. Winnie, put your boots and coat on over your pj's. Felicity, get ready to go and make sure you and Win both have hats and gloves. It's freezing." Then I looked at Millie. "Go get the bun stuff. I'll get snow everywhere and I don't want to take all my crap off."

Felicity pointed at me as she slid off the couch. "That's another fifty cents, Daddy."

"Crap isn't a swear word," I argued.

"Can I say it at school?"

"No."

"Then it's a swear."

I sighed heavily as Millie came down the stairs with a hairbrush, ponytail holder, and a dish of hairpins. Five minutes later, I'd managed to wrangle her thick honey-colored hair into something resembling a ballerina's bun. I frowned at it. "Not my best work today, Mills. Just gonna admit it."

"My bun is always the worst one there, Daddy. The other girls laugh at it."

Something tugged at my chest. "Sorry. I do the best I can."

"We're ready," said Felicity. "But my boots are so tight, I can barely get them on. And Winnie can only find one mitten."

I closed my eyes for one moment and took a breath. "We'll get you some new boots this week, and there are a million mittens in that bin. Go get me one, please."

"It won't match."

"It doesn't matter. Hurry, or your sister will be late."

"I'm late every week, what's the difference?" Millie muttered, slinging her bag over her shoulder. She was about to move past me out the door when I caught her by the elbow.

"Hey. I'm sorry. I'll try harder to get you there on time from now on, okay?"

She nodded. "Okay."

I let her go, hurried Felicity out the door in her too-small boots, and stuck a random mitten on Winnie's hand before picking her up and carrying her out into the snow, pulling the door shut behind us.

I'd had way more disastrous mornings in the last nine months, but I'd had more successful ones too—although not many. I really was doing the best I could, but goddammit, Millie deserved a better bun and Felicity deserved boots that fit, and Winifred deserved a dad that had remembered to dress her and get the syrup out of her hair before taking her out of the house.

And they all deserved a mother who hadn't deserted them—she'd only seen them twice in the last nine months.

As for me, I'd take a morning to myself. One morning without being entirely responsible for anyone else. One morning to feel like a man and not just Daddy. One morning to curse without putting money in a jar, to remember there was life beyond laundry, lunches, and little girls. Was that horrible of me?

Probably.

But still.

One morning. That's all I wanted.

Two

Frannie

THE BRIDE HAD TOILET PAPER STUCK TO HER SHOE.

I was at the reception desk of the Cloverleigh Farms Inn, which the wedding couple had rented out for the entire weekend, when I saw her exit the lobby bathroom, trailing six or seven embarrassing white squares behind her. Quickly, I scooted out from behind the desk and hurried toward her before she could re-enter the inn's restaurant, where the reception was taking place.

"Excuse me, Mrs. Radley?"

The bride, a forty-something woman with deep chestnut hair and a slender figure, turned to me and smiled at the use of her married name. "I guess that's me, isn't it? That will take some getting used to."

I returned her smile. "Congratulations. Um, I just wanted to let you know you've got some toilet paper stuck to the bottom of your shoe."

She looked down at her feet, clearly visible beneath the knee-length hem of her ivory bias-cut dress. "Oh, my goodness. Thank you so much—that would have been very embarrassing."

"No problem."

She reached down to grab it, and right as she did, one of the dress's tiny satin spaghetti straps popped. Gasping, she tugged it up and held it in place. "Oh my God, I'm a mess!" she whispered. "And we're about to do our first dance. Help!"

"Don't worry," I said, taking her by the arm. "Come with me. We'll fix it."

Pushing open the door behind the reception desk, I led her down a hallway lined with the inn's administrative offices. First, I tried my mother's, but the door was locked. Next I tried my sister April's—she was the inn's event planner and always prepared in case of an emergency. Right now she was in the restaurant overseeing the dessert service, but her office door was open.

However, a quick search of April's desk didn't turn up anything I could mend a dress with, not even a safety pin. "Shoot," I said, glancing up at the fretful bride. "You didn't happen to pack a sewing kit in your purse, did you?"

Mrs. Radley shook her head, her expression guilty. "No. I didn't even think of it."

I closed April's top desk drawer. "Okay, I have one more place to look, and if that doesn't work, I'm going to run up to my apartment and grab a pin."

"Oh, do you live here?"

"Yes," I said, pulling April's office door shut. "I'm Frannie Sawyer. My family owns Cloverleigh Farms."

"Oh my goodness, of course," she said, following me down the hall. "My husband James is one of your father's golf buddies. And I met your mother yesterday. Such wonderful people. Now there are five of you girls, right? Which one are you?"

"I'm the youngest. Okay, let's try this one," I said, pushing open the last door on the left and switching on the light.

As I entered Mack's office, I couldn't help feeling a little swoosh in my belly. It smelled like him—a manly combination of wood, leather, and charcoal. It sounds weird, but I'd always loved the smell of a hardware store, and that's what Mack's office smelled like to me. Maybe it was because I had fun memories of tagging along with my dad to the hardware store as a kid, and he always bought me an ice cream cone afterward.

Or maybe it was because Mack was hot as fuck, and I fantasized about him endlessly. There was that.

"Is this your dad's office?" Mrs. Radley asked, glancing around as I went over to the desk.

"No, it belongs to Mack, the CFO. But I think he might have a little sewing kit in here. I gave him one for Christmas as a joke, because twice last year I had to sew a button on his shirt after he popped it off at work."

Feeling slightly guilty to be rummaging around in his desk while he wasn't here, I pulled open his top drawer and shuffled things around: pens, pencils, a yellow highlighter, a torn-out page from a Disney coloring book one of his daughters must have done for him, Post-It notes, Life Savers mints, his Cloverleigh Farms business cards. Momentarily distracted, I picked one up.

Declan MacAllister, Chief Financial Officer and Business Manager

I always forgot that his real name was Declan, since everyone called him Mack, but I liked it. Sometimes I whispered it to my pillow in the dark.

"Are these his girls?" She gestured to a photograph of his daughters on his desk. There were more pictures of them on the shelves behind me too. He was *such* a devoted dad. I knew firsthand because after his wife left last year—she *had* to be crazy—I became a part-time nanny to the kids. They were adorable, smart, and sweet.

And Mack was just ... everything.

"Yes," I said. "Aren't they cute? Aha!" At the back of the drawer I found the tiny sewing kit I'd given him. I held it up triumphantly, remembering the way he'd laughed and thanked me with a hug that I still hadn't recovered from. His chest was *so hard*.

Mrs. Radley looked relieved. "Oh, thank God."

Grabbing Mack's scissors, I came out from around the desk and stood behind her. "Okay, I think I can manage this with you still in the dress, but try not to move too much. I don't want to poke you. White or yellow thread? Sorry, no ivory in the kit."

"White." She stood still while I threaded the needle. "Is that him?" she asked, gesturing toward a framed photo of Mack with his daughters I'd taken last July at the staff picnic. Winifred was on his shoulders, and the other two were hanging from his thick biceps. All four were smiling and laughing. I recalled how grateful Mack had been that day because I'd organized crafts and games for the kids, showed them all the fun places to hide, let them dip their feet in the creek, taken them into the barns and let them pet the animals. He said he hadn't seen them so happy in months and had put an arm around my shoulders, giving me a squeeze. (In my fantasies, things progressed rapidly from there, but in reality, I'd simply said, "You're welcome.")

"Yeah," I said, carefully securing the edge of the strap to the dress. "That's him."

"Handsome."

"Yes." My heart beat a little quicker.

She laughed a little. "That was a very emphatic *yes*. Are you two a thing?"

Only in my dreams. I cleared my throat. "No."

"Is he married? I don't see a wife in any of his photos."

"He was. Now he's divorced and a full-time single dad."

"Are *you* married?" the bride asked.

I laughed. "No."

"Boyfriend?"

I shook my head.

She inclined her head toward the photo of Mack and his girls. "I bet this guy could use a Saturday night out sometime. You should ask him."

"He's more likely to hire me to *babysit* on a Saturday night," I said wryly, knotting the end of the thread.

"Are you that much younger?"

"Ten years. I'm twenty-seven, and he's thirty-seven."

She waved a hand in the air. "That's nothing. James is *twelve* years older than I am. Age is just a number."

Maybe, but I was 100 percent certain that Mack looked at me and saw a kid. Not once in the five years he'd worked here had he ever given me any indication otherwise, despite the fact that I could hardly breathe when we were in a room together.

It was a hopeless crush, and I knew it.

I snipped the thread and made sure my handiwork didn't show. "Speaking of the groom, we'd better get you back there for that first dance."

"You're right. Don't want to let him off the hook. He's dreading the dancing." She laughed and faced me. "How do I look?"

"Beautiful. All lit up inside."

"No lipstick on my teeth? No wine stain on my dress?" She glanced at her shoes. "No toilet paper?"

I laughed and shook my head. "You're good to go."

"Thank you so much, Frannie." She gave me a quick hug. "You're a doll."

"You're welcome. Give me one sec to put this stuff away and I'll walk you back."

"I can find my way, no worries." She headed for the door. "And I'd better hurry—those macarons on the dessert table looked divine. I don't want them to be gone when I get there."

"Oh, I made those. I can always get you some extra if they are."

She turned around, her mouth falling open. "*You* made those? They're *beautiful!* And absolutely delicious! I tasted one when we visited the first time—no joke, they were one of the things that sold me on having the wedding here."

Blushing, I smiled. "I'm so glad."

"You're really talented. Are you a pastry chef? What on earth are you doing at the reception desk?"

I shook my head. "I'm not a pastry chef. But I was taught by one who worked here years ago—*Jean-Gaspard*. He was kind enough to tolerate my constant presence and endless questions in the kitchen, and I memorized everything he said."

She laughed. "Well, it paid off. Do you sell in stores?"

"No. Just here."

"You need to be in business!"

"Maybe someday," I said, tucking the needle back into the kit.

"What are you waiting for?" she cried, tossing her hands up.

"I don't know. A lightning bolt?" I suggested, laughing self-consciously. In truth, I'd imagined it a thousand times—just a tiny little storefront with a couple glass cases lined with rows of beautifully-colored macarons. But would it succeed? What if it was too specialized? What if tourists up here just wanted fudge and ice cream? What if I failed and lost tons of money? It's not like I had any experience or know-how when it came to business—I was just a girl who loved to bake.

"Listen, I don't have a business card on me right now, but when I get back from Hawaii, I'm going to send one over to you. I'm in commercial real estate, and sometimes I invest in local businesses as well—especially those started by female entrepreneurs. If you ever want to talk about this some more, you let me know. It'll be my way to show my appreciation for your saving me from eternal embarrassment at my wedding."

"Okay," I said, although it didn't seem too realistic. "Thanks."

She gave me one last grin and disappeared down the hall, leaving me alone in Mack's office.

I packed up the sewing kit and replaced it in the top drawer along with his scissors. I knew I should get back out to the reception desk, but I couldn't resist taking a moment to sit in his chair. Lowering myself into the worn leather, I placed my arms on the rests, closed my eyes, and inhaled deeply.

His ass sits here every day. It's like my ass is touching his.

"Frannie? What are you doing?"

My eyes flew open and I saw my sister Chloe staring at me from the doorway.

I jumped up. "Nothing," I said quickly, coming out from

behind the desk. "I was just looking for something,"

"In Mack's office?"

"Yes." After flipping the light switch off, I edged by her into the hall, shutting the door behind us. "The bride broke a strap on her dress, and Mack has a sewing kit in his desk. I fixed it."

"Yeah, I just saw her rush by." Chloe glanced over her shoulder. "Hey, have you seen Dad? Is he around tonight?"

"He was earlier. He's not in the restaurant?" I began walking back up toward reception.

"No. Maybe he went to bed already. He's been so tired lately. I'm worried about him."

"Same," I admitted, pulling open the door at the end of the hall and letting Chloe go through first. "He should slow down a little."

"I agree. I wish he'd let me ..." She sighed. "But he never will."

"Let you what?"

"Never mind. It's nothing. I'm heading out."

"Okay. Night." As I watched her head out the front door, I tried not to feel disappointed she hadn't confided in me. But it was nothing new—although Chloe was the closest to me in age, only five years older, we had never been particularly tight.

Part of me thought maybe it was because of all the attention I'd gotten as a child due to the problem with my heart. She'd been the baby until I'd come along needing all kinds of attention and care, including three open-heart surgeries before age ten. Maybe she'd gotten ignored.

Or maybe it was the age difference. She was always growing out of things just as I was growing into them— Barbies, friendship bracelets, boy bands. Our interests never seemed to align, and she was off to college before I even hit high school.

I often wished things were different between Chloe and me—between all my siblings and me, actually. *The Sawyer sisters*, people called us.

There was Sylvia, the oldest, who lived with her husband and two children in a big, beautiful home near Santa Barbara. I'd never visited, but Sylvia posted lots of pictures on her social media accounts with hashtags like #blessed and #mylife and #grateful. All my sisters were pretty, but I'd always thought Sylvia was the most striking. Her husband Brett, an investment banker, was attractive and successful, their children were adorable and smart, and they seemed to have the perfect life. Which was why it was always a little strange to me that Sylvia never seemed to be smiling in any photographs *she* was in.

April was thirty-five and had her own condo in downtown Traverse City, not too far from Cloverleigh. She'd moved to New York City after college and worked there for seven years. After that, she'd come home and taken over event planning here, single-handedly turning Cloverleigh Farms into *the* destination for luxury weddings in a rustic setting. Her eye for design and her ability to anticipate trends and adapt to them was incredible. She was a romantic like me—and she *lived* for weddings—so it was sort of odd to me that she wasn't married, but whenever our mother hinted around, April always just shrugged and said she hadn't met the right person yet.

Our middle sister, Meg, was thirty-three and lived in Washington, D.C. She'd always been wildly passionate and outspoken about her causes, from preventing animal cruelty to women's rights to fighting poverty. After graduating from law school, she'd taken a job working for the ACLU but now worked on staff for a U.S. Senator. She was so busy she didn't get home much. I thought she still lived with her boyfriend, a high-powered government something-or-other, but I wasn't sure.

Chloe, who lived in Traverse City, handled all the marketing and PR for Cloverleigh and helped manage the wine tasting rooms. She was ambitious and smart and creative, always coming up with new ideas, and she worked her ass off. It never seemed to me that my mom and dad recognized all the work she put in on a daily basis. I sometimes wondered if it was because Chloe had been a really difficult teenager—defiant and headstrong, an unapologetic rule breaker who loved pushing boundaries and sometimes forgot to think before speaking. The *total* opposite of me. Even as an adult, she often butted heads with our parents, and never seemed to back down. I often wished I was more like her.

I often wished I were more like *any* of them. I envied Sylvia's happy marriage and family, April's confidence and creative instincts, Meg's fiery passion, Chloe's outspokenness … they all seemed fearless to me. Sometimes I felt I was a Sawyer sister in name only. After all, I was the *only* one who'd never left the nest, not even for college.

It's not that I hadn't wanted to go away to school like my sisters had, but my parents, especially my mother, had encouraged me to attend classes locally so I could live at home. "That way, you'll be close to doctors you're familiar with," she told me. "And you'll be more comfortable and less stressed. I know you feel like you'd be fine, but why take the risk?"

How many times had I heard that question in my life—a thousand? A million? My mother put it to me constantly, regarding any number of things she wasn't comfortable with me doing. And I could have answered any number of ways.

Because I'm an adult and want to make my own decisions? Because I'm tired of being treated like I'm made of glass? Because I don't want to end up with zero mistakes and a thousand regrets?

But I never said those things.

Deep down, I knew that my parents only sheltered me because they loved me so much, and I couldn't really complain about anything. I loved the farm and the inn and the nearby small town of Hadley Harbor—I couldn't really imagine myself living anywhere else. I had my own suite with plenty of privacy, and there was nothing I needed that I lacked. My job at reception wasn't hard, my hours gave me plenty of time to bake, and I liked meeting new people, greeting the guests, showing off everything we offered. I knew this place like the back of my hand.

Of course, it might have been nice to have a few more friends my age, but we lived in a rural area without much economic or social opportunity for young people, especially during the winter. And because I'd missed so much school and gotten behind due to surgeries and hospital stays—not to mention my parents' fears about infection—my mother had decided to homeschool me after second grade, so I didn't have any childhood besties to call up, either.

But I had my parents and my sisters and the people I worked with. I'd even had a few flings during the summer tourist season, when the inn and the town were packed with people, and I *definitely* wasn't the innocent lamb my parents thought I was. If I sometimes felt a little lonely, I supposed it was a small price to pay for having such a comfortable life.

Still.

I slipped my hand into the pocket of my black work pants and pulled out the business card I'd tucked in there earlier.

Declan MacAllister.

It would be nice to have someone to share it with.

Three

Mack

MY ALARM WENT OFF AT SIX-FIFTEEN AS USUAL, AND I jumped into the shower. By six-thirty I was dressed for work and heading upstairs to wake the girls.

It had taken me a while, but I finally had the school morning routine down pat, and today went off with downright military precision.

Millie and Felicity showered at night and laid their clothing out before going to bed, so all I had to do was make sure they were fully awake before rousing Winifred. She could be slow to wake up, so I always helped her get out of her pajamas and into her school outfit. Like her sisters, she set her clothes out the night before, so it was usually a pretty quick thing, especially since she'd stopped wetting the bed.

By six-forty-five, I was downstairs putting breakfast on the table and guzzling coffee. By seven, the girls were eating while I packed snacks, water bottles, and cut the crusts off sandwiches, one peanut butter and jelly on wheat, one almond butter and honey on gluten-free white. (Why Millie still insisted on eating gluten-free these days was beyond me—it had been her mother's thing. Did it make her feel closer to her mom somehow?) Winnie would eat at home with the sitter after preschool.

By seven-fifteen, backpacks and boots were lined up by the door and the kids were upstairs brushing their teeth. By seven-thirty, we were bundled up at the bus stop. By seven-forty, I'd kissed them all good-bye, told them I loved them, and to have a good day. I could tell by the look on Millie's face today that she wasn't going to stand for such public displays of affection much longer, but I planned to torture her as long as I could. They had no mother around, no grandparents (since my folks had retired to Arizona years ago and Carla's lived in Georgia), and my sister Jodie's family lived two hours away in Petoskey. So it was up to me to make sure those girls knew how loved they were, and if I fucked up every other part of being a single parent, I was not going to fail at that. It wasn't their fault their mother and I couldn't make things work.

By eight, I was on my way to Cloverleigh, feeling pretty damn smug. No one had cried, fought, or spilled their juice this morning. No one had reminded me at the last minute about a permission slip I'd forgotten to sign or money I'd forgotten to send in or asked me to please chaperone a field trip I didn't want to go on, and I was like ninety-nine percent sure all of them had brushed their teeth. I hadn't managed to get Felicity new boots yet, but I had found Winifred's missing mitten.

"Fuck yeah, I'm awesome," I said to myself, sipping from a travel mug Felicity had gotten me for Christmas with a picture of a Petoskey stone on it that said **Dad, You Rock**.

Taking another sip from the mug, I remembered how surprised I'd been when each of the girls had handed me a gift perfectly wrapped with holiday paper I didn't recognize. How had they gone shopping for presents without me?

Later, Felicity let it spill that Frannie Sawyer had helped them pick out a couple little gifts for me online one afternoon while she was watching them. She'd had them shipped to her, then brought them over to be wrapped and placed under the tree. Frannie was like that, quick to step in when someone needed something, and always with a smile on her face. It was Frannie who'd offered to cut back her hours at the inn last summer in order to help me out with childcare after Carla took off. I'd nearly fallen to my knees with gratitude. She'd been a godsend.

At Christmas, I'd had them pick out a box of chocolates for her, which they gave to her at the staff holiday party. That was the night she'd given me the small sewing kit, and I'd felt guilty I hadn't put my name on the card with the chocolates.

She'd looked even prettier than usual that night, and she'd smelled good too. I remembered impulsively hugging her (after a couple beers, no doubt) and thinking how long it had been since I'd had my arms around a woman, or held one close enough to catch the scent of her neck as she hugged me back. I didn't have any female friends outside work, and I certainly didn't date. Being that close to Frannie had been a shock to my senses, and I'd let her go quickly before my body betrayed my thoughts, which were something along the lines of *Hey, I know you're the boss's daughter and the nanny (also my kids are right over there), but you smell amazing and your body looks perfect in that dress and I haven't gotten laid in a reallllly long time, so what do you say we sneak into my office and fuck? I promise it will be quick, probably shamefully so, and not at all awkward to see you at work on Monday. Thanks.*

Later that evening, she'd had the idea to take the kids for a ride in Cloverleigh's old-fashioned horse-drawn sleigh. It was a refurbished antique Portland, with a curved dash and one single, red velvet-lined seat onto which the five of us squeezed, our laps covered with thick wool blankets. Somehow she'd ended up wedged in right next to me, and the scent of her perfume as well as the feel of her leg alongside mine kept me warm even as our noses and fingers and toes grew numb from cold.

Long after I'd taken the kids home and said goodnight, I lay in my bed thinking about her. I could still hear her laughing right along with the girls, see the roses in her cheeks and the snowflakes clinging to her long, wavy hair. It had made me wish she was still there next to me. How long had it been since I'd had someone warm and soft and sexy to mess around with in the dark?

Before I could help it, I was frantically getting myself off to the thought of her naked body beneath mine. Her breath on my lips. Her gray-green eyes closing. Her hands clutching the sheets. Her moan in my ear. I felt so guilty about it, I could barely look her in the eye the next time I saw her.

Didn't stop me from doing it again, of course. In fact, she'd sort of become my go-to fantasy. I shook my head and finished what was left in my mug. What a pathetic fucking cliché I was: Divorced Dad Lusting after the Babysitter. As if a girl like her wanted anything to do with a guy like me— one with three kids and a bitter ex-wife.

But this morning, I was doing all right.

I pulled into the drive at Cloverleigh, parked in my assigned spot and headed into the inn through the front door, passing Frannie at reception on the way back to my office.

I *may* have done that on purpose. There was a back door

closer to the administrative offices, but her smile had a way of making a bad morning good and a good one great.

She gave me one, her whole face lighting up. She'd been fidgeting with the ends of her sandy-colored hair, but she dropped her hands when she saw me. "Morning, Mack."

"Morning, Frannie. How was your weekend?"

"Pretty good. We had that wedding party here the whole time."

I paused with my hand on the door to the back hall. "Oh, that's right. How did everything go?"

"Good." She nodded enthusiastically. "Except the bride broke a strap on her dress and I had to use that little sewing kit I got you to fix it." Her expression turned nervous. "I hope that's okay."

I smiled to reassure her. "No problem. It's there when you need it."

"Thanks."

"Have a good one." I pushed the door open and disappeared down the hall just as my cell phone vibrated in my pocket.

"Hello?"

"Hello Mack, it's Mrs. Ingersoll."

Miriam Ingersoll, a widowed friend of my mother's, was my other babysitter. Monday through Wednesday she picked up Winifred from pre-school at eleven-thirty, met the older two at my house after they walked from the bus stop, then watched them all until I got home around five or six. On Thursdays and Fridays, Frannie was on duty.

"Hi, Mrs. Ingersoll. Everything okay?" I asked.

"I'm afraid not. I fell on the icy sidewalk this morning and broke my leg."

"Oh, no." I felt like an asshole, but immediately I

thought about what this would mean for me and the kids. Then I remembered my manners. "Are you all right?"

"Not really. I'm at the hospital now, and my daughter is with me. I may need surgery."

Closing my eyes, I set my messenger bag with my laptop in it on my desk. "I'm sorry to hear that."

"It's me who's sorry, Mack. What about the kids?"

"Don't worry about them. I'll figure something out."

"Are you sure? I could send my daughter to get them. She's here with me now."

I pressed my lips into a grim line. "No, that's okay. You just focus on recovering. Have your daughter call me and let me know how you're doing, okay?"

"Okay. Please tell the kids I'm sorry, too."

"That's all right. Get better soon." We hung up and I sank into my chair. "Shit."

"Everything okay?"

I looked up and saw Henry DeSantis, the winemaker at Cloverleigh in my office doorway. "Yes. No." I set my phone down and ran a hand over my jaw. "My sitter broke her leg and can't drive. I need to figure out what I'm going to do with my kids this afternoon."

"Sorry. That sucks."

"I'll figure it out. What's up?"

"Wanted to run some numbers by you before we meet with Sawyer regarding the repair of the bottling lines versus the purchase of new ones."

I frowned. Sometimes the promotion to CFO seemed like more trouble than it was worth. But I'd needed the salary bump, and I liked the challenge. Plus, it was good to actually put my business degree to work. "Oh, right. What time is that meeting?"

"Ten." He paused. "Need to reschedule?"

"No, I just need to—"

"Morning, Henry! Hey, Mack." Chloe Sawyer ducked around DeSantis and edged into my office. "Got a second?"

"Actually, I—"

"I wanted to talk to you about the distillery idea I mentioned to you last week. I keep trying to talk to my dad about it, but I swear to God he's dodging me."

"Yeah, we do that when we know our daughters are about to ask for things we can't afford." I reached for my mug and found it empty. "I need more coffee. Preferably with some whiskey in it."

Chloe laughed. "If we had a distillery on site, I'd have some for you. Are you having a bad morning?"

"Kind of. My sitter is out of commission and I need to find a replacement before Winifred gets out of preschool at eleven-thirty."

"Just have Frannie pick her up."

"Frannie's working. I don't want to do that to her."

Chloe rolled her eyes. "She's at *reception*. On a *Monday* morning. In *February*. It's not like she'll be busy. I'm sure Mom can cover for her."

"I'll come back a little later, Mack," DeSantis said, backing out of my office. "If you get time, great. If not, no worries."

I gave him a grateful look. DeSantis was a good guy. "I'll find the time. Give me thirty minutes to make a few phone calls and get the kids squared away."

"I'll go get you some coffee," Chloe said.

"Thanks." I picked up my phone again. Who could I ask to bail me out? My mother had a few friends left around here, but I didn't have contact info for any of them. Mrs.

Gardner next door was an option, although I wasn't sure I wanted her driving my kids around in the snow at her age. While I was still sitting there frowning at my phone, I heard a voice.

"Knock, knock."

I looked up and saw Frannie coming into my office with a steaming mug of coffee in her hands. "Here you go," she said, setting it on my desk.

"Thanks."

"Chloe said you need someone to watch the kids this afternoon?"

"Yeah." I frowned. "Mrs. Ingersoll broke her leg and can't drive."

Frannie shrugged, tucking her hands in her back pockets. "I can do it."

"What about the reception desk?"

"I'm only scheduled until one, and my mom is working too. We're not that busy today. I have some social media stuff to do, but it's nothing urgent." She shrugged. "I don't mind, really."

"Are you sure?" I asked slowly. "I was trying to think of someone else who could help, but not having much luck. I could even run and pick her up and bring her back here so you don't have to leave the desk too early."

"That's perfect. I'll get her some lunch here, and then we'll head back to your house in time to be there when Millie and Felicity get home."

Picking up the cup of hot coffee, I looked at Frannie, half expecting her to sprout wings and a halo and float away. "You're the best. I owe you one."

Her cheeks went a little pink. "It's nothing."

"Right now, it's actually everything. Thanks, Frannie."

Blushing deeper, she smiled at me once more before leaving my office.

I tried not to look at her butt as she left, but her black pants were kind of tight and her shirt was tucked in. She had a great little figure—petite but curvy.

Alone again, I got to work, but Frannie's smile stayed on my mind throughout the morning. And her pink cheeks. And her cute little ass.

Jesus, what was wrong with me? She was practically a kid, for chrissake. No way could she even be thirty, and soon I'd be pushing forty. And she had an innocence about her that made me feel even worse … yet it also made her more appealing.

For fuck's sake. Stop it, you perv. She's doing you a huge favor and doesn't need you drooling over her like a starving dog. It's not her problem you haven't had sex in over a year.

Truth—I couldn't even *remember* the last time Carla and I had done it. The sex had been so blah for so long, so disconnected and rote, that neither of us had bothered to initiate it much toward the end.

But that didn't make it okay for me to get all worked up over Frannie. Even if she did seem like she might be a hell of a lot of fun in bed. Playful. Energetic. Eager to please.

Christ, MacAllister. Enough.

If ever there was a girl off limits, it was Frannie Sawyer. Shifting in my chair, I adjusted the crotch of my pants and put her out of my head.

Four

Frannie

"**H**I, WINNIE!" I GAVE HER A SMILE, MY HEART thumping hard at the sight of Mack holding his little girl's mittened hand as they walked through the lobby. "How was school?"

"Good," she said.

"My goodness, you're getting big." My mother shook her head as Mack brought his daughter around the desk. "You're going to be as tall as Frannie soon!"

I groaned. "She probably will. Millie only has another couple inches to go."

"Good things come in small packages." Mack winked at me, and my belly fluttered. He had the most beautiful deep blue eyes.

"Would you like to come up to my apartment for lunch, Winnie?" I asked.

"Sure!" She grinned happily.

"Great. You can help me make it." I held out my hand and she dropped her dad's to take mine. Then I looked at Mack. "Can I bring you something? A sandwich? Soup?"

He looked guilty. "I'll probably work through lunch."

"You shouldn't work through lunch," my mother scolded. "Let Frannie bring you something."

"That's okay." He gave me a tired smile and put a hand on my shoulder. "Thanks, though. For everything. You're an angel."

He was touching me. He'd called me an angel. I could hardly speak. "You're welcome."

Quickly, I turned and led Winnie out from behind the desk and across the lobby toward the stairs to my suite, so he wouldn't see the goofy grin on my face.

I lived above the inn's garage in an apartment my mother liked to refer to as the "old carriage house," which made it sound bigger and fancier than it was. "Did you hear Mrs. Ingersoll broke her leg?" I asked Winnie.

"Yes," she said, trudging up the stairs next to me. "What does it feel like to break your leg?"

"I don't know." I unlocked my door and pushed it open. "I've never had any broken bones."

"Me neither," she said as we went in.

My place wasn't very big, but it was enough room for me. My bedroom and bathroom were off to the right, and the kitchen was open to the living room. I did have a tiny fireplace, which I loved, and my oversized couch was crazy comfortable.

"Need to use the bathroom?" I asked Winnie.

She shrugged off her backpack and dropped it to the floor. "No. Is this where you live?"

"Yes. Do you like it?"

She nodded. "It's like a doll house."

I laughed. "It *is* kind of like a doll house. A little bigger, maybe, but not much. Are you hungry?

"Yes."

"Me too. Let's see what we can find."

In the kitchen, Winnie and I opened my fridge and took out a big container of chicken noodle soup I'd made over the weekend. In my tiny pantry, she found some Ritz crackers, and counted out four for each of us while I rinsed and sliced an apple.

When everything was ready, we sat at the counter next to each other. While we ate, I asked Winnie about school, about her sisters, and as usual, I snuck in a question or two about her dad. That was how I'd learned that he wasn't a very good cook and they were used to eating a lot of chicken nuggets and fish sticks for dinner, that he never got mad when Winnie wet the bed, and that he was okay at brushing hair but terrible at styling it. Today I learned that over the weekend, he'd accidentally turned everyone's white socks pink, even his own.

I laughed. "Did something red get in the white load of laundry?"

She slurped her soup. "I don't know."

After lunch, I asked Winnie if she'd ever had a macaron.

"What are those?" she asked, wiping her mouth on her sleeve.

I gasped in mock horror as I stood, collecting our bowls. "What are those? You mean you've never had a macaron?"

"No." She smiled and asked hopefully, "Is it a treat?"

"It's only the most beautiful, most fancy treat ever!" I carried our dishes to the sink and grabbed the bakery box sitting on the counter. Inside were a few macarons I'd set aside Saturday when preparing for the Radley wedding. I had hazelnut, white chocolate malt, and rosewater cream. "Peek into this box."

I set it in front of her and she leaned over to look inside. "Ooooh! Can I have one?"

"Sure. Which one would you like?"

"The pink," she said, pointing at the rosewater cream.

"Good choice." I took one from the box and put it on a plate for her, along with a white chocolate malt for me.

"Did you make them?" Winnie asked.

"I sure did. I can make about twenty different colors and flavors, and I'm always testing out new ones."

"Really? Can you make a gold one? That's the Hufflepuff color." She tucked her legs underneath her on the stool and picked up the pink macaron.

"Yes. It's lemon chiffon, another one of my favorites." I took a tiny bite of the white chocolate malt, thinking again about what Mrs. Radley had said to me Saturday night about my own business. Since then, her offer to discuss the possibility had crossed my mind a hundred times. I hoped she'd get in touch.

Winnie gobbled hers up and licked her fingers. "Mmmm. Can you teach me how to make them?"

"Well, they're a little complicated and take a lot of practice. But we can work on it. Tell you what—if you're a good girl and take a little rest now that you're done with your treat, we'll make some lemon chiffon macarons at your house this afternoon when your sisters get home, okay?"

She nodded eagerly, her mouth full. "Can I watch Sofia the First when I rest?"

"Sure," I said. "I'll find it on my TV for you. And I have this really fluffy blanket you can use. It's so soft, it feels like a cloud."

Her face lit up. "Okay."

A few minutes later, she was snuggled up in my white faux fur blanket, her eyes drifting shut almost immediately. I sat at the other end of the couch with my phone and posted a few things on Cloverleigh's social media—a graphic on Facebook advertising an upcoming wine dinner that Chloe and Henry DeSantis had organized, a photo on Instagram I'd snapped of the macarons on the dessert table at the weekend's wedding, and a tweet congratulating Mr. and Mrs. Radley along with a picture from their ceremony.

Finally, I returned direct messages from a few brides, answering their questions if I could, and forwarding April's information if they'd requested specifics on availability or pricing. I was just finishing up when I got a text from Mack.

How's it going?

Great. She's sound asleep on my couch.

I snapped a quick picture of her and sent it to him.

Awesome. I'm jealous.

I smiled, imagining him all wrapped up in that fluffy white blanket stretched out on my couch. Then my stomach whooshed—what would it be like to lie with him like that on a cold winter afternoon, his arms around me, snow falling softly outside the windows, the heat between our bodies keeping us warm …

Omigod. Stop it.

I forced myself to calm down and type something more acceptable.

Did you get some lunch?

Not yet.

I've got homemade chicken soup if you want some. Come on up.

The three dots appeared, and as they faded in and out,

I held my breath. I was always offering to make dinner on Thursdays and Fridays when I watched the kids, but he never took me up on the offer, so I figured he'd turn down lunch, too.

That sounds really good, but I'm swamped.

I'll heat some up in a container.

You can take it with you.

You are tempting me …

LOL ask my mom how to get up here. I'll heat the soup!

It took him a minute to reply, but when he did, he said okay.

I almost squealed. He was coming up to my apartment! He'd never done that before! Setting my phone aside, I hurried into the kitchen, ladled some soup into a plastic container, and stuck it in the microwave. Then I ran into the bathroom and looked in the mirror over the sink. I was still wearing my work clothes, a dark green Cloverleigh collared shirt and black pants. Nothing I could do about that now, but I fussed with my hair and put on another coat of mascara. At the last second, I gave one wrist a spritz of perfume and rubbed it against the other.

You are tempting me …

If only! God, what I wouldn't give to be the kind of woman who could *really* tempt him.

The microwave beeped and I went back to the kitchen, took the soup out, stirred it up, then pressed the lid into place. In a second little container, I placed some crackers and a couple macarons, then tucked everything into a brown paper bag with a spoon and a couple napkins.

A minute later, there were three soft knocks at my door, echoed by three hard ones in my chest. Inhaling and exhaling slowly, I put my hand on the knob and pulled.

"Hi," he said quietly, a sheepish half-grin on his face. "I heard you're feeding the hungry today."

I smiled, positive he could hear my heart thwacking against my ribs. "Come on in."

He entered my suite and glanced around, sticking his hands in his pockets. "This is nice."

"Thanks. It's small, but it suits me. Winnie's on the couch if you want to peek at her." I nodded over my shoulder.

"Okay." While he wandered toward the couch, I took the brown bag with his lunch in it off the kitchen counter. After a quick look at her, he turned around smiling. "If only they were always so sweet, right?"

"Your girls are pretty sweet all the time." I handed him the bag, one hand on the bottom, one holding the handles. "Here you go. Careful."

"Thanks." He took it from me, and both our hands touched. "I appreciate this."

"No problem. If you like it, I can give you the recipe. It's easy."

He shook his head. "You don't know who you're talking to. Ask my kids what a terrible cook I am."

I couldn't hide a smile. "They've already volunteered that info."

"Did they?" He chuckled. "Little shits."

"Don't feel bad. If I were as busy as you, I probably wouldn't know how to cook either."

"I keep thinking I'll learn, but I suppose I should actually make an effort at it," he said with a sigh. "Thanks again for everything. I don't know what I'd do without you. I mean that."

"No problem." I followed him to the door. I felt like skipping. "I'll head over to your house when she wakes up."

"Perfect. God, this smells good." He sniffed the bag. "You better be careful not to spoil me, or I'll be hanging around your door like a stray dog all the time."

I laughed. "I wouldn't mind."

He gave me a rueful, boyish grin that made my insides melt and disappeared down the hall.

Twenty minutes later, my heart was still pounding.

"What's got you so smiley?" my mother asked when Winnie and I came downstairs to say goodbye.

"Oh, I don't know," I said airily, watching the little girl dart down the hall toward her dad's office.

"Frannie Sawyer, you're a terrible liar." She crossed her arms. "What's in that head of yours?"

I could hardly tell her how happy it had made me to pack a lunch for Mack, so I decided to confide in her about Mrs. Radley's suggestion.

"You know the bride from last weekend? She had an idea for me." Thirty seconds into the story, I was sorry.

"I don't know, Frannie," my mother fretted, shaking her head. Then she hurled a million questions at me without giving me a chance to answer them. "A bakery? Where would it be? Who would run it?"

"I would."

"Don't be ridiculous. Running a business would be much too hard and stressful for you. You don't know anything about it."

"I could learn," I bristled.

"But why would you need to? You already have a job here. And your macarons are so popular for weddings."

"It would be nice to have my own thing for once, Mom," I said testily. "Do you have to shoot this down before we even talk it over? Just like you shoot down everything I've asked to do on my own?"

She looked offended. "What are you talking about?"

"It's the same old thing. I don't know why I even bothered to think you'd be excited for me."

"Frannie!"

"It's the truth, Mom. I wanted to do all the things my sisters did, but the answer was always no. Play sports. Go away to college. Backpack through Europe. I've never even been out of the country!"

She looked around to make sure no guests heard me shout, then lifted her chin. "You can't compare yourself to your sisters. You were different, Frannie. Special. There were limits to what your heart could handle."

"Not anymore."

"You don't know that for sure," she said, her eyes welling up. "We only worry so much because we love you, honey. You're still our baby, and—"

I groaned, holding up one hand and pulling open the door with the other. "Enough. I'm sorry I even brought it up. I need to go get Winnie."

Simmering with anger, I moved down the hall toward Mack's office.

Five

Mack

I DEVOURED THE LUNCH FRANNIE HAD PACKED FOR ME—EVERY last cracker crumb, drop of soup, and sugary bite of whatever kind of cookie that was. I'd never tasted anything so fancy and delicious. In fact, when I was done, I kept looking in that empty brown bag, hoping for more to magically appear.

I'd pay her extra this week, so I wouldn't feel like I was taking advantage of her kindness. Normally I'd have refused her offer to pack me a lunch, but it was such a cold day and homemade chicken soup had sounded so good. When was the last time I'd eaten soup that hadn't come from a can?

Carla hadn't been much of a cook even before things fell apart with us, but she'd been better than me.

Which wasn't saying much.

I glanced at the photo of the girls on my desk and fought off the quick stab of guilt, always sharpest when I worried I hadn't done enough to fix the marriage, hadn't tried hard enough to make it work for the sake of the kids. It was a constant knife in my heart.

"Daddy!"

I looked up to see Winifred darting into my office, dressed to go outside. "Hey, you! Did you have a nice nap?"

"Yes." She climbed onto my lap and looped her arms around my neck, telling me all about the lunch they'd made, the cookies they were going to bake this afternoon, and napping on Frannie's "cloud blanket."

She was still rambling when Frannie appeared in the doorway wearing snow boots, a puffy white winter coat and a burgundy hat with a furry ball on top of it. It was adorable on her. I wished she'd come and sit on my lap too.

"Sorry, got stuck talking to my mom," Frannie explained, tugging on her gloves. She didn't sound too happy about it.

"Everything okay? Does this still work for you, or does she need you here?"

"This still works." But her expression remained tense.

"I don't believe you."

She sighed, shaking her head. "Sometimes my mother drives me nuts."

"Yeah, mine too. They know how to push our buttons." I wanted to cheer her up a little, she looked so down. "Hey, thanks a million for lunch. It was delicious."

Her features eased into a smile. "You're welcome. Winnie liked it too—she ate two bowls of soup. And I meant what I said about the recipe. I'd be happy to share."

I looked down at Winnie. "What do you think? Can I handle making homemade chicken soup?"

She giggled and shook her head. "No way."

I sighed. "But I need to be feeding you guys healthier stuff. I should at least try."

"Frannie says we can make lemon macaroni today," Winnie announced.

Frannie laughed and stuck her hands on her hips. "*Macarons*, not macaroni. Not that *those* are very healthy. Those were the cookies in your lunch," she said to me. "Did you like them?"

"Yeah. I kept looking for more in the bag. I'm not a huge dessert person but those were delicious. Not overly sweet."

"If they're done right, they shouldn't be too sweet. *And*," she added with a smile, "they're gluten-free."

"Thanks. Hey, how did you get to be so good in the kitchen?" I asked her, genuinely curious.

She shrugged. "I spent a lot of time at home with my mom growing up. She always made sure I ate really healthy because of—well, just because. And winters are long up here. Cooking and baking filled the time."

"Winters *are* long up here." I glanced out the one window in my office. Snowflakes continued to fall lightly, but it was supposed to get heavier tonight. "You better get moving. The driving isn't going to get any better."

"Do you know how much snow we're going to get tonight?" she asked. "I heard eight to ten inches."

I'd like to give you eight to ten inches tonight, I thought. What I said was, "I think that's about right, but it's not supposed to start *really* coming down until five or six. You okay to drive in this?"

"Oh, yeah. I'm fine. My dad gave all of us extensive lessons in driving in the snow."

"True story," said a gruff male voice.

I looked up to see John Sawyer's tall, thick frame appear in the hallway behind Frannie. He put an arm around his daughter's neck, getting her in a headlock.

"*Dad*," she complained, pulling at his arm. "Let go."

"Never." He kept her there and looked over her shoulder

at me. "Got time to go over a few things?"

I nodded, kissed Winnie's head and pushed her gently from my lap. "Yep. Be good, Winn. I'll see you later." To Sawyer, I said, "Your daughter has rescued me by agreeing to watch my kids this afternoon."

"She's a good egg," said Sawyer, squeezing her tightly.

"Thanks, Dad. Now let me go before I choke to death."

Sawyer laughed as he released her. "You be careful out there. And call me if you don't want to drive home later. I'll come get you."

"I can bring her back," I offered. "Millie's old enough to stay with the younger two, or I can toss them in the car."

Sawyer hitched up his jeans and leaned down to talk to Winnie, hands on his knees. He never wore dress clothes to work—said he was a farmer more than anything else and was happiest outside in the dirt. "And how are you, peanut?"

"Good."

"No school today?"

"I already went," she told him.

"Ah. Well, if it keeps snowing like this, maybe you won't have to go tomorrow."

I groaned. "Don't jinx us, Sawyer. I've got work to do tomorrow."

"I can always watch them here if they want to come into work with you," offered Frannie.

"Don't *you* have to work?" I asked.

"My parents own the place," she said, giving her dad a poke on the shoulder. "I don't think they'd fire me for taking a day off. And maybe we could take the sleigh out again, Winnie. Would you like that?"

"Yes!" Winifred exclaimed.

"What we should do is put up a sign selling rides on that

thing," Sawyer said. "We could probably make a fortune this week."

"Dad!" Frannie was outraged. "The idea was just to have the sleigh for the guests to ride for fun. And to use for weddings."

"Fun has a price, doesn't it?"

She rolled her eyes at her father. "It's not all about the money, Dad. Jeez."

Sawyer looked at me and shook his head. "My daughters are going to break me, Mack. If it's not April with her heated wedding barn, it's Chloe with her distillery, or Frannie giving everything away for free. And those are just the three that live here!"

I laughed. "Frannie's got a soft heart. But I hear you—my daughters are going to break me as well. Probably with the swear jar."

Frannie clucked her tongue and reached for Winifred's hand. "Come on, Winnie. We don't have to take this abuse."

"Bye," I called as they walked out hand in hand. "Thank you!"

Over her shoulder, Frannie stuck her tongue out at me. But then she winked, and my chest felt tight.

Sawyer came toward me and sat down in one of the chairs across from my desk, launching into his financial concerns about purchasing the new bottling lines and wondering what I thought about Chloe's distillery idea, then complaining about how his wife was always nagging at him to slow down and consider retirement.

I heard him, but in all honesty my thoughts were on Frannie. Was she okay driving in this snow? Was the house clean enough that I wouldn't be embarrassed? Had I left any piles of my underwear folded on the dining room table?

As the afternoon hours dragged by, the snow falling faster and heavier, I kept wondering what everyone was doing. Had the girls finished their homework? Had Millie practiced piano? Had Felicity conned her way into more iPad time? Around four thirty, I got a text from Frannie.

Making dinner and dessert.

A few seconds later, the message was followed by a series of pictures showing each of the girls in the kitchen, sleeves rolled up, hair tied back, grins on their faces, hands busy with kitchen tools. Apparently, I owned a mixer.

Then there was one photo showing something simmering in a big pot on the stove—was it chili? Just looking at it warmed my belly.

Wow. Is that really happening in my kitchen?

It is! And your girls are doing all the work. Almost. :)

I didn't want to be at work anymore. I wanted to be home with them, hanging out in the kitchen and smelling that chili, drinking a beer and listening to my daughters laugh. We never had fun like that on school nights, which always felt to me like a list of things to tick off—homework, dinner, piano, reading, baths, bed. Piano on Tuesdays. Therapy every other Wednesday. Ballet on Thursdays.

Homework done? I asked, feeling a bit like a curmudgeon.

Yes. And Millie says to tell you she practiced piano already, and Felicity wants you to know she read two chapters in her book.

Sounds like you have everything under control. Was the driving bad?

Roads were slippery. I went slow. Be careful!!

I assured her I would and tried to get a few more things done at my desk, but found it hard to concentrate. I was about to call it a day when my phone vibrated.

Ryan Woods calling, it said on the screen.

I smiled and picked it up. "I thought you were dead, asshole."

Woods laughed. "Nah. Just busy."

"I bet. How's everything going with the wedding plans?"

"Pretty good. Although what the fuck do I know?"

"You ready to do this thing?"

"Yeah. *That*, I know."

I laughed. "Good."

Woods was a buddy from the Marines, although by now he was like a brother to me. We'd been deployed together in Afghanistan and had remained tight. Like me, he'd struggled to adjust to his old life once he got back for good, and I got him a job at Cloverleigh as well as a place to live. The house had been a mess before he moved in and refurbished it.

Despite being busy, he'd found time to fall in love with Stella Devine, the granddaughter of Mrs. Gardner next door. She'd come up from Detroit for a visit, Woods had taken one look at her and that was that. When he moved down to Detroit to be with her, the girls and I moved into the house. He and Stella were getting married at Cloverleigh in a few weeks. I was the best man.

Hopefully I wouldn't jinx him.

"So when are you coming up?" I asked. "Am I supposed to be planning some kind of bachelor night?"

"*No*," he said emphatically. "Neither Stella nor I want anything like that. I'd settle for a few beers somewhere. We're coming up on the Wednesday before the wedding, and Thursday is the day Stella and her sisters are doing some kind of all-day girl thing, so maybe we can hang out that night."

"Done," I said. "My parents get in that day, and God knows I'll need to escape the house. I'm looking forward to it."

"Me too." He lowered his voice. "All this wedding shit is driving me crazy. I'm trying to be interested and involved, but Jesus fuck."

I laughed. "I can imagine."

"And the cost—my God, we want to pay for everything ourselves, but I had no idea how expensive things are. And her sister Emme, who's a wedding planner, has talked her into all these extras. It's insanity. Stella has lost her mind, I swear."

"Well, we knew that. She's marrying *you*, isn't she?"

He laughed. "Fuck off."

"I'd better go. We're getting a ton of snow tonight," I told him. "The roads will probably be bad."

"Yeah, we're getting some here too, but not like you guys are up there. Can't say I miss it."

We hung up, and I packed it in for the night. Up at reception, I said goodbye to Frannie's mom, who looked anxious.

"Oh, there you are," she said, knotting her hands together. "I've been texting Frannie. It's so bad out there, I don't want her to drive in the dark. The roads will be icy."

"I'll bring her back, Daphne," I assured her. "Don't worry."

"Okay." She glanced over her shoulder. "I'd send John to come get her, but I worry that his eyesight isn't great for night driving."

"No problem. Really. My tires are good in the snow, and it's a short ride."

She smiled in relief. "Thanks, Mack. You have daughters, so you know how it is."

"I do. Have a good night."

But as I hurried out to the parking lot and impatiently brushed off my car, I realized it wasn't only *my* daughters I was so eager to get home and see—it was her daughter too.

Six

Mack

THE BLIZZARD WAS IN FULL FORCE. THE ROADS WERE AWful, and traffic crawled. Normally, the ride between my house and Cloverleigh was only about fifteen minutes, but today it took nearly two white-knuckled, curse-muttering hours. Not only did the snow and ice slow me down, but twice I had to pull over and help out other drivers. One lady had gotten herself stuck in a ditch, and some guy had spun out onto the shoulder trying to take a curve too quickly.

By the time I pulled into the garage at the back of the property where we lived, Frannie's little Volkswagen was pretty well buried at the curb, and I was tense and irritated and *starving*.

But the moment I stepped through the back door, the smell took the edge off my mood. My stomach rumbled with anticipation as I inhaled.

"Daddy!" Felicity shouted, running over to me. "You're home!" She wrapped her arms around my waist and squeezed.

I hugged her back without telling her to wait so I could

take off my coat and boots and gloves, even though I was getting snow on the floor. Whenever I was late, the girls reacted this way, and I often wondered if part of it was worry I might not come home—if I'd abandon them the way their mother essentially had. "I'm home. Wow, it smells good in here."

"We made chili." Felicity looked up at me and gave me a smile. "And macaroni."

"Maca*rons*," said Frannie from the stove with exaggerated French pronunciation. "And if you don't stop calling them macaroni, I'm never coming over to make them again."

From the way the girls all giggled at once, which was my favorite sound in the world, I got the feeling it was already some kind of joke between them. My mood lifted further. "Well, whatever it is, it smells so good my belly sounds like a bear."

Felicity pressed her ear to my stomach. "It does. You're right." Then she looked over at Frannie. "Did you know my dad has hair on his belly?"

Frannie burst out laughing while I considered strangling my middle child. "Thanks, Mavis. Have I mentioned you have a goofy haircut yet today?"

She shook her head. "No."

"Well, you do. Now let me get my boots and coat off so I can eat, okay?"

"Okay."

I yanked off my boots and left them on the back hall rug next to four other pairs, tossed my gloves and hat on the little bench near the door, and hung up my coat. While I was out of sight, I ran my fingers through my hair, attempting to repair the damage done by wearing a hat for two hours.

When I stepped into the kitchen, Winnie was there wanting a hug. "Hi, Daddy."

"Hey you. Long time, no see." I picked her up, squeezing her against my chest. Over her shoulder, I surveyed the scene in disbelief. The kitchen was definitely cleaner than I'd left it this morning. No one was looking at a screen. A platter of pale yellow macarons was on the kitchen counter, where Millie was sitting.

"These things are amazing," she told me, her mouth full. "And they're gluten-free! We used almond flour."

"I had almond flour?" I asked, surprised.

"Winnie and I stopped at the store on the way here," said Frannie as she stirred the chili.

My stomach growled again. "Let me know what I owe you for groceries."

"Don't worry about it." She winked at me over one shoulder, making my nether regions tingle.

"Daddy, did you know that macarons have *feet*?" Winnie asked, making Frannie laugh.

"Imagine that," I said, setting her down. "You girls ate dinner already?"

Millie nodded, rolling her eyes. "Yes, and did my homework *and* practiced piano."

Frannie's back was to me, and I watched, a little starstruck, as she ladled chili into a bowl. "Where are my real daughters and who are these imposters?" I asked.

She turned to face me, a smile on her face and a steaming bowl in her hands. "Here. This is for you."

"Thanks. It looks awesome." Taking it from her, I went around the counter and slid onto the seat next to Millie.

"Can I get you something to drink?" Frannie asked, setting a napkin and spoon in front of me.

What I really wanted was a beer, but I thought I'd better not since I was going to have to drive her home. "Maybe some water, but I can get it." I started to get up again.

"I've got it. Sit." She gave me a sympathetic look. "You just got here, and that drive had to be stressful."

"It was." Forgetting how hungry I was for a moment, I watched her take a glass from the cupboard and fill it, looking perfectly at home in our kitchen. She set the water in front of me as Winnie and Felicity bounced around the kitchen, telling me about all the cooking they'd done.

"I got to help slice the bell peppers," Felicity said proudly. "And there's pumpkin in the chili!"

"I swifted the flour," announced Winnie.

"Sifted," corrected Frannie.

"And I separated the egg yolks from the whites for the macarons, but I messed up the first couple and wasted some eggs," Millie said, her expression guilty.

"That's okay, Millie." Frannie leaned her elbows on the counter across from us and smiled at my oldest. "It's tricky and takes practice. I used to mess that up all the time too. And you did a great job making sure the batter was mixed enough. Our meringue was perfect, and that's quite a feat for your first time." She'd changed out of her work shirt and was wearing a loose-fitting gray top that sort of fell off one shoulder, revealing something white and lacy underneath.

Quickly, I dropped my eyes to my food and concentrated on eating. In fact, I scarfed down the first bowl of chili Frannie had given me so fast I burned my tongue, but I didn't care. It was hot and delicious, thick with chicken and vegetables.

"Daddy, can we watch Andy Mack?" Millie asked,

hopping down from her chair. "Frannie said we had to wait until you got home to have screen time."

I nodded to the girls. "It's okay."

The kids wandered into the front room and turned on the TV while I scraped the bottom of my bowl. When every last bite was gone, I set down my spoon and put my hands on my stomach. "God, that was good."

"There's more," Frannie offered.

"Sold." Grabbing my empty bowl, I slid off my chair and went around the counter. "One more bowl and then I'll drive you home."

"Oh, you don't have to drive me home," she said as I moved past her to the stove, taking care not to let my body brush against hers.

"I promised your mother I would." I took the top off the pot of chili and scooped more into my bowl. "And the driving's bad. I wouldn't feel right putting you out on the roads, especially not when you've done so much for me today." Although the last thing I wanted to do was hit the roads again. I'd have to take the girls with me, since the blizzard made the drive time too long to leave them alone.

"It was no big deal. I enjoyed it. My days can be pretty monotonous at the desk, especially in the winter when the inn gets slow."

I put the top back on the pot and moved around her again, taking my chair at the counter. "Do you like working reception? Is there another job you're interested in at Cloverleigh?"

She shrugged and leaned on the counter again. "Chloe offered to let me manage the Traverse City tasting room, but I actually don't know that much about the wine. I'm better off at the inn. I like working with food, especially baking."

"From what I hear, you're amazing at it—and from what I taste, of course. Have you ever thought about opening a bakery?"

Her eyes dropped to her hands. "A little."

"And?"

She didn't answer right away. "I don't know. It takes a lot of time and money to start a business, and I'm not very … adventurous. I don't think I'd make a very good entrepreneur."

"I think you could do anything you set your mind to," I told her.

"Really?" She looked up and smiled softly, making my heart skip a few beats.

"Really."

"I guess I could talk to my dad," she said with a sigh. "But my mother would have a problem with it."

"Why?"

She straightened up and leaned back against the island, rolling her eyes a little. "It's not a big deal, really, but I was born with a heart defect that puts me at a *slightly* higher risk for a heart attack, believe it or not, so she's always worried about stress."

"I never knew that," I said, realizing there were probably a lot of things about her I didn't know, and wanted to. "Are you okay now?"

"Yeah, I had surgeries to correct the problem when I was younger, but my mother has always been overly protective—both my parents, actually. Even though the doctors say I'm fine, I feel like my parents look at me and see a sick kid."

Placing my spoon in the empty bowl, I carried it to the sink. "As a father, I can understand that. We can't help seeing our kids as innocent, helpless babies who need our protection."

"Well, I'm not a baby," she snapped. "And I don't want to be treated like one."

I turned around and looked at her in surprise. I'd never heard her speak angrily. "I'm sorry, Frannie. I didn't mean *you're* a baby. I meant that it's hard for a dad to let go. Mentally, we know our kids need us to, so they can make their own way in the world, but in our hearts, we can't stop trying to prevent them from making mistakes. We never want to see them get hurt."

She took a breath. "Sorry. I didn't mean to snap at you. I had an argument with my mother earlier, and … I just get a little tired of being seen as a kid all the time. I want to be seen as an adult capable of making my own decisions. You know?"

What I knew right then was how good she looked standing in my kitchen, feisty and worked up, a little color in her cheeks, a little skin showing where her top had slipped off that shoulder. I wanted to bite it.

I leaned back against the sink, gripping the edge of the counter. "I hear you."

"I mean, I'm twenty-seven years old." She took a step closer. "Don't you think I should be allowed to make a few mistakes?"

Talk about mistakes. In two strides I could have covered the distance between us. Taken her in my arms. Crushed my lips to hers and felt her chest pressing against mine.

But I wouldn't do it.

Maybe she wasn't a baby, but she was only twenty-seven—*ten whole years* younger than I was. She was the boss's daughter. She was the nanny. She was here doing me a favor.

And she trusted me.

There was no way.

Seven

Frannie

I WAS HOLDING MY BREATH.

I wasn't even sure why, but it was something about the way Mack was looking at me. And the tension in his body—the taut muscles in his neck. The grip of his fingers on the edge of the counter. The set of his jaw. It gave the impression of *restraint*. Like he was holding himself back.

Something unfamiliar hummed in the air between us. I could *feel* it—he wanted me the way I wanted him.

No wonder I couldn't breathe.

Then he cleared his throat and turned away from me, cutting off the current. "Sure. Everybody needs to make mistakes now and then."

I'd forgotten I'd even asked the question.

He turned the sink on, rinsed his dishes, and placed them in the dishwasher. I stood there staring at his muscular back, at the width of his shoulders, at the snug fit of his jeans on his butt. *If I were his and he was mine, I'd go over and wrap my arms around his waist, press my cheek to his back. Then he'd turn around, winding his arms around me. He'd lower his lips to mine, and—*

"I should get you home," he said, interrupting my fantasy. "Want to grab your coat?"

"Sure." But I didn't really want to leave. I wanted to stay in this warm, chaotic house with him and the girls. Pretend I belonged here. Pretend I belonged to him.

"Want me to put the chili in the fridge?" I asked.

"I can do it when I get back."

"Okay. I'll say goodnight to the girls."

"Actually, they should probably come with us. It's late." He went over to the back door and pulled on his boots, leaving them unlaced. "Can you tell them to put on their stuff? I'll warm up the car."

"Yes." I went into the front room and rounded up the kids, and we were zipping up our coats when Mack came in the back door again, a frown on his face. "Of course, my fucking car won't start."

One of the girls clucked her tongue. "That's a dollar, Daddy."

He glared at them. "I should get a freebie for car trouble."

"Is it the battery?" I asked, pausing with one glove on.

"Maybe. But the way it's parked in the garage, we wouldn't even be able to get your car close enough to jump it."

"What about using my car to drive me home? You can drop me off and borrow it for tomorrow. Or for as long as you need. I can always use my mom's SUV if I need to go somewhere."

His brow furrowed. "I could try, but your car is pretty well buried. Might take me a while to dig it out. Was it okay on the roads earlier? The streets haven't even been plowed here yet."

"It wasn't awesome," I admitted. My Beetle was adorable and fun in the summer, but every winter I regretted not choosing something bigger and better in the snow.

Mack sighed, rubbing the back of his neck. Snowflakes were melting on his shoulders, scarf, and hair—he'd gone out without his hat. The tips of his ears were red from the cold.

As we were standing there, the phone rang, and Millie whooped. "Snow day! Please, please, please!"

Felicity made it to the phone first and picked it up. "Hello?" Then she nodded excitedly and did a little dance. "Snow day tomorrow! No school!"

While the girls cheered, Mack looked at me over their heads, his expression grim. "I need a beer."

I laughed, shaking my head. "I don't blame you."

"Dad, can Frannie spend the night?" Millie asked.

"She can sleep in my room!" shouted Winnie, clapping her hands.

"She doesn't want to sleep with *you*," said Millie. "You wet the bed."

"Do not!"

"Do too!"

"Dad, Millie said I wet the bed and I don't anymore!"

"Enough!" Mack put out his hands. "I need to think."

"But can she sleep over, Daddy? Please?" Felicity clasped her hands beneath her chin.

He looked at me. "I hate to say it, but I think you might be stranded at the zoo for the night."

"I don't mind. I just need to call my mom and let her know." I rolled my eyes, thinking that at twenty-seven, it shouldn't have been necessary and probably made me sound even more like a child. "Otherwise she'll freak out."

"I get it," he said.

"Yay! Then we can bake something in the morning for breakfast. Frannie knows how to make gluten-free monkey bread!" Millie danced around the island.

He unwound his scarf. "Well, I guess that settles it. I can't turn down monkey bread."

My heart was thumping hard as the girls crowded around me. Which was silly—I wasn't staying because he wanted me to. I was *stuck* here.

Still. We were going to sleep under the same roof. It gave me a thrill I hadn't felt in a long time.

Was that pathetic?

I removed my coat and boots and took my phone out of my purse to text my mom.

Going to stay at Mack's house. His car won't start and mine is buried on the street.

She called me immediately, and I imagined she'd been waiting nervously with her phone in her hand. Gritting my teeth, I answered it.

"Hello?" I moved into the dining room, where it was less noisy.

"Do you want Daddy and I to come get you?" she asked right away.

"No, that's okay." I glanced up and saw Mack pull a beer from the fridge, then hold it up as if to say, *You want one?* I nodded. "I'm fine here."

"Are you sure?"

"Yes. The girls are all excited about baking something in the morning. And I don't want Daddy out driving tonight. The roads are terrible and you know how bad his eyes are in the dark."

"That's true," she conceded.

"I'll text you in the morning. The kids don't have school, so Mack and I will probably bring them over to Cloverleigh." *Mack and I.* That was fun to say. "We might be a little late, though."

"That's all right. Just be safe."

"We will."

"Goodnight, dear."

"'Night."

I wandered back into the kitchen, where the girls were putting a bag of popcorn in the microwave. After I tucked my phone into my bag, Mack handed me a beer. I took it, and he clinked his against mine. "Cheers."

"I told my mom we might get to work a little late tomorrow. At least we can sleep in." As soon as I said it, I was embarrassed because it sounded kind of like I thought we'd be sleeping in *together.*

"Ha," he said with a grin. "I can tell you don't live with kids. I don't even remember what sleeping in feels like."

"Daddy, can we watch a movie?" Felicity asked.

He took a pull on his beer. "What movie?"

"Hotel Transylvania!"

Millie groaned. "No. We always have to watch that. It's not her turn to pick."

"Whose turn is it?" he asked.

"It's Winifred's, I think," Millie answered, "but since we have a guest, maybe we should let her pick it."

They all looked at me. "Oh!" I bit my lip. "Uhhh, what about something classic like The Wizard of Oz?"

"Winnie's scared of the wicked witch," Felicity said with a snicker.

"I don't like her," Winnie confirmed dolefully. "That witch is *mean.*"

"Well, what if I sit right next to you the whole time?" I suggested. "You can close your eyes during the scary parts."

She beamed. "Okay."

With that settled, the girls dumped popcorn into bowls and poured themselves some lemonade. Mack went into the living room to see if he could find the movie on demand, and I put the leftover chili into a large plastic container and stuck it in the fridge.

"Found it!" he called a moment later.

The girls all shouted with excitement, and we carried the snacks into the living room. Right away, Winnie hopped up on one end of the L-shaped sectional couch. "Sit here," she directed, patting the cushion next to her.

I did as she asked, briefly wondering where Mack would end up and if it was too much to hope for that he might sit next to me. Turns out he had no choice, because Millie stretched out on the floor with a big pillow and Felicity lay down along the shorter section of the couch. That left only one place open, right next to me.

He glanced at it as the opening credits to the movie began. "Girls," he said, "I'll be right back. I just want to check on Mrs. Gardner, okay?"

"Okay," they chimed.

"Hey Dad, turn off the lights when you leave!" Millie called, making herself more comfy on the floor.

He saluted her, switched off both living room lamps, and headed for the kitchen. From my spot on the couch, I watched him set his beer on the island and step into the back hall.

He was gone for about ten minutes, and when he came back, he was carrying a plate covered with foil. After taking off his winter stuff, he picked up his beer and brought the plate into the living room. "Anyone want a brownie?"

"Oooh," said Felicity. "Me!"

"And me," said Millie, popping to her feet. "Although they're not as fancy as macarons."

"Delicious doesn't have to be fancy," I assured her. "Is she okay over there?"

Mack nodded and set the plate on the end table next to Winnie. "Yeah. I checked her furnace and it's working fine."

Then he dropped onto the cushion adjacent to mine, and I thought I might die.

But I played it cool. "That's good. This would be a terrible night to be without heat. It's freezing."

"Are you cold? Here." Reaching behind me, he took a thick, crocheted blanket off the back of the couch and set it in my lap.

I wasn't that cold—actually my body was heating up with him so close—but I couldn't resist the idea of sitting beneath a blanket with him in the dark. "Thanks. Here, I'll share." Unfolding the heavy knit throw, I spread one end over Winnie's folded legs and gently tossed the other onto Mack's lap.

"Hey, I want a blanket," Felicity whined.

"Me too," said Millie.

Mack grumbled but set down his beer and got up again. He disappeared up the stairs and came down a moment later with two fleece blankets. After dropping one onto Millie, he shook out the other and draped it over Felicity. "Anything else while I'm up?"

"Shhhh," Millie admonished.

Mack nudged her ribs with his foot before taking his seat next to me once more, and if I wasn't crazy, it felt like he sat a little closer this time. I could totally feel the length of his thigh alongside mine beneath the blanket.

We watched the movie and sipped our beers while the kids munched popcorn and slurped lemonade. At one point, Millie wanted more snacks, Felicity needed a bathroom break, and Winnie wanted a stuffed animal, so we hit pause. All three girls got up and took off in various directions, leaving Mack and me alone in the dim living room.

"Another beer?" he asked, rising to his feet.

I hesitated. I was kind of a lightweight, and I didn't want to get goofy. I wanted him to see me as an adult and not a kid, so getting tipsy wouldn't help. That said, I was so aware of his body next to mine that I was having trouble relaxing. One more beer couldn't hurt. "Okay."

"Good. I thought you were going to be all responsible and say no and I was going to feel shitty for being a bad influence."

I smiled up at him. "You're not a bad influence."

"We'll see." He looked toward the kitchen, where someone had turned on the light and an argument had begun over how much time the popcorn needed. "Oh, Jesus. I'll be right back."

While he was gone, I grabbed my purse and darted upstairs to use the bathroom, blinking at the bright light. In the mirror over the sink, I checked my reflection, trying to imagine what he saw when he looked at me. A kid? A co-worker? An employee? How could I get him to see me differently?

Give it up, I told my reflection. Then I dug my birth control pills out of my purse and took one for today, turned off the light and returned to the living room, where Mack was already sitting on the couch. The girls were still making a racket in the kitchen.

"Here you go," he said, handing me another beer.

"Thanks." I took the bottle and settled onto the couch again, sitting with my legs criss-crossed beneath the blanket this time. I hadn't done it on purpose, not *exactly*, but my left knee now rested on his right thigh, and he didn't move away. My pulse picked up.

Mack's eyes were on the kitchen as he tipped up his beer. "Sometimes I can't believe I haven't totally fucked this dad thing up yet."

"Are you kidding? You're a great dad."

He took another sip. "I don't know. Sometimes I think I'm doing right by them. Sometimes I'm convinced that I'm doing irreparable harm. Most days, I have no fucking idea *what* I'm doing."

The confession touched me, and his insecurity squeezed my heart. I put a hand on his arm. "Does anyone? I mean, I know you've got a lot more to worry about than I do, a lot more responsibility, but I think the same thing sometimes."

"You do?" He looked at me in surprise.

"Absolutely. I look at my sisters or other people my age and think, what the hell am I doing still living on the family farm with my parents? Why don't I have more ambition? What's wrong with me that I'm not out there in the world being a badass?"

He shook his head. "You don't need to be a badass. You don't need to be anything other than what you are. And frankly, the world could use more people like you."

"What am I like?" I asked, surprised and flattered by his words.

"Sweet. Genuine. Kind."

I stared at the label on the beer bottle. Those were all nice things, and I was glad he thought them of me, but none of them were very exciting or sexy. "Thanks."

"Did I say something wrong?"

Embarrassed, I laughed a little. "No. I just sometimes wish I wasn't so ... scared."

"What are you scared of?"

"Lots of things." I took a drink. "But lately I've been worried about life passing me by."

"What do you mean? You're so young."

"But I never take any risks. Never take any chances. I think about the fact that there was a decent chance I wouldn't even survive childhood, and here I am. So what am I going to do to prove I'm worthy? To make sure I live life to the fullest?"

Mack was silent for a minute. Sipped his beer. "What would that look like for you? To live life to the fullest? What chances would you take?"

I took a breath and was about to answer when the light in the kitchen went out and the girls trooped back into the living room.

"We're ready," Felicity said, hopping back on the couch with her bowl, spilling popcorn onto the cushions and floor.

Mack groaned. "Felicity, look what you're doing."

"Sorry," she said, picking up the pieces and putting them back in her bowl.

"Don't eat the ones from the floor." He got up and took care of the pieces on the carpet, taking them to the kitchen to throw away while Winifred and Millie settled in again and someone hit play on the movie.

I had to laugh a little, imagining that this was probably what a typical Saturday night looked like around here—a movie, some blankets, some popcorn and lemonade. A little bickering, a little mess here and there, a couple beers for

Mack after a long week of being CFO and Daddy. It seemed cozy and comforting to me, but that was from the outside. Was he happy? I wondered, maybe for the first time. I spent tons of time fantasizing about him, but I really didn't *know* him, not intimately.

Was he lonely? Did he feel like *he* was living his life to the fullest, or was that some stupid idea that only someone in my situation worried about? After all, what choice did he have? His children were entirely dependent on him for everything from where they slept to what they wore to what they ate to how they felt about themselves. He was 100 percent responsible for their physical and emotional health. He didn't have the luxury of wondering, *Gee, am I living my best life?*

I felt silly for saying something so frivolous to him while at the same time admiring his devotion to his children. By his own admission, he wasn't perfect, but he was here, he was trying, and he loved them with his whole heart.

It was inspiring. It was humbling. It was *hot*.

Even his dirty mouth. For a moment, I wondered just how dirty it got, and felt my face get warm.

When he came back from the kitchen and sat next to me again, I moved my leg to give him more room. "Sorry," I whispered. "I'm taking up too much space."

"You're fine." Then, to my complete shock, he put his hand on my leg and nudged it back where it had been, resting against his. *And left it there.*

It was on top of the blanket, and it's not like he was intimately caressing my inner thigh or anything, but still. *Still.* My heart thundered. My breath caught. My skin hummed.

That's when I felt his thumb slowly start to move back and forth just above my knee.

Eight

Mack

WHAT THE FUCK ARE YOU DOING? MY INNER DAD VOICE barked at me. *Stop touching her!*

But I left my hand right where it was, enjoying the feel of Frannie's knee pressed against my thigh, imagining what it would be like if my hand were beneath the blanket.

I knew it was wrong. I knew I'd probably go to hell for having impure thoughts about the babysitter. I knew I'd definitely get fired if Sawyer saw me groping his daughter, but I left it.

After all, I wasn't really *groping* her, was I? It was more of a *graze*. Innocent. Over the blanket. Out in the open. She probably hadn't even noticed. She wasn't even looking at me.

And it felt so nice to sit close to her this way. To touch her. To have her in the room on a winter evening—another adult, someone I could talk to, someone who understood. Maybe she couldn't fully comprehend what it was like to be a single parent, but it wasn't as if she hadn't struggled. She knew what it was like to fear you were falling short, to worry you were fucking up the one chance at life you'd been given. Like I had when I was deployed, she'd been forced to consider her own mortality—and she'd been only a child.

My gut churned, imagining what that must have been like for her and for her parents. Frannie appreciated life. She appreciated little things like good meals and kindness and sleigh rides in winter. She was sweet and beautiful and generous—more than worthy of the life she'd been given. I wished I could tell her that. I wished she wasn't my boss's daughter. I wished my kids weren't in the room. I wished I could share not only this blanket and this couch and this snowy evening with her, but more. A hell of a lot more.

But this was as close to her as I could get.

By the time the movie was over, Winnie had fallen asleep. I carried her upstairs, managed to get her clothes off, her pajamas on, and wake her up enough to use the bathroom and brush her teeth. A few minutes later, Millie and Felicity came up the stairs to put their pajamas on, arguing about whose room Frannie was going to sleep in. Once I'd tucked Winnie into bed and kissed her goodnight, I went into the bathroom where they continued to bicker while they brushed their teeth, toothpaste and spit flying everywhere.

"I have bunk beds," said Millie. "That way she won't have to sleep with one of us."

"But my bed is big enough for two," argued Felicity. "It's a double."

"It's actually only a full and not big enough for you and an adult," I told her. "Millie's bunk makes more sense in terms of space." Actually, what made the *most* sense in terms of space was to offer her the other side of my king-size bed. *And if she wandered over to my side, I wouldn't complain one bit.*

"Hey," Frannie whispered from the hallway behind me.

I turned around and felt my face get hot, as if she might have guessed what I was thinking.

"Hey," I said quietly. "I'm just going to put some clean sheets on Millie's bottom bunk for you. And maybe she can lend you something to sleep in." She was so petite, I figured Millie's clothes might fit, although she had a lot more curves.

Frannie smiled. "Ah, I think her things will be too small for me."

"Yeah. Geez, Dad. Do you think she's a kid?" Behind me, Millie's tone was pure eye roll.

I frowned over my shoulder at my firstborn, then turned back to Frannie. "I'll get you a T-shirt. Would that be okay?"

She nodded. "Perfect. And really, don't go to any trouble about a bed. I can sleep on the couch with the blankets."

"Will you be comfortable?"

"Totally," she assured me.

I scratched my head. "Okay. If you want to. I'll get you a pillow."

"Thanks. Oh, and if you by any chance have an extra toothbrush …"

"We do. Millie, can you get her a new one from the drawer?"

"Sure, Dad."

"Do you need a towel or anything?" I asked Frannie, although I panicked a little at the thought of her taking a shower at my house.

She thought for a second. "Maybe just a little one so I can wash my face."

"I'll get her one," said Felicity, bolting out of the bathroom and going to the linen closet at the top of the stairs.

"Thanks, Felicity. I'll be right back," I told Frannie. "Girls, finish up and get in bed. I'll be up to say goodnight in a minute."

Downstairs, I went into my room and searched for a clean T-shirt for her to sleep in. Unfortunately, my nicest white ones were either dirty or freshly laundered but pink. Cursing, I hunted through my drawers and found a dark gray one with USMC written across the chest in thick black letters. It was faded, but had minimal fraying and no pit stains. She would swim in it, but at least it would be more comfortable than sleeping in her clothes.

Oh, fuck. Don't think about her without clothes on.

I grabbed an extra pillow from my bed, tossed it onto the couch on my way through the living room, and hurried back upstairs, where the bathroom door was closed. With the T-shirt in my hand, I said goodnight to Millie and Felicity, kissing their foreheads and telling them I loved them.

"Can we really go to work with you and Frannie tomorrow?" asked Millie, yawning.

"Sure. If we can get ourselves there." Grimacing, I remembered how my engine refused to turn over earlier. Assuming it was a dead battery, I'd have to get a jump tomorrow. "Go to sleep now."

When I left her room, Frannie was coming out of the bathroom, and we met in the hall. She'd left the light on, thank goodness, otherwise we'd have been alone in the dark. Her face was freshly washed, and she looked even younger and sweeter without any makeup on.

Because she is young and sweet. So stop thinking about

putting your dick in her mouth.

I thrust the shirt at her. "Here."

She took it from me. "Oh—thanks."

"I put an extra pillow on the couch. I just need to grab a spare pillowcase for it from the linen closet. I'll do that right now."

"Okay."

"All the blankets are still down there too."

"Okay. Thanks." She smiled at me, and my chest got so tight I could hardly breathe.

Go, asshole. Get the pillowcase. Get downstairs. Leave her alone to change and get the hell into your room where you belong. Then shut the door and don't even think about coming out again.

But I stood there staring at her for ten more seconds, my hands clenched in fists at my sides. I wanted to kiss her so fucking badly. Just once, to know what those sweet little lips would feel like on mine. To hold her in my arms. I found myself wondering, on a scale of one to ten, exactly *how* wrong it would be. A seven? An eight?

I shoved my hands in my pockets.

She glanced over her shoulder into the bathroom. "Guess I'll get changed."

I nodded. "Okay. 'Night."

"'Night." She went into the bathroom and shut the door, and I slumped over with a sigh of relief.

Fuck. That was close.

Then I ran to the linen closet, grabbed a spare pillowcase, and descended the stairs three at a time. I had to be out of the living room by the time she came down.

The problem was, I'm *shit* at changing pillowcases. I can get the old one off just fine, but fuck if I can get the new one on. Three minutes in, I was flustered and sweaty and still trying to shove that fat fucking pillow into the case—why the hell was this so difficult? Why was it sideways? Had the case shrunk in the dryer? Cursing, I switched on a lamp and tried again.

Of course, she came tiptoeing down the stairs in time to see me struggling with it. Giggling, she set her clothing on the couch and reached for the pillow. "What's happening here, is it fighting back?"

"Yeah." Gladly, I handed it over, groaning inwardly at the sight of her in my shirt. It was huge on her—the hem nearly reached her knees—but that was probably a good thing. I did *not* need to see any more of her bare legs.

"There." She slipped the pillowcase on with no trouble at all.

I shook my head. "What's the secret? And why do only women seem to know it?"

She hugged the pillow and gave me a devious smile. "I'll never tell."

God, she was cute. And sexy. And really, really close. The curtains were closed and only one lamp was on, making the room feel intimate. The house was sleepy and silent under the snow, and we were alone—whatever happened would be our secret. My mind went to a dangerous place. My heart was doing something scary in my chest.

Nothing can happen, I told myself. *Nothing.*

But instead of backing away from her and going to bed like I was supposed to, I reached for the pillow she held and tossed it onto the couch.

Her smile faded.

I moved closer to her. I took her face in my hands. I rubbed a thumb over her soft pink lips.

"You should tell me to go to bed," I said quietly.

"Why?" she whispered.

"Because if you don't, I'm going to kiss you."

Her hands slid up my chest as she rose on tiptoe. "Mack. Kiss me."

I lowered my mouth to hers, vowing that I'd only kiss her once—*one time*—just to know what it was like. Of course, that was before she opened her lips and invited my tongue between them. It was before she slipped her arms around my neck and pressed her chest to mine. It was before my hands moved down her sides and crept beneath the bottom of my shirt. And it was well before she jumped up and wrapped her legs around me, entreating my hands to slip beneath that ass I'd been thinking about all day.

Because after that, I was fucked.

My dick was hard as a rock. My adrenaline was pumping. My willpower had disintegrated.

I stumbled backward onto the couch and set her on my lap so she straddled my thighs. My hands stole underneath her shirt and hers slid into my hair. She sighed softly, pleadingly, as I covered her breasts with my palms and stroked her nipples with my thumbs. Her head fell to one side, and I moved my mouth down her throat, tasting her skin. My cock twitched, trapped between us.

She took my head in her hands and brought my lips back to hers, rocking her hips, rubbing herself against me.

Oh, God. This was getting precarious. Another minute of her grinding on me like that and I was going to embarrass us both by going off like a rocket, and I *really* didn't want to do that.

"Frannie." I put my hands on her shoulders and gently pushed her back. "We have to stop."

"Because of the kids?" she asked breathlessly.

"Because this is wrong." Actually, I'd forgotten all about the kids, which was yet *another* sign that this was not a good idea. It was killing my brain cells. "Because you're my co-worker and babysitter. Because you're my boss's daughter. Because I'm so much older than you. And because if you don't stop moving like that, something is going to happen."

"I don't mind."

"In my *pants*."

She laughed a little. "I knew what you meant. But it doesn't have to happen like that. We could …" She hesitated, and when she spoke again her voice was softer, shyer. "We could go to your bedroom."

I groaned. "No. We can't."

"But I want to. I've wanted this for a long time."

"Fuck, don't tell me that."

"Why not? It's the truth."

I shook my head, vowing to stay strong. "No."

"But—"

"*No*." Summoning up every ounce of willpower I had, and some I didn't, I lifted her up, set her down beside me, and stood up. "No buts."

She looked up at me. "You don't want to?"

"Christ. Of course I do." In fact, my hard-on was refusing to give up, and I had to adjust myself in my pants.

Her expression was amused as she watched me, her eyes taking in the obvious bulge at my crotch. "Then what's holding you back?"

"All the things I just said!" It was a struggle to keep my voice down. I was angry and wanted to yell—not at her, exactly, but just in general. At the situation. And definitely at myself. I ran a hand through my hair. "I'm sorry, Frannie. I shouldn't have kissed you. This is my fault."

She sighed resignedly and shook her head. "No, it's not."

"It is." I could barely look her in the eye, but I forced myself to. "I had *one job*—put the fucking pillowcase on the pillow and go to bed. Instead I took advantage of you."

She surprised me by rolling her eyes. "Please, Mack. You did not take advantage of me. If I hadn't been dying for you to kiss me, I'd have stayed upstairs until I was positive you were in your room. Or at least kept my pants on."

"You probably should have."

She nodded and looked down at her knees, which were pressed together. "Sorry."

I tried to take the edge off my voice. "You're too young, Frannie. And if we'd let this go any further tonight, we'd both have been sorry."

"Too young! I'm twenty-seven."

"And I'm *thirty*-seven."

She lifted her chin. "I don't care about the age difference."

I struggled with how else to communicate what I was thinking. "I'm only trying to protect you."

"Don't," she said tightly. "Don't say that. I'm so sick and tired of being denied something I want for myself and being told someone is doing it for my own good. I'm not a child, Mack. I don't need your protection." With that she angrily grabbed the pillow, stuck it at one end of the couch and lay back, throwing the blanket over her legs.

I was simultaneously sad to see them disappear and glad they weren't visible any longer.

"Goodnight," she said, pulling the blanket up to her chin and closing her eyes.

Accepting the fact that there was no way to exit this

situation gracefully—especially not with a massive, stubborn erection—I switched off the lamp and left the room.

Inside my bedroom, I shut the door and sat down on the foot of the bed, hands propped on my knees.

"Fuck," I whispered, squeezing my eyes shut. Why was my gut churning? Hadn't I done the right thing? Hadn't I put my own urges aside? Hadn't I done exactly what I'd have wanted another man to do if Frannie were one of my daughters, years from now? I flopped back on my bed and threw an arm over my eyes.

Christ. I didn't want to think about my daughters in the future. I didn't want to think about them *now*. And I didn't want to treat Frannie like she was one of them—because that's not how I saw her at all. But it was wrong to want her this way. I couldn't get past it.

Eventually, I dragged myself off the bed and into the bathroom to brush my teeth. Then I undressed down to my underwear, pulled on some sweatpants, turned off the light, and crawled beneath the covers alone, which I would probably do for the rest of my fucking life.

Except … I couldn't stop thinking about her. Those bare legs beneath the hem of my shirt. The taste of her kiss. The scent of her hair. The hard little tips of her breasts beneath my palms. The way she straddled my body and moved above me.

My dick was so hard, and it would feel so good to be inside her. My body was desperate for the release. And she'd wanted it too, hadn't she? Maybe she was just as lonely as I was. Maybe she was only looking for a little companionship. A little fun. A connection.

I found myself wavering. What would be the harm? We were two consenting adults, weren't we? Maybe once would be okay. Maybe we could have this one moment of insanity, and then go back to normal. Maybe all I needed was to get this out of my system.

And I was so sick and tired of feeling like my entire purpose in life was to be a Responsible Person. I used to be unpredictable. I used to be bold. I used to take risks and act on instinct and say *fuck the consequences*.

My feet touched the floor, and before I knew it, I was opening my bedroom door and moving through the dark.

Nine

Frannie

I STARED AT THE CEILING IN THE DARK, ALTERNATELY ANGRY AND humiliated.

He'd wanted me, hadn't he? Of course he had—I'd felt it between his legs. And he'd kissed me first! He'd put his hands all over my skin! My breasts ached as I recalled his touch, and the unrequited longing in my body refused to ease up. I was restless and irritated, with him and with myself.

Although it *was* kind of nice that he was trying to be noble and heroic about the whole sex thing. I understood his point—he worked for my dad, so technically, yes, I was the boss's daughter. And his part-time nanny. And ten years younger.

But dammit, I'd been harboring this crush on him forever. I didn't care about those other things. I wanted to *be* with him.

And now he knew it. Ugh.

I squeezed my eyes shut, feeling like a kid who'd made a total ass out of herself in front of her teacher crush. Had I really suggested he take me back to his bedroom? Shaking my head back and forth, I tried to erase the memory of his rejection.

So much for seduction.

But the longer I lay there, awake and shivering a little beneath the blanket, the more I realized I wasn't sorry for trying. At least I'd taken a risk. Acted on an impulse. Granted, it hadn't gone as well as I'd hoped, but still—*Mack had kissed me.*

I turned onto my side, pulling the blanket up over my shoulder and closing my eyes.

I wasn't sure how long I'd been lying there when I felt a hand on my hip. I opened my eyes and saw Mack crouched next to me, balanced on the balls of his feet. Shirtless.

My breath caught.

He put a finger to his lips.

My heart started to pound. Was this real or a dream?

Without wanting to know for sure, I put my hand in his and rose from the couch. He led me through the dining room and into his bedroom, closing the door soundlessly behind me.

"Mack. What are you doing?" I whispered.

Instead of answering, he pushed me back against the door and kissed me hard and deep, his arms caging me on either side. "I changed my mind."

"Why?"

"Because I've been lying here for fucking hours and I can't stop thinking about how much I want you." His voice was quiet but gravelly, more growl than whisper.

"But you said—"

"I know what I said. But I've decided I'd rather be reckless than responsible tonight. If you're in, I'm in."

I put my hands on his chest and pushed him back. "I'm in."

Then I grabbed the bottom of the shirt I wore and whipped it over my head. Immediately our bodies came together, our bare chests pressed tight, our mouths sealed. Somehow, we managed to make it over to the bed, where he worked his pants off and stretched out above me. My heart was pumping so furiously, I was nearly afraid the doctors were wrong and there *was* something it couldn't handle—getting naked with Declan MacAllister.

I shivered.

"Are you cold?" he asked.

"Are you serious?"

He smiled down at me in the dark. The warmth and weight of his masculine, muscular body was like heaven, and I wrapped my arms and legs around him. His erection pressed hard against me.

"We have to be quiet," he whispered, his breath on my lips.

"I can be quiet," I promised.

"Good." He kissed me then, sending stars shooting throughout my body, to the ends of every finger and toe. I kissed him back like I'd never kissed anyone before, like he was the air I needed to breathe. I loved the warmth of his skin on mine, the way he smelled, the thickness of his chest.

Mack, Mack, Mack.

He put his hands on my breasts, making me arch into his touch and bite my lip to keep from sighing too loudly. He moved his mouth down my throat and chest, stroked my tingling nipples with his tongue, teased them into unbearably hard peaks that he sucked and flicked and caught between his teeth. I wove my hands into his hair, writhing rapturously beneath him. When he kissed a path down my belly, I began to panic that I wouldn't be able to keep my promise about being quiet.

He barely lifted his mouth from me as he dragged my underwear from my legs. Then his head totally disappeared beneath the blanket, and he pushed my thighs apart.

At the first sweep of his tongue, I yelped. I couldn't help it. Immediately, I slapped a hand over my mouth. I heard him laugh before he gave me another long and luscious stroke across my clit. I yelped again and clapped the other hand over the first.

Mack pushed the blanket off his head. "Should I stop?"

I shook my head. Vehemently.

"Then you have to be quiet, angel. Shhhhh." He returned to what he'd been doing, and I whimpered helplessly behind my palms. He slid a finger inside me, and I covered my face with a pillow. He sucked my clit into his mouth while he fucked me with one finger, then two, causing my body to hum and tighten and fill with uncontrollable longing, until finally it was too much for me to contain and everything burst wide open in an explosion of stars that rained down around me.

I *might* have been quiet. I wasn't really sure.

With one last kiss on my inner thigh, Mack moved up my body again. "Jesus Christ," he said, his voice raw.

"Was I too loud?" I whispered.

"I have no idea. I was too busy trying not to come from the way you taste." He kissed my neck. "And the way you move." He kissed my jaw. "And the way it's going to feel when I get inside you." He covered my mouth with his, and I twined my limbs around him, desperate for the very same thing. I could feel how big and hard he was as he rocked his hips above me.

"Yes," I said against his lips. "I want you inside me. Now."

Mack leaned over me to open the nightstand drawer. Ten seconds later, he'd shoved his underwear off his legs and was kneeling between my legs, rolling a condom on. I'd seen other guys do this twice before, but it was always awkward and fumbling, like they hadn't wanted me to even look at them. Granted, those had been skinny adolescent boys compared to the man in front of me now. He was mature and confident, rugged and strong. Everything about him exuded masculinity, from the stubble on his chin to the hair on his chest, to his muscular arms and thick, hard cock.

But I barely had time to admire his silhouette in the shadowy dark before he was above me again, positioning himself between my legs, then easing inside me. Slowly. Inch by hot, rock-solid inch.

I took a few deep breaths and closed my eyes as my body got used to being stretched so tight and filled so completely.

"Are you okay?" he asked. "You can tell me to slow down." But he was already starting to move, his hips undulating over mine in deep, unhurried strokes.

Echoing his rhythm, I moved my hips beneath his, sliding my hands down his back and whispering in his ear. "I'm more than okay. I want this so much."

He kept the rhythm slow and steady, his voice low in my ear. "Do you know how many times I've thought about fucking you right here in this bed?"

"Tell me." I struggled to speak

"So many nights." He changed the angle, making me gasp and sink my teeth into his shoulder. "But you're even better than my fantasy. Sweeter. Hotter. And I fucking love how wet you are for me. It feels so damn good."

God, I loved his foul mouth. I'd donate every cent I had into the swear jaw if he'd just keep talking to me that way.

And the way he moved, oh my *God* ...

Already aroused from my first orgasm, my body was more than responsive to a second one. Within a few minutes, I felt myself at the edge of the cliff once more, and every deep, hard thrust of his cock pushed me closer to jumping off. And if Mack's strangled moans and ragged breaths were any indication, he was just as close.

I clawed at his skin. I choked back cries. I grabbed his ass and pulled him into me, wanting *more, more, more*, even though I knew my body couldn't take it. "Mack," I begged. "*Mack* ..." Just saying his name, feeling it on my lips as he moved inside me, was a kind of ecstasy.

Sex with Mack was unlike anything I'd ever experienced before. Rougher. Deeper. More intense. It felt like the *real thing*, like the times before were silly imitations. And every sensation was heightened by the fact that we couldn't be loud. It was damn near impossible! All my effort was needed to keep from crying out—in pleasure, in pain, in total disbelief that this was actually happening.

Then he was cursing into the pillow beneath my head and his muscles clenched and I felt his orgasm rippling through his body into mine. It sent me spiraling over the heights, head over heels, spinning and falling and pulsing and holding him close as we shared this insanely powerful, extraordinary thing.

A few moments later, he lifted his chest off mine and pulled out. "I'll be right back."

"Okay," I said, disappointed he wanted to get up so fast.

While he was in the bathroom, I lay there clutching the blankets beneath my chin. I couldn't believe this! Just to be sure it wasn't a dream, I pinched myself. Hard.

Nope. It's real.

But now what? I couldn't actually sleep in here, could I? No, I should go back out to the couch. We did not need his kids discovering me in his bedroom in the morning. I found my underwear at the bottom of the bed, yanked them on, and was hunting around on the floor for my T-shirt when Mack opened the bathroom door. Light spilled into the bedroom.

"Hey," he said.

"Hey." Spying the shirt on the floor, I straightened up and slipped it over my head.

"Um, do you want to use the bathroom?"

"Oh … sure." He stepped aside as I passed him, giving me way more space than I needed to get by, which seemed kind of weird since his sweaty, naked body had been tangled up with mine for the last thirty minutes. That was a move you made passing someone in the hallway at work, not in the bedroom after sex. Were we going backward now?

In the bathroom, I shut the door behind me and cleaned up a little, trying not to read too much into it. But something felt off. I dried my hands and paused for a moment before reaching for the doorknob. After a couple deep breaths, I turned off the light and opened the door, hoping I'd been wrong.

My eyes weren't used to the dark, and I wasn't sure where he was at first. It took me a moment to realize *he wasn't even in the room.* I stood there for a minute, confused and blinking at the empty bed, when the bedroom door opened. Mack entered, holding the pillow I'd been using on the couch. He wore sweatpants and a T-shirt.

"Hey," he whispered. "I was just switching pillows."

"Switching pillows?"

"Yeah. Moving mine out there and bringing yours in here. I'll sleep on the couch and you can have the bed."

"That's not necessary. I can sleep on the couch."

"I'll just tell the girls I offered you the bed when I realized how cold it was out there."

It actually hadn't been that cold out there, but suddenly it felt damn near Arctic in here. "Mack, I—"

"Do you want clean sheets on the bed?"

"What? No."

"Okay. Keep this closed, and hopefully the kids aren't too loud when they come down. You can sleep in a little." He grabbed the door handle and began pulling it shut behind him. "Night."

"Wait a minute. Mack." I walked toward the doorway. "Come back in here a sec."

He hesitated, but then did as I asked and entered his bedroom again, closing the door. "What?"

"Well …" I folded my arms over my chest. "What now?"

"What do you mean?"

"I mean, are we just going to pretend this didn't happen?"

"I think that's best. Don't you?"

Of course not. I wanted to ride off into the sunset with him. Cue the music. Roll the credits. "I … I don't know. I guess so."

"It is. Trust me on this, Frannie." He'd adopted a sort of I'm Older And Wiser tone that made me feel five years old. "Tonight was a nice break from the norm but it can't happen again."

Nice break from the norm?

Nice?

I'd just experienced the most unbelievable, mind-blowing, earth-shattering sex imaginable. My life would never be the same. And he'd thought it was *nice*?

I wanted to die.

"Right," I said, glad the lights were off so he couldn't see how mortified I was. "Okay. It didn't happen."

"Good. We agree." He sounded relieved. "And now that it's out of our system, we can just go back to the way it was before. 'Night."

He was out the door before I could even say it back.

Confused, hurt, and embarrassed, I crawled back into the bed, which smelled like him. Curling up on my side with a pillow in my arms, I fought off the lump swelling in my throat.

Then I was angry.

Grow up, Frannie. You wanted to be treated like an adult? Free to make your own mistakes? Here you are—a great big plate of THIS IS WHAT IT FEELS LIKE, served cold with a side of humiliation. And it won't do you any good to cry over it.

What, did you think he was going to confess his undying love just because he gave you a couple orgasms in the middle of the night? Did you think you two would be a couple now? What a joke.

Sometimes sex is just sex, and you're acting like a teenager, sniveling into a pillow in the dark. No wonder he thinks you're too young for him. You knew your feelings for him were pointless from the start, so don't pretend otherwise.

Only a child believes in fairy tales.

Ten

Mack

I HURRIED OUT TO THE COUCH AND STRETCHED OUT, TOSSING the blanket over my legs.

Jesus, that had felt good. Even better than I'd imagined—and I'd imagined it a lot. Everything about it had been really intense—the heat, the chemistry, the connection. I hadn't felt that in years, if ever. Maybe it was the whole forbidden aspect, maybe it was the fact that I'd been fantasizing about her illicitly for months, or maybe my dick was really that starved for attention after a year of celibacy, but honest to God, I could have wept after that orgasm.

For a moment, I let myself imagine what it would be like if I were younger and didn't have kids. If I were free to pursue her. Win her. Keep her. Christ, I'd fucking spoil her rotten all the time. She was that perfect combination of sexy and sweet—it drove me crazy in the best possible way. In another life, I'd have done everything possible to make her mine.

But as it stood, I'd meant what I said. As good as the sex had been, we couldn't do it again. She was still too young, she was still the boss's daughter, she was still the nanny, and

I was in no position to pursue *anyone.*

Thank God she agreed with me that we should just pretend it never happened and go back to the way things were.

I really didn't know what I'd do without her.

In the morning, the girls came down in their pajamas and asked where Frannie was.

"She's in my room," I told them, yawning and pulling the blanket over my shoulder. "It was too cold out here, so I told her to take the bedroom and I slept on the couch."

None of them batted an eye. "Can we wake her up now?" Felicity asked. "We want to make the monkey bread."

"No. Don't." Reluctantly, I sat up. Scratched my stomach.

Winifred giggled. "I saw Daddy's hairy belly."

"Ewww!" the older two chorused.

"Hey," I said, grabbing Winnie and throwing her across my lap. "I do not have a hairy belly."

"Yes, you do," squealed Felicity. "And some on your chest!"

"Hey, listen. Where I come from, a man should have some hair on his chest. And I'm a man."

But for a second, I wondered what Frannie had thought of my body. I wasn't in my twenties anymore, and while I was physically fit, I didn't have one of those carefully groomed, perfectly smooth, manscaped male bodies. She hadn't seemed to mind, and I'd been too turned on to give a fuck about it last night, but now I hoped she hadn't been disappointed ... I found myself saying a quick prayer. *Please, God, let it have been even half as good for her as it was for me.*

Shoving last night out of my head, I rose to my feet and threw Winnie over my shoulder like a sack of potatoes. "Be quiet now, and we'll go find something for breakfast."

They whined and protested, but they followed me into the kitchen and watched as I began opening the fridge, the freezer, and multiple cupboards. Of course, they rejected everything I offered them—waffles, oatmeal, pancakes, eggs, toast, cereal, granola bars.

"Come on, guys. You have to pick something. It's going on eight, and I have a lot of snow to get rid of before we can go anywhere."

"But we want monkey bread," Felicity insisted.

"Well, I don't fucking know how to make it."

That's when I heard my bedroom door open, and then footsteps on the dining room's creaky oak floor. Frannie tiptoed into view, hair mussed, arms crossed over her chest. "Morning," she said.

I wasn't prepared for the sight of her. My heart skidded. My throat went dry. My dick twitched in my pants.

I moved behind the island and cleared my throat. "Morning."

"Daddy doesn't know how to make anything good for breakfast," Millie complained. I felt like pinching her. "Can you make breakfast?"

Frannie smiled at her. "Sure. Let me just get dressed real quick, okay?"

"Yay! Okay."

Without another look at me, Frannie went into the living room to retrieve her clothes. Then she must have gone upstairs to the bathroom to change, because she didn't come back to the kitchen until she was fully dressed.

Our eyes met only briefly before she looked away.

"So," she said, pushing up her sleeves. "In all honesty, girls, I don't think we have the right ingredients for monkey bread. But from what I remember seeing in the pantry yesterday, I think we can make some awesome gluten-free banana muffins with chocolate chips. Does that sound good?"

"Yes!" Millie rubbed her hands together. "Can I help?"

"Definitely." Frannie set to work, giving the girls small, age-appropriate tasks. "Millie, you peel and sort of chop up two bananas. Felicity, can you grab the sour cream and eggs from the fridge? And Winnie, can you help me remember where the chocolate chips might be hiding?"

I put on a pot of coffee and stayed out of their way, checking messages on my phone, texting Sawyer that I'd be late, glancing out the front window to see if the street had been plowed yet (it had), and the back to see how much snow the blower would have to handle (a lot). When the coffee was ready, I poured a cup and asked Frannie if she'd like one, too.

"Sure, thanks," she said without taking her eyes off what she was doing.

"Milk? Sugar?" I asked, wishing she'd look at me like she had last night, with adoration in her eyes. Or at least warmth.

"Just black."

I poured her a cup and left it on the island while I sipped mine standing on the dining room side of the breakfast bar. The girls were happily following her directions, not arguing, and working harder than they ever worked in the kitchen for me. They were even rinsing the dishes as they went along, and putting them in the dishwasher. A few times, I tried to catch Frannie's eye and smile, but she never seemed to look in my direction.

After a while, I gave up and went into my room to get dressed. I tried not to look at the bed and think of her bare limbs between my sheets, but it was impossible. Not only did I look, but I went over and grabbed a pillow, lifting it to my face and inhaling deeply. Her scent lingered on the cotton, sweet and sexy at the same time, just like she was. My stomach muscles tightened, and I—

"Daddy?"

I glanced at the door, which apparently I hadn't shut all the way. Felicity had pushed it open and stood there blinking at me with owlish eyes behind her glasses. "What are you *doing*?"

"Nothing." I tossed the pillow onto the tangled sheets. "I was going to make the bed. What do you need?"

"We can't find the vanilla extra. Do we have any?"

"Vanilla *extract*?" I frowned. "I have no idea. It's not in the pantry? Or the cupboard above the fridge? Sometimes I stick stuff up there we don't use that often."

"We can't reach that cupboard."

"Ah. Okay, I'll look." I followed her back to the kitchen, where Frannie was doing her best to reach the handle above the fridge without much luck.

I puffed my chest out a bit, feeling like a Man Coming to Save the Day. "Here. Let me." Coming up behind her—way closer than necessary—I reached over her head and pulled the cupboard open.

She immediately ducked out of my way.

I stared into the cupboard without seeing anything for a moment, then refocused. "Is this what you need?" I grabbed a small brown plastic bottle and handed it to Frannie.

She inspected the label, then twisted off the cap and sniffed it. "Yes. It actually expired this month, but it smells fine. Okay, girls ..." She turned away from me and resumed baking with the kids. I realized she hadn't looked at me once.

Fine. Be that way.

Irrationally angry, I stomped off to my room, got dressed, then stomped into the back hall to put on all my winter crap—boots, coat, scarf, hat, gloves—without looking at anyone. When I was ready, I risked a glance at her and caught her looking at me. Immediately she turned in the opposite direction.

I went out the back door and closed it with a bang.

After snow blowing my driveway and Mrs. Gardner's next door, I shoveled both front walkways and porch steps, then moved on to the back. When I was done there, I grabbed a shovel and went out to the curb to dig out Frannie's car, although what I really felt like doing was marching into the house and demanding to know why she was giving me the cold shoulder.

Because the more I thought about it, the more I decided this was *not* what we had agreed on. We said we were going to pretend it never happened and go back to the way things were before.

This wasn't how things had been before!

Full of furious energy, I finished the job and stomped back into the house. The kitchen was blissfully warm and smelled heavenly. But I was grumpy as fuck. "Can I have your keys?" I asked Frannie, who was loading the dishwasher.

Without answering, she went over to her purse and took them out. Then she handed them to me without meeting my eyes or saying a thing.

I glanced toward the living room, but didn't see the kids. "Where are the girls?"

"Getting dressed." She put a detergent pod in the dishwasher, closed the door, and started it.

"Are you mad at me?" I blurted, unable to stand it anymore.

She began wiping down the counter. "What would I be mad about?"

I rolled my eyes. "Last night."

"Last night didn't happen, remember?"

I stared at her back for a moment, then stormed out the back door, slamming it behind me. Hard.

Her car started fine, so after I'd taken a quick shower and gotten dressed, we all piled into it for the drive to Cloverleigh. I was behind the wheel, Frannie was in the passenger seat, and the girls were squeezed in the back. The tension in the front seat was icy and thick.

"Daddy, what are we going to do at Cloverleigh?" Felicity asked. "Can we see the animals?"

"I don't know," I said tersely.

"Can we take a sleigh ride?" Winnie asked.

"I don't think so."

"But Frannie said we could."

"We can't take up all Frannie's time."

"It's fine," Frannie said stiffly.

"Will we have lunch there?" Millie wondered. "I'm kind of hungry."

"I don't know," I snapped. "Stop with all the questions already."

"Jeez, why are you in such a bad mood?" Millie asked.

"I'm not in a bad mood!" I roared. From my right I could

feel Frannie's eyes on me. I clenched my jaw and gripped the wheel tighter.

When we arrived at Cloverleigh, Daphne Sawyer came rushing out from behind the desk. "There you are! I was so worried about you all on these roads. Was the driving awful?"

"It wasn't too bad," I said. But I couldn't seem to unclench my jaw.

She hugged Frannie. "I'm so glad to see you. And you, too, girls," she added, smiling at my daughters. "Mr. Sawyer said you can take the sleigh out this afternoon."

"And how about lunch up in my apartment?" asked Frannie.

The girls jumped up and down with excitement at both ideas. After thanking Daphne and Frannie, and warning the kids to behave, I went back to my office and tried to get things done, but it was tough going.

My dark mood refused to lift. I barked at DeSantis when he checked with me about his new bottling line. I skipped lunch to punish myself and my stomach growled hungrily all afternoon. I swore at the guy from the towing company when he told me they were backed up because of the snow and he wasn't sure when they'd be able to get to my car. And all day long I kept glancing out the window, wondering if the kids were out in the sleigh with Frannie and whether she hated my guts for last night. Sure seemed like it this morning.

But I knew I hadn't forced her to do anything she didn't want to do. Had she faked her orgasms? Maybe I wasn't the stud I thought I was.

The thought did *not* sit well with me.

Or had I hurt her feelings somehow? Slighted her in

some way? Had I said something insensitive without realizing it?

Goddamn, I was fucking clueless about women.

Around four-thirty, my ex called. Of course.

I winced when I saw her name on my phone and gave the screen the finger, but I took the call. "Hello?"

"It's me," she said.

"I know." I pinched the bridge of my nose with two fingers. "What do you want?"

"I'm fine, thanks. How are you?" Her voice oozed sarcasm.

"Fine."

A heavy sigh. "I'm coming up this weekend."

"Have you told the kids?"

"No. I want to surprise them."

"Do you have a ticket already?"

"Not yet."

"Do me a favor, and don't say anything to the kids until you're sure you're coming," I said. "Last month, you didn't make it and they were devastated."

"I won't," she snapped. "That's how a surprise works, Mack. You don't say anything beforehand. And it's not my fault that I couldn't come last time. I was sick."

"Whatever. I just don't want them disappointed again."

"They won't be," she snapped. "I'll be there Friday."

"Fine." I ended the call and tossed my phone onto my desk. I felt like throwing it out the window. Why the hell did she bother coming at all? She didn't really care about them. And she'd probably spend the entire weekend badmouthing me.

Suddenly my office door swung open, and the girls came running in. They were red-cheeked and runny-nosed from the cold, and their hair was matted from their hats.

"Daddy!" Winnie said excitedly. "I got to drive the sleigh!"

"Me too," said Felicity, taking off her glasses to wipe the fog off them. "The horses' names were Scout and Cinnamon!"

"Frannie says we can make real hot chocolate in her apartment if it's okay with you," Millie bubbled. "So can we?"

I checked my watch. It was going on five and getting close to dinner time, but I still had some things to finish up. "That's fine. But come back down when you're done. We need to get going soon, although I have no idea how we're going to get home."

"Do you need a ride?" Frannie asked from the doorway. She'd changed clothes, and her long hair was in two gold-streaked braids over her shoulders. They made her look even younger than she was, and my heart sank even lower. She had no idea what she did to me.

"I might," I admitted. "I called the towing company, but they haven't gotten back to me yet. But I hate to put you out again."

"It's no big deal," she said, but there was still none of the warmth in her face that had been there yesterday. "I can take you. Come on, girls." She gathered them up and steered them into the hallway. "Let's go make our chocolate."

"Frannie, wait."

She looked back at me, her expression blank. "Yes?"

But what could I say with the kids right there within earshot?

I'm sorry, I mouthed.

She shrugged. "Don't worry about it."

"I don't mean about the ride home."

"I know what you mean." Then she disappeared, pulling the door shut behind her.

Cursing, I flopped back into my chair.

Two knocks on my door, and then it opened.

For a second, I thought maybe it would be Frannie, but it was DeSantis.

"Oh. Hey," I said despondently.

He laughed. "Not the warmest welcome I've ever received."

I sighed and rubbed my face with my hands. "Sorry. I'm having a shit day. What can I do for you?"

"I was going to ask if this was an okay time to talk about H.R. needs for spring, but it can wait."

"No, it's fine. Sit down."

DeSantis shook his head. "Let's talk tomorrow. Why don't you take off for today?"

"I can't even do that." Suddenly I looked up at him. "Hey, can I ask you for a favor?"

"Sure. What's up?"

"Could you drive me and the kids home? Whenever you're ready to go is fine."

He nodded. "Ready whenever you are."

"And if it's not too much trouble, could we try giving my car a jump? It's in my garage, so we'd have to get it out."

"No problem."

"Thanks. Give me about twenty minutes to round everybody up."

"I'll be in my office."

I picked up my phone and texted Frannie. **Thanks for the offer, but no need to drive us back. DeSantis can take us.**

OK.

I glared at my screen and typed another message.

I'll come get the kids in fifteen minutes.

OK.

I sat there stewing for a moment, then set my phone aside and tried to answer some emails. But only about three minutes had gone by when I gave up on concentration, slammed my laptop shut, and marched out of my office.

What the fuck did she want from me? I'd apologized. I'd asked her if she was mad. If she had something to say, why didn't she say it?

She was being immature and ridiculous, and I was going to tell her so.

Eleven

Frannie

WE'D BARELY GOTTEN UP TO MY SUITE WHEN HE TEXted me that I didn't have to drive him home.

Good, I thought. The less I had to see him, the better.

All day long, I'd done my best to pretend nothing had happened, but it was useless. He was all I could think about. And I didn't know how to act around him now—there was this weird tension between us that hadn't existed before. He didn't seem too comfortable around me, either. I'd never seen him as grouchy and mad as he'd been by the time we'd left the house.

I wanted to ask him what was wrong, but I couldn't. Every moment in his presence was torture for me. All I wanted was to get to the end of this day so I could curl up in a ball on my couch and have a good ugly cry. I'd thought being with him that way would be a dream come true, but this felt like a nightmare.

When the hot chocolate was done, I ladled it into mugs for the girls, then let them squirt it with whipped cream and decorate it with sprinkles.

"This is like dessert before dinner," said Millie, licking whipped cream off her spoon.

As soon as I got them situated at the counter, there was a knock at my door. I glanced at my phone, which told me it had been little more than five minutes since he'd texted he'd be up to get the kids in fifteen.

I went to the door and pulled it open, and there he was in the hallway, looking restless and agitated. His hair was kind of a mess, and his hands were fisted at his sides. Still, my heart went crazy at the sight of him.

"They're not quite done yet," I said.

"That's fine. Can I talk to you?"

Shrugging, I opened the door so he could come in, but he shook his head.

"Out here in the hallway."

"Oh." I glanced at the kids. "Okay." Making sure the door was unlocked, I went out into the hall and pulled it shut behind me. Then I leaned back against it and folded my arms. "What's up?"

"Frannie." He was in no mood.

"What?"

"Stop it."

"Stop what? I'm doing exactly what you told me to do—pretending nothing happened. Going back to the way things were before. You're the one who's angry."

"I'm angry because ..." He gestured back and forth between us. "This isn't how it was before."

"What do you mean?" I asked, although I knew exactly what he meant.

"You didn't freeze me out like this before. You didn't refuse to look at me. We could joke around and talk."

"Maybe I don't feel like joking around."

He crossed his arms. "Why not?"

I decided to be honest. Pretending was clearly *not* my thing. "Because, Mack. Last night meant everything to me and nothing to you."

His arms came uncrossed and his solid chest stuck out. "That's not true. It *did* mean something to me, Frannie."

"Then why do we have to pretend it never happened? Why can't it happen again?"

"Because there are too many complications. You know I'm in an impossible situation."

"No, I don't. Last night, you asked me what chances I would take if I wasn't scared. I didn't get the opportunity to answer you then, but I'll tell you right now—I'd take a chance on you."

His face softened, and his aggressive posture deflated a bit. "You don't know what you're saying."

Tears blurred my eyes, but I smiled. "Maybe I don't. Maybe I *am* too young and immature. Maybe I'm stupid to think that you and I could ever be more than friends."

"You're not stupid, Frannie. And in another life, we could be."

I shook my head. "There is no other life, Mack. This is the only one we get. Look, you probably have sex like that all the time, but—"

Mack's jaw dropped. "Are you kidding me? I haven't had sex in over a year. And last night was fucking amazing. I haven't been able to think about anything else all day long."

Braver now, I came off the door and stood up taller. "Then I don't understand why you can't give me a chance. I *feel* something for you, Mack. I have for a long time—I've just been too scared to act on it."

"You were right to be scared." He came toward me,

and for a moment, I thought he was going to take me in his arms. But at the last second, he reached beyond me for the door handle. Then he spoke low over his shoulder. "Don't waste your chances on me, Frannie. I've got nothing to offer you in return."

An hour later, I was a solid twenty minutes into my ugly cry when I heard knocking on my door. For God's sake, now what? I grabbed a handful of tissues on my way to the door and blew my nose before opening it. My sister Chloe stood in the hall.

She'd been about to say something, but at the sight of me, her eyes went wide. "Jeez Louise," she said. "What happened to you?"

"What do you want?" I asked, a little angrier than intended.

"Well, I was gonna ask your opinion on some new label designs, but maybe now's not a good time."

"It's not." I stomped back over to the tissue box on my kitchen counter and yanked another one out.

"What's wrong?" My sister came in and shut the door behind her.

It was on the tip of my tongue to say "nothing," since I didn't usually confide in her about stuff like this, nor did she in me, but while I blew my nose, I figured, *what the hell?* Maybe we'd have a closer relationship if I *did* tell her these things. And maybe she'd have some advice.

"You can't tell anyone," I said.

She held up three fingers. "Scout's honor."

"I slept with Mack," I told her.

Her chin about hit the floor. "You *what*?"

"I slept with Mack."

"Holy shit. *Holy. Shit.* I gotta sit down." She sank onto a chair at my table as I stuffed soggy tissues into the trash. "*You* slept with Mack? Like you …" She made a fist with one hand and punched the palm of the other a few times.

I rolled my eyes. "Yes, Chloe. I had sex with him. You can say it."

"Whoa. I mean—whoa." She blinked at me. "Sorry, I'm just really surprised."

"That I did it?" I asked, marching over to the table and dropping into the seat next to her. "Or that I'm telling you about it?"

"Both." Then she shrugged. "Actually, I'm surprised you have sex at all."

"Of course I have sex," I snapped. "I'm a grown woman, not that anyone around here seems to realize it."

"Hey, relax," she said, reaching over to pat my arm. "You don't have to get mad. I'm glad you're telling me. Frankly, it's a relief. It makes you human. It's just a surprise, that's all."

"It's a surprise that I'm *human*?" I screeched.

"Kind of." She lifted her shoulders. "You've always been such a Mommy's girl. So well-behaved and just … *good*. I never knew there was another side to you. You've never shown it to me."

I felt more tears coming and fought them off. "Well, I'm tired of being treated like a little girl, so I guess I'd better stop acting like it."

"You're off to a good start," she murmured wryly. "So, Mack, huh?"

"Mack." Hard to believe that less than twenty-four

hours ago, I'd been whispering his name while he was inside me.

Chloe shook her head. "You want to hear something funny? At the Christmas party last year, April *swore* something was up with you two."

"She did?"

"Yes. She kept seeing you guys talking and looking at each other, and she asked me what I thought, and I said no way." She laughed. "Guess I was wrong."

"Yeah," I said miserably. "I've had a crush on him forever."

"So when did *this* happen?" Chloe punched her fist again.

"Last night. I was watching the girls and stayed overnight because of the weather. After the girls went to bed, one thing kind of led to another."

"Got it. So what happened afterward? Was he a jerk?"

I wiped my nose on my sleeve. "Yes and no. He said we had to forget it happened and go back to being just friends—I'm too young, I'm the boss's daughter, blah blah blah."

My sister shrugged. "He's not *wrong*, exactly."

I glared at her. "Yes he *is*, Chloe. I'm not that young. And I can't help who my father is."

"So what did you say?"

"I agreed, because I didn't want to seem like a baby, and because I was scared to say how I really felt. So I tried to pretend like I didn't care. But it was so awkward." I cringed, shaking my head. "We had to bring the kids to Cloverleigh because they had a snow day, and when he came up here to get them, he said he wanted to talk to me in the hall. Then he accused me of freezing him out."

She rolled her eyes. "Of course. He wants it both ways."

"I gave up pretending and told him my feelings were hurt. That I couldn't just forget it as easily as he could." I got up and went for the tissue box again, trying to recall what else he'd said. "He claimed it wasn't easy for him either, but that he's in an impossible situation. And he said he had nothing to offer me."

"Hmm." Chloe leaned her elbow on the table and propped her chin in her hand. "Maybe he's right. I mean, he just got divorced and he's got three little kids. He probably doesn't want a girlfriend."

I blew my nose. "It's not like I'd be demanding. And I love his kids."

"I'm sorry, hon." She gave me a sympathetic look. "I don't know what to say."

Sighing, I lowered myself into my chair. "I'm curious about his divorce. Like what happened. Do you think Sylvia would know anything?" Sylvia and Mack had gone to school together, and they'd been pretty good friends.

"It's possible. They used to be pretty good friends. But she's been gone for so long." She shrugged. "You could ask her."

I shook my head. "I can't."

"Why not?"

"Because we don't talk like that. She'd think it was weird."

My sister sat up straight and nodded slowly. "Frannie, I'm just going to say this out loud because I'm thinking it and even though I have worked *very hard* on my filter over the years, I feel like it's something you should hear."

"Okay," I said hesitantly.

"I've never been in here like this before. Sitting down with you, just the two of us. Having a really personal conversation. Sharing secrets." She leaned forward. "And the reason is because you've never invited me."

"Well ..." I felt embarrassed all of a sudden. "You're always so busy. And I didn't think you'd want to talk to me. I don't really feel like any of you want to talk to me. You'll think this is stupid, but I feel like you're all part of this secret sister club and I'm not in it.

"I don't think it's stupid at all," she said seriously. "It feels that way to us too, sometimes. And a lot of it stems from when we were little. Mom and Dad were always so worried about you. They kept you apart from us a lot. We felt like you were in this bubble and we all had to be so careful."

"I hate that," I said, my teeth clenched. "I know I can't be mad that they were so protective of me, but do you know how lonely it was, growing up like that? I wasn't close to you guys, I didn't have school friends, I spent tons of time in the hospital with only my parents and the nurses for company, and even after I was perfectly healthy, Mom and Dad wanted to *keep* me in that bubble. They *still* do!"

"I'm sorry," Chloe said. "Now I can see that it must have been lonely for you, but back then, we were all just trying to get some attention, and it didn't seem like there was enough to go around."

"You must have resented me," I said. It was a relief to finally say these things out loud. "You were the baby until I came along."

Chloe thought about it. "It wasn't so much about not being the youngest anymore as it was just basically feeling ignored. My therapist thinks that's why I got into the pattern of acting out."

I nodded, my eyes filling. "I'm sorry, Chloe. I've thought about it a lot as I've gotten older and wished things were different, but I didn't know how to approach it."

"Hey." She put her hand over mine. "It wasn't your fault. I think my therapist is wrong about that anyway—I think being a shithead teenager was just in my blood. And we can't change the past, but I definitely think we can be better in the future about talking openly and letting each other in a little."

I sniffed. "I'd like that. You guys have such great relationships with each other."

She shrugged. "Sometimes. I mean, April and I are pretty close. Sylvia's been kind of distant for a while, but she's all wrapped up in her perfect life. And Meg, who the hell knows what she's thinking? We're the closest in age, but I haven't spoken to her in months. Mom's always complaining that she never calls."

"Mom and I had an argument yesterday."

She looked surprised. "What about?"

I filled her in on my hopes to start my own business, the offer I'd had from Mrs. Radley, and our mother's immediate dismissal of the idea.

"I think it's a great idea," she said excitedly. "Fuck Mom on this one. Really. I love her, but she needs to let go of you or eventually you're going to hate her."

I didn't think I could ever hate my mother, but I knew what Chloe meant. "Maybe I'll try talking to her again."

She nodded thoughtfully. "Do you *need* their help? Because you certainly don't need their permission."

I sighed, fitting the tips of my thumbnails together. "I might be able to do it on my own. Get a small business loan from the bank, or see what Mrs. Radley would be willing to invest. But it would be really hard for me to take on such a big venture without their support—and I'm not talking only about financial support." I peeked at her. "You probably think that's childish of me."

"Not at all." She reached over and patted my arm. "There's nothing wrong with wanting your family's support, and I agree it would be better for you to have it. So talk to Mom again. And get Dad in the room this time. I think he might be more willing to see your side. He's more logical— Mom's emotions get the best of her."

I nodded. "Thanks, that's good advice. I also think it would help if I went in armed with some actual numbers and statistics. Maybe even some possible locations."

"Definitely," Chloe agreed. "I can help you there. Hey, have you eaten yet? Why don't we get some food and just hang out here tonight? Do a little research."

"Okay." I felt my mood lift a little at the prospect of spending an evening with my sister. Something had shifted between Chloe and me—it felt like a barrier had been removed. And it would be good to have an ally in the battle for my parents' support.

Something good might come out of this day yet.

Twelve

Mack

AFTER TALKING TO FRANNIE IN THE HALLWAY, I GATHERED up the kids and got them into their winter gear as quickly as I could. I avoided eye contact with her the entire time. She had no idea the effect her words had on me, how hard it had been to shoot down the idea of being more than her friend, how badly I wanted to take her in my arms and say *yes, please give me a chance. Give me a thousand of them, because that's how many I'll need.* She had no idea about any of it.

And that's how it had to stay.

My first priority in life was my children, and my second was my job, so that I could provide a good life for them. That left no room for anything else. She couldn't possibly understand how thin I was already stretched, trying to be two parents. She'd end up hating me.

So when the door closed behind us, I breathed a sigh of relief and hustled the kids downstairs to where DeSantis was waiting. After retrieving Winnie's booster seat from my office, we trudged out to the parking lot and piled into his SUV. Felicity and Winifred started babbling immediately about their day and kept it up the entire ride to the house, but I noticed Millie stayed silent, preoccupied with her phone. It set off an alarm bell in my head. I'd have to check in with her later.

The roads were finally decent, so it was only about fifteen minutes later that DeSantis pulled up at the house. The girls went inside while he and I managed to get my car out of the garage and into a spot where he could get close enough to hook up the cables. It wasn't easy, and our hands were about frozen by the time we were done, but it worked. I thanked him profusely and promised him a beer after work as soon as I could manage it.

Later that night, after the dinner dishes were done and showers were taken and the day's deposits were made in the swear jar, I spent some time with each of the girls in their rooms.

"So did you have a good time at Cloverleigh?" I asked Winifred, setting aside the book I'd just read aloud to her.

"Yes. The sleigh ride was so much fun."

I got off her bed and switched off her light. "Was that your favorite part?"

"Yes. Can I have a horse?"

"No."

She sighed. "I didn't think so. Can we take another sleigh ride tomorrow?"

I laughed, leaning down to kiss her. Her damp hair smelled like baby shampoo and made me want to stop time. "Maybe not tomorrow, but sometime. Goodnight."

"Wait, Daddy! Did you look under the bed?"

"Oh, sorry. I forgot." Kneeling on the floor, I performed the requisite monster check. "All clear. Just some dust bunnies."

She smiled. "Those are okay. Kiss Ned the Hammerhead from Shedd."

I dutifully planted a kiss on her stuffed shark, which she'd gotten from Shedd Aquarium in Chicago last summer and never let out of her sight if she could help it. "That thing does not look cuddly."

"I know, but I love him. I don't feel right if he's not next to me."

"Then I guess he can stay. Love you, princess."

"I love you too, Daddy."

Goodnight." Leaving her door open the way she liked it, I went into Felicity's room. Her nightlight glowed in the dark, and she was under the covers. "Tired?" I asked, sitting on the bed.

She yawned. "Yes."

"Did you have a fun snow day?"

"Yes. I love Frannie. She's so nice."

"She is." I thought of her hurt expression from earlier and my chest felt tight. What would happen if she decided she didn't want to nanny for me anymore? Then the girls would lose her, and it would be my fault completely. God, I'd really fucked this up.

"She's my favorite babysitter ever. She said she used to have nightmares too when she was my age."

"Really?"

"Yes. And then someone told her how certain rocks can help you relax and sleep better. She even gave me one, see?" She brought her hand out from under the covers and opened her fist. On her palm lay a small, smooth stone.

I switched on the lamp on her nightstand and looked closer. It was a crystal of some sort, with streaks of purple and green and lavender running through it. The perfect gift for Felicity. "That was nice of her."

She closed her fist and tucked her arm beneath the blankets again. "Can she sleep over again sometime?"

"Uh … we'll see." I switched off the lamp, leaned over and kissed her cheek. "Night, Mavis."

She giggled. "Night, Daddy."

"I love you."

"I love you, too."

Millie's bedroom door was closed, and I knocked gently. "Come in," she said.

When I opened the door, I saw her reading in bed by the light of the lamp on her nightstand. I went in and sat by her feet. "Hey."

"Hey." She didn't lift her eyes from her book.

"Everything okay?"

"I guess."

"You guess?" I took her paperback from her hands and closed it. "That's not very convincing."

"Dad, you lost my place," she said, annoyed.

"I'll find it again. Tell me what's wrong."

"Nothing." She played with some loose threads on her quilt.

"I don't believe you."

She shrugged. "I have a stomachache."

Concerned, I set her book on her nightstand. "Your stomach hasn't bothered you for months. Did something happen?"

"No."

I didn't believe her. Clearly there was an issue, but she wasn't going to tell me what it was. For a moment I panicked that it was something related to puberty, and I got lightheaded and sweaty. What the hell was I going to do when all those changes set in? God, why couldn't they stay young forever?

"Millie, do you ..." My voice cracked, and I cleared my throat. "Want the heating pad? Some Advil?"

"No. I'm fine, Dad." She rolled away from me onto her side. "'Night."

"'Night." I leaned over, kissed her head, and switched off her lamp. Her hair smelled sweet, too, but not like baby shampoo. More fruity. Like women's shampoo. Then I stood there a moment looking at her, wondering where the years had gone. It seemed like only yesterday that—

"Dad?"

"Yeah?"

"What are you doing?"

"Looking at you. Thinking that you're growing up too fast."

"Quit it. It's weird."

I laughed. "Sorry. I'm going now. You're sure you don't want the heating pad?"

"I'm sure. Goodnight."

"Goodnight." I reached her doorway and turned around. "I love you."

"Love you too."

I felt a little better as I went downstairs, but not much. Millie's stomachaches, like Felicity's nightmares and Winifred's monsters, had begun after their mother left and usually flared any time Carla said she was coming to visit, even though she rarely followed through.

In the kitchen, I went over to where Millie's phone was plugged in, picked it up, and entered her passcode. She and I had an agreement—I allowed her to have a phone, and she allowed me access to it at any time to make sure she wasn't on social media or texting with serial killers. Every now and then, I glanced at her messages, but mostly there were just long threads full of emojis between her and a few friends, and occasionally texts from her mother.

When I saw that Carla had been in touch today, Millie's stomachache made sense.

Hello darling, I just wanted to tell you how excited I am to come see you! Remember not to say anything to your sisters so the visit can be a surprise! I'm only telling you because you sent me the note saying how much you miss me. It was so sweet of you to write me, but hearing that you are sad because of me made me feel sad too. I had a migraine for days afterward. I really wish I could be there for the mother daughter fashion show you mentioned, but that date isn't good for me. But I will see you Friday and we'll have such a good time!

I set the phone down, my blood boiling. I'd specifically asked Carla not to tell the kids about her visit, and she'd gone behind my back immediately and messaged Millie. And how fucking dare she make Millie feel guilty for telling her mother she misses her! Seething, I paced the kitchen. I wanted to punch something. Throw something. Destroy something. Opening the back door, I took a few gulps of icy air to calm myself down, but it barely had an effect. Then I came in the house and downed a shot of whiskey.

Ten seconds later I was going up the stairs three at a time, then opening Millie's door. "Millie? You still awake, honey?"

"Yeah."

"Can I talk to you for a sec?" I asked, fighting for composure.

"Okay."

I walked over to her bed and sat down at her feet. "I saw the message from Mom on your phone. Is that what's bothering you?"

Silence. "She said she's coming to visit."

"I know."

"Is she really coming this time?"

"That, I don't know."

Millie rolled over and looked up at me. "Sometimes I really miss her and wish she was here. And sometimes I wish she would just stay away."

My throat got tight. "It's okay to wish that, honey. Everything you feel is okay."

"There's a mother-daughter fashion show at school," she went on sadly.

"I saw that. What's it for?"

"It's some kind of fundraiser. You get to make your own outfits. All my friends are doing it."

"Well, that's stupid and unfair," I snapped. "Not everybody has a mother around."

"All my friends do. Even if their parents are divorced, their mothers are still around."

I exhaled, guilt weighing heavily on my shoulders. "I'm sorry, Mills."

Millie was silent a moment. "Does she even love us anymore?"

"Of course she does." I leaned over her, bracing a hand above her shoulder and brushing her hair back from her face. "And so do I."

"I know you do."

It should have made me happy, but I still felt like somehow, it wasn't enough. I tried again. "Sometimes moms and dads decide they don't want to be married anymore, but they always love their children."

"But if you love someone, you want to *be* with them, don't you?"

"Well … yes. Usually. But love is complicated."

"It shouldn't be," she said with ferocity. "If you love someone, nothing else should matter. You should do everything you can to be with them as much as possible."

"I agree."

She was quiet for a moment. "Mom says you didn't love her enough and that's why she had to leave."

My composure slipped. "That's fucking ridiculous." Then I sighed. "Sorry. I'll put a dollar in the jar when I go downstairs."

"It's okay. You don't have to. I was mad when she said that too. It made me feel bad."

"You have *nothing* to feel bad about." Leaning forward, I pressed my lips to her forehead. "Listen. Maybe I wasn't good at loving her. Maybe I didn't try hard enough. I don't know. In all honesty, honey, I just felt confused most of the time. But what matters to me now is that you and your sisters know how much I love you and want to be the most awesome dad possible, even if your college funds are being depleted by the swear jar."

That brought a little smile.

"Hey, I've got an idea."

"What?"

"What if *I* did the fashion show with you?"

"*You?*"

I sat up tall and puffed out my chest. "Yes, me. I'm a good-looking dude, don't you think?"

She giggled. "I guess."

Getting off the bed, I did my best John Travolta

Saturday Night Fever strut across her room. "And I've got *moves*, Millsy."

"Oh my God, Dad. Please do not walk like that in front of my friends. Ever."

"Hey, listen. It is a dad's solemn duty to embarrass his children in their adolescent years as often as possible. So no promises."

"Are you really going to do the show with me?"

"Do you want me to?"

"Yes. But I need to ask and make sure it's okay to have a dad in the mother-daughter fashion show."

"If it isn't, we're suing them for discrimination," I said, pointing a finger at her.

She smiled, and I almost felt like things were okay in the world again. Maybe I wasn't Superdad, but I was doing this.

"'Night, honey." I blew her a kiss and headed for the door.

Downstairs, I folded some laundry, stacked everyone's piles in baskets, and opened up my laptop on the dining room table. I emailed Sawyer and DeSantis that I wouldn't be in tomorrow because of childcare issues, asked if meetings could please be rescheduled, and apologized for the late notice. Then I tried to tackle some of the work tasks that I'd been unable to finish during the day, but I still found it hard to concentrate.

At midnight, I finally gave up and went to bed, but even though I was tired, I couldn't fall asleep. I was mad at Carla, worried she wouldn't show, worried she *would* show, concerned about Millie, fearful I wasn't handling her questions right, anxious about the future, and desperate to make things right with Frannie again. But how?

I couldn't go backward and undo what we'd done. I

couldn't unhear the words she'd spoken. I couldn't unfeel this longing for her. But I couldn't act on it, either. My girls aside, Frannie deserved someone who could put her first, someone at the same stage of life she was in, who had all the time and energy in the world to dedicate to making her happy.

I was awake half the night wishing that someone could be me.

Thirteen

Frannie

A T THE RECEPTION DESK THE NEXT MORNING, I BRACED myself every time someone came in the front door of the inn, but Mack never showed up for work. Around noon, I casually asked my dad where he was, and he informed me that Mack had taken the day off.

Even though I should have been glad I didn't have to see him, I found myself wandering past his empty office anyway, feeling sad and lonely and torn. Had I made a mistake telling him how I really felt? Had that only made things worse? What if I'd ruined things between us forever and we could never look each other in the eye again?

Later that evening, he texted me.

Carla is coming to visit the kids on Friday. Can you still cover tomorrow?

There were so many other things I wanted to say to him, but in the end I replied with only one word.

Yes.

Three dots appeared on my screen, as if he were typing another message, but a few seconds later they disappeared, and no additional texts came through. Disappointed, I set my phone aside.

Then I opened my laptop to do a little digging around about small business loans and read whatever advice I could find about being a young female entrepreneur. It felt good to spend my energy on something other than obsessing over Mack, but he was always there at the back of my mind.

I spent the night hugging my pillow and trying not to cry into it.

Thursday I picked up Winnie from school and went through the usual afternoon routine with the girls. I helped Millie with her bun for ballet class and waved her off when her carpool ride picked her up. She'd seemed a little melancholy today, but her forehead didn't feel hot, and she said she was fine.

At about quarter after five, I was standing at the counter helping Felicity with her spelling words when I heard the back door open. My heart jumped into my throat.

"Hi, Daddy," Felicity called.

"Hi, everyone." A moment later, Mack entered the kitchen. My back was to him, but I felt short of breath, as if he'd sucked up all the oxygen in the room.

"How was school?" he asked.

"Good. I lost another tooth." Felicity grinned, proudly displaying the new hole in her smile.

Mack examined her teeth closely. "Good job. Where is it?"

"I put it in a little baggie on her dresser." I faced him, but I couldn't bring myself to meet his eye. Instead I looked at his chest. "Millie's at ballet. Winnie is in her room."

"Okay."

Quickly I turned and headed for the back hall, shoved my feet into my boots, and threw on my coat. Without even bothering with gloves or a hat, I called a fake-cheerful "see you tomorrow" and rushed out.

I couldn't even breathe until I was in my car, engine running.

Later, I got a text from Mack.

You left so fast I didn't get a chance to pay you. I'll bring you a check tomorrow and leave it at the desk.

I didn't usually work at reception on Fridays. If I had orders for macarons for a weekend event, I got up early and spent the morning baking before picking up Winnie. However, there was no event scheduled at Cloverleigh that weekend and I didn't even have to get Winnie, so my time would be totally free. I could easily go down to pick up a check from Mack.

But that would necessitate a face-to-face conversation, and I wasn't sure I could handle it.

That's fine.

He didn't write back.

I used Friday to clean, do laundry, catch up on social media work, make some soup, and check in with April regarding the wedding schedule for the next few weeks. Ryan Woods's wedding was coming up, and originally I'd been looking forward to the event—all the family on staff were invited since Ryan used to work for us—but now I found myself dreading it, since I knew Mack was the best man. I'd probably spend the entire night staring at him across the room.

April confirmed that they did want macarons as favors, and Stella's wedding colors were navy, cranberry, ivory and gold. "She trusts you with the flavors and asked for velvet ribbons on the boxes that complement her color palette."

"That sounds beautiful. I'm on it."

I was looking through recipes and trying to decide on flavors when my mom called to ask if I'd mind taking the evening shift as hostess at the restaurant, since someone had called in sick. I said I'd be glad to. What else did I have to do besides sit around and mope?

The thought annoyed me. I was only twenty-seven years old. Why didn't I have a more interesting social life? Or at least somewhere to go on a Friday night? Valentine's Day was coming up next week. The inn would be full of romantic couples, which normally made me happy, but I found myself dreading it. I stayed good and aggravated as I showered and got ready for work. As I made my way down to the restaurant, I noticed it was snowing again. For fuck's sake, even *snow* reminded me of Mack now. Would winter never end?

I checked in with the floor manager at the restaurant and assumed my post at the hostess stand, trying not to frown at all the couples coming in for a romantic dinner. Evidently, I wasn't doing a very good job at it, because after a while my mother hurried across the lobby from the reception desk with creases in her forehead.

"Frannie, would you mind taking that sour expression off your face? It's very off-putting."

"I don't have a sour expression," I snapped.

She folded her arms. "I can see it clear across the room. We want people to feel welcome when they come in. Look a little warmer, please."

"Sorry." I fought the urge to roll my eyes. "I'll try."

Suddenly her annoyance turned into concern. "Are you feeling okay?"

"I'm feeling *fine*," I said through my teeth, plastering on a smile as a few guests approached. "And I have to seat these people, so excuse me."

I made a better effort to be warm and welcoming after that, and I was doing okay until I heard Mack's voice. Looking up from the stack of menus in front of me, I locked eyes with him as he and Henry DeSantis crossed the lobby. My heart beat faster as they approached.

"Hey, Frannie," Henry said. "They've got you out here tonight, huh?"

"Yes." I offered Henry a smile, tearing my gaze from Mack. "Working late tonight?"

"We were, but we just decided to knock off for the night and grab a drink at the bar."

Mack spoke up. "I left a check for you at the desk, Frannie."

My smile faded as I forced myself to meet his eyes again. "Thanks."

"We'll just grab a couple seats at the bar if that's okay," Henry said. "No need to seat us."

"Okay." I tried hard to sound cheerful. "Enjoy."

They moved past me, and I caught a whiff of Mack's scent—it nearly made my knees buckle. And he looked so good in that shade of blue. It matched his eyes. Why'd he have to be so handsome?

Several times over the next hour, I peeked into the bar area and spied on them. It wasn't easy since they'd taken two seats at the far end of the bar, but twice I was able to make up an excuse to go into the kitchen. That meant I had to walk by them four times. The first time, I was careful to make no eye contact whatsoever. The second time, Mack happened to notice me, and our eyes met. Neither of us smiled. The third time, I noticed they'd decided to eat at the bar, and both had ordered steaks. The final time, Henry must have gone to the bathroom or something, because Mack was sitting by himself. He looked at me as I passed him, and I refused to make eye contact. Then he said my name.

I pretended like I hadn't heard him and walked faster, my heels clacking on the wood floor. Next thing I knew, a hand was on my shoulder.

"Frannie," he said again. "Stop a minute."

I turned to face him, reluctantly meeting his eyes. "Yes?"

"Are you—I mean, how are you?" He shoved his hands in his pockets.

"Fine." I crossed my arms. "Are the girls with their mom?"

He grimaced and shook his head. "She didn't show."

I gasped, although it didn't surprise me. "She didn't?"

"No, she texted me this morning to tell me she wasn't coming because of the weather. She didn't want to fly into a snowstorm."

"Were the girls upset?"

"They didn't even know she was coming. Well, Millie knew it was a possibility, but she's getting to the point where she knows she can't believe anything her mother says."

"That's tough." I felt myself softening. "Poor Millie."

"Yeah." He rubbed the back of his neck. "I felt so bad I picked them up from school and drove them all the way to my sister's in Petoskey to hang out with their cousins. Then Jodie invited them to stay the night, so I came back here to get some work done because I'm so behind, but ... I couldn't concentrate."

"Why not?"

He lowered his voice. "Because you're upset with me."

"No, I'm not," I said, glancing around at the other

patrons in the bar.

"Then why are you avoiding me? You've hardly said two words to me since Tuesday. Yesterday at the house you wouldn't even look at me."

I took a breath and squared my shoulders. "I'm not *upset* with you. I'm just trying to get over my stupid feelings. Talking to you doesn't help."

He nodded slowly. "Does that mean you don't want to nanny for me anymore?"

"No." I sighed, feeling embarrassed that I'd turned this into a *thing* that was making us both feel awkward. "I'll be fine, Mack. Don't worry about it. I should get back to work."

"Okay." He opened his mouth like he might say something else, and I could have thought of any number of things I wanted to hear. *Don't go. I'm sorry. I changed my mind.*

But a second later, he closed it again, and I walked away. What else could I do?

The inn's dinner crowd was a pretty early one in the winter, so the floor manager let me go by nine-thirty. Mack and Henry still hadn't come out of the bar, and I was glad I didn't have to see him again before I left.

After finishing up the hostess's side work, I said goodnight to my mom at reception, picked up Mack's check, and went up to my suite. Tossing the check onto my dresser, I changed from my work clothes into flannel pajama pants, a giant gray sweatshirt with a sherpa-lined hood, and fuzzy socks. After throwing my hair into a sloppy bun on the top of my head, I went into the kitchen to warm up a bowl of the squash soup I'd made earlier. But I wasn't very hungry and only ended up eating about half of it.

I was rinsing out the bowl when I heard a knock at my door.

That's weird, I thought, checking my phone to see what time it was—after ten—and whether someone in my family had tried to get ahold of me. No one had.

My heart tripped a little faster as I made my way to the door, and I held my breath as I pulled it open.

Mack stood in the hall, his hands fisted at his sides, his expression tense. He was breathing hard, as if he'd just run up a steep flight of stairs.

Suddenly I *was* mad at him. How dare he show up here? He *knew* I was trying to avoid him. This just felt mean. "What do you want?" I asked, not bothering to disguise my anger.

"I want you to tell me to leave." He spoke quietly, but firmly.

"Leave," I told him, folding my arms over my chest.

Without another word, he rushed toward me and crushed his lips to mine.

Fourteen

Mack

THINGS HAPPENED FAST.

I kicked the door shut with my heel. I backed her into the room. I tore at her clothes, and then my own, although I only succeeded in removing her hoodie and pants, and though I was shirtless, my jeans were still tight around my knees.

Didn't matter. Within five minutes of arriving at her door, I was fucking her mercilessly on the living room carpet, driving my rock-hard cock into her soft, warm body again and again and again. It was almost like I was punishing her for refusing to let me be.

And she clearly wanted to punish me too.

She wrapped her legs around me and clawed at my back. She whispered my name against my lips and cried out with every deep, hard thrust. She moved beneath me, rocking her hips in tandem with mine, pulling me closer to her body until we were gasping and shuddering and clinging desperately to each other through a simultaneous orgasm so intense, I couldn't breathe, couldn't see, couldn't think.

It was obvious the other night hadn't been a

fluke—whatever this thing was between us was real. And powerful. And not going anywhere.

When I finally opened my eyes, I saw her face beneath mine. She turned her head to the side, giving me her profile, chin slightly raised. Then I realized she wasn't holding on to me anymore.

Fuck. I was *such* an asshole.

I detached myself from her and sat back on my heels, head hanging low. "Jesus. I'm sorry."

"Don't be. I could have stopped you."

I wasn't so sure about that. "Why didn't you?"

She didn't answer.

I leaned over her again, bracing myself above her shoulders. "Hey. Look at me."

She didn't, so I put two fingers beneath her chin and turned her head. Her lower lip trembled, and I had to kiss it.

"Stop," she said softly.

A smile hooked up one side of my mouth. "*Now* you want me to stop?"

"Yes. You're confusing me."

"I know. I'm sorry. I'm confused myself."

"Why did you come up here, anyway?"

"Because I've been fucking miserable all week. Because that night with you was the best I've felt in years. Because it doesn't matter why I should stay away from you—I can't."

"Don't tease me. Do you really mean that?"

I nodded. "I got all the way out to the parking lot tonight. I got in my car. I turned the fucking engine on, and I sat there, getting more and more furious with myself that I couldn't go."

"Really?"

"Really. Finally I gave in. But I knew it wasn't fair after

what I'd said, so I promised myself that if you told me to leave, I would."

She looked amused. "I *did* tell you to leave."

"Uh, yeah." I cleared my throat. "Clearly that was a promise I should not have made."

"It's okay." Her hands swept up and down my back, her touch sending warm shivers across my skin. "I want to be with you."

"I want to be with you too." I brushed some hair back from her forehead that had come loose from the knot on top of her head. "But I'm not going to be able to make *any* promises, Frannie. I meant what I said—I've got nothing to offer you."

"That's not true," she said with that irresistibly stubborn tilt of her chin.

"You say that now, but just wait. My life is complete chaos. Most days I feel like I'm hanging on by a thread."

"You don't need to worry about me, Mack. I don't want to be another responsibility in your life. And I don't need promises or labels." She took a breath. "I just want to feel like I'm *somebody* to you."

I smiled down at her. "You are. But we'll have to be careful. I don't want the kids to—" Suddenly I realized something—we hadn't been *careful* tonight. I panicked, backing off from her again. "Oh, shit, Frannie. I didn't even think. I—"

She silenced me with one hand. "No worries. I'm on the pill, and I'm very, very good about taking it."

I relaxed a little. "Okay. Whew. That's good." The last thing I needed was another baby right now. Or ever.

"Give me a few minutes, okay?" she asked, getting to her feet. "If you want a drink or anything, help yourself. I don't have any beer, but I've got wine, whiskey, vodka, te-quila …"

I raised my brow. "Should I be worried about you?"

Laughing, she gathered her clothing and headed for her room. "No. I'm not a huge drinker, but I do like a little whiskey by the fire now and then."

"Whiskey by the fire it is." I looked around and noticed the fireplace at the far end of the room. Scooping up my clothing, I threw on my underwear, jeans, and shirt and wandered into the kitchen.

By the time Frannie came out of her bedroom, dressed the same way she had been before but with her hair loose around her shoulders, I'd poured two glasses of whiskey and lit the gas fireplace, which lacked the romance of real wood in my opinion, but it warmed the room.

She smiled as she joined me on the couch, tucking her legs beneath her. "This is nice."

I took her glass from the little coffee table and handed it to her. "It is. Much nicer than what I was heading home to, which was an empty house."

She took a sip of her whiskey. "So the girls are with your sister?"

"Yeah. Jodie. She's got a daughter a year older than Millie and a son Felicity's age. They all get along really well. I wish they lived closer."

"I wish Sylvia lived closer too. I hardly know my nieces and nephew." She smiled sadly.

"How is Sylvia? I haven't spoken to her in a while."

"Good, I guess. I don't talk to her much, either." Frannie tipped up her glass again, then stared into it. "That's something I'd like to change, though. I should reach out to her. Are you close to your sister?"

I nodded. "Pretty close. I mean, we're both busy with kids and jobs, but we were tight growing up. She's only seventeen months older than me. And she's married to a great guy. They make it look easy."

She looked up at me, her expression curious. "Can I ask what happened with your marriage, or is it too personal?"

I exhaled and tossed back some more whiskey. "My marriage was tough from the start. Carla got pregnant with Millie right before I was set to deploy, and we got married fast before I left. We'd only known each other for a few months."

"Marines, right?" she asked.

"Yeah."

"What made you join?"

"I was kinda lost for a while in my early twenties, didn't really know what I wanted to do yet. I'd dropped out of college because I was too immature to handle the responsibility and my parents told me they weren't going to pay for me to fuck around anymore." I took another drink. "I needed to burn off some energy and I wanted to get out of here. One day I decided being a Marine sounded kind of badass. So I signed up."

"And you were in Afghanistan?"

I nodded. "Twice. And I was in Iraq too. So I was gone a lot during the early years of our marriage, while the older two girls were little. That didn't help. Then, when I got out, I wanted to move back up here where I'd grown up, and she wanted to move to Georgia, where she was from. She said she'd agree to come here if I agreed to have another baby. So we did both." I paused to take a drink. "But it didn't matter where we lived. We never really made each other happy. Eventually resentment set in."

"Resentment over what?" She took another small sip.

"Oh God, you name it. She resented feeling like I'd married her out of a sense of duty more than anything else. She resented being left alone with kids while I was deployed. Then when I came home and struggled to readjust to civilian life, she resented me for not bouncing back faster. She also felt abandoned again because I worked during the day, managing a hardware store, and went to classes at night so I could finish my degree."

Frannie nodded slowly and took another sip. "How'd you end up at Cloverleigh? Did Sylvia get you the job here?"

"Yeah. I'd finished my degree and was looking for a better job, and I ran into her one day when she was home. She introduced me to your dad."

"Did things get better once you had a good job?"

"Not really. We fought all the time, and when we weren't fighting, there was a lot of angry silence."

"That must have been awful."

"It was." I frowned. "I tried to make it work, I really did—especially for the kids' sake. But nothing I did or said was right, and I got tired of being the bad guy. Eventually I stopped trying, and she ran off with someone else."

"I'm sorry."

I shook my head. "Don't be, not for me, anyway. It's not like Carla and I had some great love affair. But our kids deserved better. I feel horrible every day that I failed them."

"You didn't fail them, Mack." She put a hand on my leg. "Sometimes marriages don't work out. It wasn't your fault."

I'd heard the same from my sister, from Woods, from my parents ... but I couldn't convince myself of it. Rationally I knew it wasn't fair for Carla to blame me for the divorce, but her words had a way of eating at me deep down. Maybe I *hadn't* loved her the way I was supposed to. Maybe I didn't know how.

Frannie swirled the amber liquid in her glass. "The girls don't talk about their mother much."

I shook my head. "Not anymore. They missed her a lot at first, but since she's only seen them a couple times since, the separation anxiety has eased. I'm sure somewhere in each of them is a gaping wound and a permanent fear of abandonment, but day to day they seem okay."

"That's a credit to you," Frannie said.

"And their therapist." I threw back some more whiskey. "I'll be paying those bills for years to come. Millie's been asking some tough questions lately, wondering if her mother even loves her."

Frannie gasped. "What did you say?"

"I said yes, and I *think* that's the truth, but fuck if I know what's in Carla's head." I took another big swallow and ran a hand through my hair. "I'm sorry, Frannie. I didn't mean to unload all that on you."

"Hey," she insisted, putting a hand on my leg again. "I *want* you to unload on me. You can tell me anything."

I smiled at her. Her cheeks were flushed and her hair was a mess, and some of her eye makeup from earlier was smudged under her eyes, but it didn't matter. She still made my heart beat faster. And the way she was sitting there so patiently while I dumped out all my emotional garbage, the way she gave me all of her attention and said all the right things … it made me feel validated and understood in a way I hadn't in a long, long time. I *did* feel like I could tell her anything.

But I'd had enough talking.

"Thanks," I said. "But you know what? Nights like this

are going to be few and far between, possibly nonexistent, and I don't want to waste any more of it complaining about my ex. Tell me about *you*."

Light danced in her eyes and she lifted her shoulders. "What do you want to know?"

"Hmmm." I took one last sip of whiskey and set the empty glass on the table before reaching for hers too. "Mostly I want to know why you're not closer to me right now."

She giggled, letting me put her drink aside and pull her onto my lap the way she'd been the other night, straddling my thighs. My shirt was unbuttoned and she immediately put her hands on my chest. God, it felt good to be touched that way. I'd forgotten how good.

"Now what?" she asked.

"Now I want to know why you're still wearing so many clothes."

She grinned devilishly before unzipping the sweatshirt she wore and tossing it aside. Then she hesitated, glancing at the fire, which was the only source of light in the room. At first I didn't understand why, but when she tugged the little white tank over her head, I noticed the scar on her chest.

Immediately I reached out and traced the long, ragged, dark pink line that ran down her sternum, between her breasts. "Does it hurt?" I asked.

She shook her head.

"What was the surgery for?"

"I was born with a congenital heart defect called a bicuspid aortic valve. I had several surgeries as a baby to repair the valve, and eventually one to replace it when I was ten."

"That sounds scary." I looked up at her with concern,

placing my hands on the sides of her ribs. "You're okay now?"

"I'm totally fine. The worst that happens is I can get tired easily, and I have to watch my cholesterol. I have a slightly elevated risk of an aneurysm or heart failure. But I'm very good about paying attention to my body, and I eat right and exercise, and take all my meds and keep all my doctor appointments like a good little girl."

"Good." I looked at the scar again, and she sighed.

"I know it's really ugly, but I've made my peace with it."

I met her eyes. "Every inch of you is beautiful. Inside and out."

"That's how I feel about you too," she whispered.

Pulling her closer, I fastened my mouth to one perfect pink nipple, teasing the tip with my tongue. She threaded her hands into my hair and moaned softly, arching her back. My dick was hard again in no time.

Lucky for me, she was just as hungry for more as I was, and she ditched her pants and yanked mine down inside a minute. I couldn't even speak as she sheathed my cock with her fist and moved it up and down, then licked her fingers and touched herself in a way that made my chin hit my chest.

"Jesus fucking Christ," I whispered, glad this was round two or else I'd have come all over myself in seconds.

She lowered herself onto me slowly, her eyes shut, her mouth open. I put my hands on her hips and fought the urge to buck up beneath her. When I was buried inside her, she opened her eyes and looked at me as she started to move.

At that moment, I didn't care about the age difference or whose daughter she was or how I was going to add her to the chaotic mess that was my life. All I knew was how good it felt to be with her this way, to see the desire in her eyes, to watch her come apart above me, to be the man she saw when she looked at me, not the one I saw when I looked at myself.

We went a little slower this time—probably because I let her set the pace for once. She didn't race to the finish line, but the gradual buildup was just as intense, and the climax an even sweeter reward, our bodies pulsing together in perfect harmony.

When it was over, she fell forward, her head on my shoulder, her chest heaving against mine. I wrapped my arms around her and inhaled the scent of her soft wavy hair.

"Mack," she whispered.

"Yeah?"

"Do you have to go home tonight?"

I thought for a moment, realizing quickly that I didn't want this fantasy to end so soon. Tonight, I was just a man going after what I wanted. What I needed. What felt good. When I walked out of here, it was back to real life. Who knew when I'd have this chance again? The truth was, I had no clue how this was going to work—how I would balance being who I *needed* to be with who I *wanted* to be. Maybe I was just setting myself up for another failure. Maybe it was stupid to think I could make this work. Maybe in a week she'd realize that feeling like somebody to me wasn't worth the trouble and she'd move on.

But tonight … tonight could be ours.

"No," I told her. "I could stay here with you."

She picked up her head. "Do you *want* to stay here with me?"

"Yes," I said, pressing my lips to hers. "I do."

Fifteen

Frannie

I HAD TO WORK THE NEXT MORNING, ALTHOUGH I'D NEVER BEEN more tempted to call in sick. We'd been up half the night. I was exhausted and sore and so hungry I could have eaten a bear. But I was giddy too—when I woke up, the first thing I did was look at the man sleeping next to me to make sure last night hadn't been a dream.

Mack lay on his stomach with his head completely under the pillow. Suppressing a giggle, I carefully slid out of bed and jumped in the shower. The smile stayed on my face as I washed and conditioned my hair, soaped, rinsed, and dried off.

Back in my bedroom, with the towel wrapped around me, I couldn't resist sneaking over to the bed and lifting up one corner of the pillow to peek at Mack's face.

Even asleep, he was so handsome my heartbeat quickened. His profile was sharply defined and masculine, his jaw thick with scruff, his nose strong and straight. He slept with both arms over his head, and the muscles on his bare shoulders bulged thick and round. I was tempted to run my hand over them, but I didn't want to wake him up. We'd only been sleeping for about four hours.

His eyes opened.

"Hi," I whispered, smiling.

"Hi." He grabbed the pillow I was holding up and stuffed it beneath his cheek, closing his eyes again. "Was I snoring?"

"No. Do you snore?"

"*I* don't think so. But the girls tease me about it. Teasing me is their favorite thing to do."

My grin widened. "What else do they tease you about? Besides your cooking."

"My hairy stomach, my hairy chest—"

"I like the hair on your chest. It's hot."

"Thank you. Then there are my wrinkles, my gray hair—"

"You do *not* have wrinkles. And I like your gray hair, too." I brushed my fingertips over the silvery strands at his temples. "You're perfect."

Opening his eyes again, he smiled and tugged at my towel. "Come back to bed."

Ditching the towel, I scrambled into his arms, loving his bare skin against mine. "I've only got a minute," I said reluctantly, tucking my wet head beneath his chin.

He held me close and kissed my hairline. "You have to work?"

"Yeah." I sighed. "I wish I didn't. What are you going to do today?"

"Pick up the kids. Clean the house. Grocery shop. Attempt to catch up on work. Your dad's probably going to fire me for being so behind. That is, if he doesn't fire me for seducing his daughter."

"You definitely did not seduce me." I dropped a kiss on his chest and sat up. "You just kept me up late."

"Sorry."

I laughed. "Liar."

He grinned, tucking his hands behind his head. "You're right, that was a lie."

Wincing a little, I got out of bed and onto my feet. "Sheesh. I've never been so sore. My abs are killing me."

"But you feel okay?" He sat up, his brow furrowed. "I mean, your heart isn't stressed or anything?"

I grinned. "Oh, *now* I see the wrinkles."

He yanked the pillow from behind his back and threw it at me.

I caught it in two hands and whacked him across the shoulder with it, but before I could get away, he grabbed me and threw me down on the bed. I shrieked and struggled half-heartedly to get out from under him, but really I couldn't get enough of his body on mine.

"You know what I do to my girls when they make fun of me?" he said, circling my wrists and pressing them into the mattress above my shoulders.

"What?" I asked breathlessly, thrilled to be one of his girls.

"It's called the tickle torture."

"No! No, please! I'm so ticklish—don't—no, not the neck—" I dissolved into a wriggling mess, laughing and squirming as he buried his face in my neck and swirled his tongue lightly over the skin just below my ears. "I'm sorry," I gasped. "I'm sorry I made fun of you! I'll never do it again!"

"Now who's lying?" He picked up his head and stared me down. "I was serious about your heart. Are you okay?"

"Yes. Your concern is very sweet, but no amount of sex is going to cause my heart to fail, no matter how good it is. I promise." Then I laughed again. "Your dick is big, but not big enough to puncture my aorta."

"That's it." He dove for my neck again, keeping my hands immobile and torturing my ticklish spot with his tongue until I pleaded for mercy.

"I'll be good, I'm begging you," I gasped. "I'm going to be late for work. I have to be down there in like ten minutes and I haven't even combed my hair yet."

"Want me to comb it for you? I'm really good at it."

I laughed. "Stop it. Millie is always complaining about your buns."

"Okay, I'm shit at the bun thing, but I am awesome at combing hair. I'm serious." He let go of my wrists and sat back on his heels. "Go get your brush."

"Mack, you do not have to brush my hair. It's all wet and tangled. Do you know what a chore it will be?"

"I don't care. There aren't many things I can do for you, and you do so much for me. Let me do this."

I didn't really have time to mess around, but something about Mack offering to brush my hair was too sweet to resist. "Okay."

In the bathroom, I grabbed my wet brush and threw on my robe. When I came out, Mack had pulled on his pants and was zipping them up.

"Here you go," I said, turning around and presenting him with a long, wet, knotted mess.

He started at the ends and worked his way up, slowly and patiently. Since I stood facing the mirror above my dresser, I could see his reflection, and my heart beat faster at his serious expression. His long, gentle strokes across my scalp and down my back sent shivers up my spine. I didn't care if I was late. This was totally worth it.

"There," he said. "How was that?"

"Perfect." We caught each other's eyes in the mirror. "You were right—you're awesome at combing hair. Thank you."

He wrapped an arm around me and kissed the top of my head. "You're welcome."

A few minutes later, we said goodbye at the door. He pulled me against his chest, hugging me tight. "This was so much fun. Thank you."

"You don't have to thank me, silly." I looped my arms around his waist and pressed my cheek to his chest. "I had fun too."

"I hope no one catches me sneaking out of here."

"You know, I really don't care what my parents think about us. We don't have to hide."

"But *I* care." He pulled back and looked down at me, his expression serious. "Your family is good to me. And this complicates not only our working relationship, but also things with my kids. Can we keep it to ourselves for a little while? Is that okay?"

"Of course."

"Thanks." He tugged a strand of my wet hair. "I want to do this again. But I have no idea when that will be."

"It's okay, Mack. I meant what I said last night. I don't need promises and I won't make demands. Whenever we can steal a little time together is good enough for me."

He kissed my forehead. "You're too good to be true."

"You're in a good mood today," my mother remarked after she caught me humming a tune at the reception desk.

"I am, actually." I'd spent the entire morning at work

mooning over him, replaying last night in my mind, and wondering when I'd see him again. I'd meant what I said to him about not wanting to be another responsibility. The last thing Mack needed was one more female making demands on his time and attention. But I also couldn't help the way I felt—every cell in my body was radiating with happiness.

Near the end of my shift, Chloe poked her head out the door leading to the offices. "Hey. Mom around?"

I shook my head. "She was, but she went up to change. She and Dad have dinner reservations somewhere."

She came all the way out the door and closed it behind her. Then she leaned back against it and crossed her arms. Her eyes gleamed. "So."

I looked expectantly at her. "So?"

"So last night I had a private tasting in the winery for some industry people, and it ran kind of late."

"Oh?" Suddenly I had a feeling I knew where this was headed, and I busied myself cleaning the computer screen in front of me.

"By the time I was done cleaning up, it was close to midnight."

"Mmm."

"And I went out to the parking lot to leave, and saw Mack's Tahoe in the staff lot."

"Really?" I wiped repeatedly at a stubborn smudge.

"Really. The restaurant was long closed. The bar was closed. The offices were dark. Any idea where he might have been?"

"No," I said, but I felt the burn in my face and knew my cheeks were going scarlet.

"Liar!" she hissed, thumping me several times on the shoulder. "I can see it in your face! He spent the night with you, didn't he?"

"Shhhhhhhh!" I admonished, glancing around to make sure no one had heard.

"Oh my God, he did!" She hopped up and sat on the reception desk, which we were not supposed to do. "Tell me everything."

"Get down from there before Mom comes down and sees you." I tossed my paper towel in the trash and tucked the screen cleaner under the counter. "And lower your voice."

She pouted but pushed herself off the desk and onto her feet. "Well?"

I scanned the lobby one more time, but didn't see anyone I knew. "Okay, yes. He did."

Chloe gasped. "I knew it!"

"But you can't say anything to anyone. I don't want to broadcast it."

"Broadcast what, that you're fucking the CFO?" She snorted. "Can't imagine why. So how was it?"

A long, slow sigh escaped me. "Magical."

Cracking up, she shook her head. "You're not going to be able to keep this a secret for long, you know. The look on your face is a dead giveaway you're in love."

"I never said I was in love," I said defensively, although the feelings I had for Mack were dizzying and breathtaking and all-consuming—exactly what I imagined love to be like.

"Whatever you say, sis." She thumped me on the shoulder before pulling the hallway door open, giving me a wry grin on her way out.

I couldn't help grinning too.

Around two, he texted me.

Hey beautiful. How's your day?

I blushed and messaged back.

Good. Not too busy. How's yours?

Good. Guess what? My sister called and said the girls can stay another night. Apparently there is a very serious Junior Monopoly tournament happening.

My stomach flipped over. Did that mean we could see each other again? With shaky fingers, I texted back.

That's nice of her.

How does dinner and Netflix at my house sound? Don't worry, I won't cook. We'll get takeout.

I laughed out loud before replying.

Why don't I cook? I'll get some groceries and meet you at your house. Seven?

Perfect. See you then.

My shift at reception finished at three, and I went upstairs to my rooms and crashed on the couch immediately. When I woke up, it was already going on six, and I jumped up to go change.

Trading my work clothes for jeans and a sweater (and my utilitarian underwear for something lacy and cute), I quickly brushed my hair and freshened up my makeup. Just in case, I packed a tiny bag with a change of clothes, my toothbrush, and makeup remover. Double checking that my pills were in my purse, I threw the bag over my shoulder and headed out the door.

On the way to Mack's house, I hit the grocery store and bought everything I'd need to make stuffed shells. Not exactly gluten-free, but since Millie wasn't home tonight, I figured I'd take the opportunity to cook pasta for him.

I also bought a loaf of fresh Italian bread and ingredients for a garden salad and lemon-tarragon vinaigrette. *Maybe* I was showing off little, but it wasn't as if I wouldn't enjoy every moment spent preparing dinner for us in his kitchen. I loved cooking and baking, and I rarely had anyone around to share meals with. Usually I ended up giving food away.

Mack's house was dark when I pulled up at ten after seven, and I wondered if he was in the shower or something. I parked on the street, got the grocery bags from my trunk, and trudged through the snow to his front door. Putting one bag down and shifting the other to my hip, I knocked a few times.

When he didn't answer, I picked up the second bag and went around to the back of the house. The kitchen appeared dark too. I knocked again and even tried opening the back door, but it was locked.

Huh.

I set down both bags, pulled off my gloves, and checked my phone. Quarter after seven and no message or call from Mack. Double checking the earlier texts, I made sure I hadn't gotten the time wrong, but I hadn't—I'd said seven, and he'd said that was perfect. I hoped nothing was wrong. Biting my lip, I looked around. Garage door was shut, so I couldn't tell if his car was in there or not.

Well, now what was I supposed to do? I didn't have a key. Should I wait in the car? Go home? Try to call him? I decided to text first.

Hey, I'm here.

Adding a smiley face emoji, I hit send.

And waited.

Nothing.

My fingers were starting to freeze, so I left the groceries on the back porch, got back in the car, and tried again.

**Are you home? I tried the front
and back door, but both are locked.**

I waited about five minutes, turning the car on for the heat.

Nothing.

Then I tried calling. Straight to voicemail.

"Hey Mack, it's me. Um, Frannie. I'm at your house, I thought we said seven, but maybe I got the time wrong? Anyway, I hope everything's okay. Give me a call when you can. I guess I'll … just head back home. I've got groceries."

I drove home slowly, stopping at every yellow light, checking my phone often, and taking a circuitous route. But Mack never got in touch.

Back at home, I unpacked the grocery bags and decided to cook the dinner I'd planned on. When the shells were in the oven, I texted both April and Chloe, asking them if they wanted to come over for dinner. But Chloe was out with friends, and April had already gone home for the night and didn't feel like making the drive.

I ended up eating alone with the television on, but even a sappy Valentine's movie on the Hallmark channel didn't ease my mind. What on earth had happened? Was everyone okay? Why hadn't he at least called?

By ten o'clock, the dishes were done and the leftovers put away, but I knew there was no way I'd be able to sleep. I was too scared something awful had happened. My dinner was not sitting well in my stomach. Throwing my coat and boots on again, I jumped in my car and drove back to his house.

As I turned onto his street, I noticed lights on in his living room window. Slowing down, I pulled up along the curb and put the car in park. What the hell? Was he home? Why hadn't he returned my messages?

I got out of the car, hurried up the driveway, and knocked on the back door.

Sixteen

Mack

I WAS PRYING THE CAP OFF A MUCH-NEEDED BEER WHEN I HEARD the knock. My gut clenched, and I went to answer it.

As expected, it was Frannie. Her usual warm, friendly expression was a mixture of relief and what-the-fuck.

"Hi," I said quietly. "Come on in."

She stepped into the house and I shut the door behind her. Crossing her arms over her chest, she eyed the beer bottle in my hand. "What's going on? Where have you been?"

"At the ER with Winnie," I said grimly.

Frannie gasped and dropped her hands. "Oh no! Is she okay?"

"Yeah. She fell down the stairs at my sister's house. Knocked a tooth out and split her lip. Luckily, it was a baby tooth, but ..." Shaking my head, I exhaled heavily. "There was a lot of blood and she needed stitches. She was pretty terrified."

"Oh my God. That's awful." Her pretty features contorted in sympathy. "The poor thing. Where is she now?"

"She's in bed upstairs. We got home about twenty minutes ago."

"And the other kids?"

"Still at my sister's in Petoskey. Frannie, I'm so sorry," I said, pinching the bridge of my nose. My head was pounding. "This day has turned into such a fucking disaster."

"It's okay, but … why didn't you call?"

"I can't find my fucking phone. I don't even remember where I had it last. I know my sister called me on it, frantic and crying, and then I jumped in the car, but I don't know if I had it with me or not. I didn't even realize it was missing until I was already at the ER."

"Did you check the car?"

"Yeah, just a few minutes ago. But it was dark in the garage, and I didn't want to leave Winn alone upstairs too long. I'll search again tomorrow when it's light out."

"Oh, Mack. I'm sorry." She slipped her arms around my waist and hugged me tight.

"I feel like such an asshole for doing this to you." I wrapped my arms around her big puffy coat and kissed the top of her head. "This is exactly what I was talking about. This is the shit that's going to happen."

"Hush. You're not an asshole. You're a dad. I get it. It's not like you stood me up on purpose."

"No, but it still sucks. Want to come in for a beer? I know it's not the night we planned, but now that you're here, I'd love it if you could stay a little."

"Sure." She stepped out of her boots and unzipped her coat, which I hung up for her.

In the kitchen, I grabbed another beer from the fridge and popped the cap off before handing it to her. "It's so fucking scary when something happens to one of them. There's nothing worse than seeing your child in pain and being helpless to make it better. And it was worse because

148

I wasn't there when it happened. I feel so guilty, especially because I'd been so glad to have them out of the house for the night."

Frannie took a sip from her beer and leaned back against the counter. "You shouldn't feel guilty, Mack. You take care of them twenty-four-seven. Anybody would be glad for a break."

"I guess." Rationally, I knew my unhinged excitement at another all-night fuck-a-thon with Frannie hadn't caused Winnie's accident, but something in my gut would not let me be. "Then once she'd been treated and my head was clear, all I could think about was you out there in the cold, knocking on the door and waiting for me to answer. I let you down too." I set my beer aside and pulled her into my arms. "Do you have frostbite?"

She chuckled. "No, silly. I'm tougher than that."

I leaned back and tipped her chin up. "I was really looking forward to tonight."

"Me too. But life happens." She kissed me and placed a hand on my chest. "I know what I'm getting into, Mack. Okay? I know there will be nights like this, where we have plans that fall through because one of the kids needs you. Yes, it's disappointing, but I understand, and I still want to be with you. You're worth it."

There was no way that could be true, but my feelings for her deepened at hearing her say it. "Thanks."

My stomach chose that moment to rumble loudly, and she glanced down at it. "Hungry?"

"Starving."

"Let me get you some dinner." Setting her beer down, she went over to the refrigerator and pulled it open. "I should have brought leftovers with me. I had a ton of food."

"What did you make?" I asked, knowing it would be torture to hear the answer.

"Spinach and ricotta stuffed shells with meat sauce."

I groaned long and loud. "That sounds so fucking good."

"It was." She rummaged around in my fridge and took out a few things I'd bought earlier today. "I'll bring you some this week. I made plenty."

"You don't have to make a real dinner for me," I told her as she set a cutting board on the counter. "I can eat something quick. I'll stick a frozen pizza in the oven or whatever."

"No, you won't." She began mincing a clove of garlic. "I enjoy cooking. When I'm done with these sliders, if you still want a tasteless frozen pizza, be my guest."

"Sliders?" I asked, eyeing the roast beef and provolone on the counter as my salivary glands went into overdrive.

"Mmhm. With roast beef and caramelized onions. Can you grab a can of beef broth from the pantry? I'm pretty sure I saw one in there last week." She turned the oven on to preheat. "Oh, and I'll write my number down on that notebook by the phone. That way it's there in case of an emergency."

As I stood there watching her, my heart began to feel like a jackhammer in my chest. Clearing my throat, I headed for the pantry before I did something crazy like tell her I loved her.

But honest to fucking God, I almost did.

Frannie sat at the dining room table with me while I ate, slowly sipping her beer and telling me about the conversation she'd had with her sister Chloe about starting her own business.

"You already know I think that's a great idea," I said between bites of the delectable roast beef sandwiches. "I'll help you any way I can."

"Thanks." She smiled gratefully. "I still have a lot of research to do, but I've been working on it here and there over the last few days."

"Have you talked to your parents?"

She sighed. "I brought it up with my mom and we argued about it. She trotted out her same old arguments about my health and the stress, blah blah blah. In the past, I've always backed down, but this time I won't."

"What have you asked for in the past?"

She pulled one leg up, wrapping her arms around it and setting her chin on her knee. "Mostly I just wanted to be like other kids. Go to school. Run around at recess. Play soccer."

I paused with a slider halfway to my mouth. "You didn't go to school?"

"I was homeschooled."

"Ah."

"Later I wanted to go away to college. Backpack around Europe like my sisters had. Do you know that I've never even been out of the United States?"

"No?" I asked, surprised.

She shook her head. "No. I have a passport and everything, gathering dust in a drawer."

I reached for the last slider. "Where would you go first?"

"Hmmm." She thought for a moment, pressing her lips together. "France. I've always wanted to go to Paris, of course, but I'd also like to visit other places. We had a French pastry chef at Cloverleigh years ago, before you came on, and he was from a little town in the Loire Valley that has the castle that inspired the fairy tale of Sleeping Beauty."

"Oh yeah?"

"Yes. Château d'Ussé," she said with perfect French pronunciation. "He'd tell me all about it, and I'd dream that one day he was going to pluck me from my humdrum life and whisk me away to his enchanted castle, where we'd live happily ever after."

I laughed as I stuck the last bite in my mouth. "Didn't happen?"

Giggling, she shook her head. "Alas, Jean-Gaspard did not prefer women. Eventually, he moved back to France, leaving me alone and heartbroken. But I learned a lot from him."

"Well, I'm no French pastry chef, but I have total confidence that you can start your own business." I sat back and tipped up my beer. "Christ, that was good. Thanks for making dinner for me."

"You're welcome." She smiled happily. "The bride from the wedding at Cloverleigh last weekend offered to help me, did I tell you that? She's a commercial real estate agent, and she said she sometimes invests in female-owned small businesses. When she gets back from her honeymoon, she's going to get in touch."

"That's awesome," I told her. "See? The universe wants you to do this. All signs point to success."

She laughed. "Maybe. We'll see."

I finished my beer, picked up my plate and took it to the sink. "I should go check on Winnie."

Frannie rose to her feet too, stifling a yawn. "Yeah, it's late. I should get going."

"Wait, don't go yet. I'll be right back down." I touched

her back as I passed her on my way to the stairs.

Hurrying up to Winnie's room, I looked in on her, double checking that she was breathing easily and her lip hadn't started bleeding again. I picked Ned the Hammerhead from Shedd up from the floor, tucked him in next to her and pressed my lips to her forehead a moment, thanking God again that she was okay. I'd never take the health and safety of anyone I loved for granted. I'd seen too much for that.

Quietly I left her room, leaving the door all the way open and the nightlight on in the hall. I'd sleep in Winnie's room tonight just in case she woke up and called for me. But first I wanted to say goodnight to Frannie and walk her to her car.

Downstairs, she was loading dishes into the dishwasher. Affection and gratitude for her overwhelmed me. What had I done to deserve the kind of devotion she showed me? I came up behind her and wrapped my arms around her waist, burying my face in her sweet-smelling hair. "You're the best thing that's happened to me in a long time, you know that?"

She placed her arms over mine. "That makes me feel good."

"And I wish you didn't have to leave." I kissed her shoulder.

"Me too. But it's late, and you've got—Mack ... what are you doing?"

One of my hands had wandered beneath her sweater, and the other had moved between her legs. The feel of her warm bare skin, of the heat beneath my palm, sent blood rushing through me. The crotch of my pants was growing tight. "Don't go," I whispered, rubbing her through the tight-fitting denim. "Stay with me a while longer."

She made one small sound of protest, but stopped when I undid her jeans and slid my hand inside her underwear, stroking her gently with my fingertips. "Oh, God," she whispered. "That feels so good."

My other hand found her breast and I filled my palm with her perfect round flesh, then teased her pebbled nipple through the lace of her bra. That's when I noticed I could see our reflection in the window over the sink. Her eyes were closed and her mouth open as she began to writhe against my hand. By now I knew exactly how she liked to be touched, and I loved making her feel good.

"You want to come for me, don't you?" I spoke low in her ear. "You want to come for me right here, standing at the window."

Her eyes flew open and she noticed our images on the glass against the darkness of night. I had no curtains or shade to hide behind.

She struggled to get loose. "Mack, stop," she whispered frantically. "Someone could see in."

"If there was anyone in my yard at this time of night, I'd break his fucking neck with my bare hands." Anchoring her in place with the arm across her chest, I slid two fingers inside her. "You're not going anywhere until I make you come."

"But—"

"Shhh." She was hot and wet, and I fucked her easily with my fingers. I knew from the way her hips were moving that her body wanted it, even as she told me to stop. "I'll stop as soon as I make that sweet little pussy come all over my fingers," I told her, rubbing her clit hard and fast. "As soon as I hear you make that sound—the soft little moan you make when I'm fucking you, and my cock is so deep it hurts, and you feel me start to come, and your body—"

Suddenly she cried out, her knees buckling, and she would have gone down if I hadn't been gripping her so tightly. I did my best to hold her up and keep my fingers moving until I was positive she'd come, while she braced herself against the counter and gasped for air.

"Good girl," I whispered, keeping her pinned against me. "Now let me taste you."

In the glass, I saw her eyes pop open and she watched as I brought my fingers to my mouth and sucked them clean. My cock bulged painfully in my jeans. "Fuck," I growled in her ear. "Do you know how hard you make me? Do you want to feel it?"

"Yes," she whispered. "Please."

I forgot all about my promise to move away from the window and yanked off her pants, and then mine. Taking my hot, swollen dick in my hand, I rubbed the tip over her plump little ass, then pushed inside her, making both of us moan.

"Fuck yes," I muttered through clenched teeth as I grabbed her hips and watched myself slide in deep.

Frannie fell forward but kept her legs together, which made her feel even tighter around me. She whimpered and clutched at the edge of the counter as I fucked her harder and faster than I'd intended to, but her ass was so perfect and her pussy so wet and her sounds were making me crazy and the taste of her was still on my tongue and in no time at all I was erupting inside her with the force of a nuclear blast. I felt young and powerful and virile—fucking invincible.

When the spasms subsided, I pitched forward, covering her back with my chest. My pulse was thundering. My body rippled with aftershocks.

"Oh my God." Frannie shivered. "That was … intense."

"Yeah."

"And I can't believe we did that in your window," she whispered, bending forward so far her cheek was resting on the edge of the sink. "Someone could have seen."

"No one saw," I assured her.

"What about Mrs. Gardner?"

I laughed. "She'd probably be thrilled. She's always threatening to set me up with a nice young lady that works at her beauty salon."

"She is?"

"Yeah. She tells me all the time how she was the one who got Stella and Woods together. She's pretty smug about it." I carefully tried to disengage myself from her without making a mess, but didn't have much luck. "Sorry. Let me get you a towel."

"It's okay," she said, scooping up her pants and hurrying for the bathroom. "I just need a minute."

While she was in the bathroom, I pulled my jeans back on and turned off the kitchen light. Standing there in the silent dark, I got a little nervous that I'd been too rough and demanding with Frannie. Hopefully she wasn't traumatized. I wasn't even sure what had possessed me to say that stuff to her in the first place—I'd never really gotten off on sexual power play. But she brought it out in me. Maybe it was the age difference or something.

Or maybe I was just an asshole. Shit.

The bathroom door opened and she tiptoed into the darkened kitchen. "Hi."

She looked so innocent and sweet, I felt even worse. "Hi. You okay?"

"Of course."

"Was I too mean?"

"*Mean?*" She laughed. "No. Why would you say that?"

"I don't know." I rubbed the back of my neck. "Because you said to stop and I didn't. I don't want to be that guy."

She shook her head. "You're not that guy, believe me."

"Good." I pulled her into my arms, loath to see her go.

"Actually, I like that you got bossy with me. It was hot." She paused. "Although you owe *quite* a bit of money to that swear jar over there."

I twisted her around in my arms, binding her arms tight against her body so she couldn't escape, and whispered in her ear. "Hush, little girl. If you want to be with me, you'll have to put up with my dirty mouth."

She giggled. "You know I like it."

I groaned. "God, I wish you could stay over. There are *so many things* I want to do to you."

"Next time," she said. "So don't forget what they are."

"Not a fucking chance," I whispered in her ear.

I warmed up her car while she put her boots and coat on, then I walked her down the icy drive, holding her hand in mine.

"You're not even wearing a coat," she said, shivering as we carefully made our way toward the street. "You'll freeze out here."

"I'm fine," I told her, watching our breath hit the frigid air in warm white puffs. "But I *am* sick of this cold."

"Me too. The snow's pretty and all, but enough is enough. I wish I could take a vacation."

"Me too," I grumbled as we reached the car.

"Somewhere hot and sunny."

"Yes! A beach with miles of white sand. Clear blue water. Tropical drinks with little umbrellas in them."

"Uh, no way am I drinking anything that comes with a fucking umbrella in it. But the beach sounds nice." I pulled open the driver's side door for her.

"Doesn't it?" She gave me a quick peck on the lips. "Let's do it. Let's escape."

I laughed. "Sure. Somewhere between piano on Tuesdays, ballet on Thursdays, and the mother-daughter fashion show I've agreed to be in."

She burst out laughing. "What? I haven't heard about that."

"Millie." I shook my head. "She asked her mother and her mother said no, so I felt bad and offered to do it."

"When is it?"

"The weekend after the wedding, I think."

"That's so sweet of you." She hesitated. "If you really don't want to, I don't mind doing it with her."

I grimaced. "You have no idea how tempted I am to say yes. But I promised her. I want her to know she's got one parent she can depend on. That not everyone she loves will abandon her."

She rose up on tiptoe and kissed me again, one hand on my cheek. "You're a good man, Declan MacAllister."

"I try."

"I'm off tomorrow. Need anything? Want me to stay with Winnie while you go get the other two? That way you don't have to drag her out in this cold."

I shook my head. "You've done so much for me already this week. You deserve one day off, at least."

She got behind the wheel and smiled up at me. "My

number is by the phone. You let me know."

"Thanks. 'Night."

"'Night." She pulled the door shut, buckled her seatbelt, and pulled away, blowing me a kiss over her shoulder.

Shoving my hands into my pockets, I stood there in the frozen dark for a moment and watched her go, imagining the two of us alone in some tropical paradise. Lying on the sand. Kissing in the ocean. Walking along the beach in the moonlight. Endless nights in each other's arms, our bodies hot and tangled up in cool sheets. Not a care in the world.

Too bad it could never fucking happen.

Seventeen

Frannie

MACK CALLED BEFORE I WAS EVEN OUT OF BED THE NEXT morning, and the number on the screen was his cell. "You found your phone," I said, my voice low and gravelly.

"It was in my car, beneath the driver's seat."

"Good. How's Winnie?"

"She's okay, pretty fucking crabby, but I don't blame her." He sighed. "I hate to ask you this, but she does *not* want to get in the car, and I have to pick up Millie and Felicity by noon."

"Say no more." I swung my legs over the side of the bed. "I'll take a quick shower and head over."

"You're the best. Back door's open."

When I arrived at Mack's my hair was still damp. He met me in the kitchen and ruffled it. "Did you miss me this morning?"

"Yes. I had to brush my own hair, and it was not nearly as nice."

He smiled. "I'm sorry for the rush. She's in the living room watching cartoons. In about an hour, she can have another dose of Motrin. It's right there on the counter, already measured out."

"Okay."

"If she's hungry, she can have some lunch, but she had a tough time eating anything for breakfast." He grabbed his coat from the back hall and slipped it on. "I should be back before two. Call if you need anything."

"Okay. Don't worry, she'll be fine." I reassured him with a smile. "I'll fix her some soup or something."

"Thanks." He gave me a grateful look and headed out.

I spent the rest of the morning sitting on the couch with Winnie, trying to keep her mind off her poor stitched-up mouth. We watched Disney's Sleeping Beauty and I told her I knew someone who had grown up near the castle.

"Really?" Her eyes went wide. "It's a real place?"

I nodded, widening my eyes too. "Yes."

"Is the story real?" she wondered.

"Definitely," I said.

"I want to marry a prince, don't you?"

I winked at her. "Definitely."

A little while later, I got her to take the Motrin but she refused to eat much more than a piece of bread with nothing on it. She did let me braid her hair, though, and she was asleep with her head on my lap when I heard Mack and the other two girls come in the back door.

"How's she doing?" Mack said, following Millie and Felicity into the living room.

"She's fine," I whispered, putting a finger over my lips so the girls would stay quiet.

Millie noticed her sister's braids right away. "You said you'd teach me how to do Dutch braids in my hair, remember?"

161

"I want braids too," piped up Felicity.

Millie rolled her eyes. "You don't even have enough hair. And it's all hacked up in the front."

Felicity started to cry, and Winnie woke up. Mack came over and helped her sit up, feeling her forehead.

"I think you have enough hair for braids, Felicity," I told her. "I can do it—they'll just be short at the ends."

"Yay! Daddy, can Frannie stay a little?"

"That's up to Frannie," he said. "If she wants to spend more time in this loony bin, I'm not gonna stop her."

I laughed. "I like this loony bin. I can stay a little longer."

When all three girls had Dutch braids in their hair, I gave them each a hug goodbye and went into the kitchen, where Mack was pouring a can of tomato soup into a bowl for Winnie.

"Hey, I'm going to head out," I told him. "Unless you need anything else."

"I'm good."

"What about this week? The usual schedule?"

"Yeah. I can't believe the weekend is over already." Covering the top of the bowl with a plate, he stuck it in the microwave. "But I spoke with Mrs. Ingersoll on the ride to Petoskey, and it turns out the break wasn't as bad as she thought. She's in a cast, but her daughter can help with the driving and she can watch the girls this week."

"That's good news."

"Hell yes, it is. I'd have been fucked without her this week. And without you last week." After setting the cook time for three minutes, he took out his wallet and placed forty dollars on the counter. "For everything extra you did, although it's not enough."

I shoved it back toward him. "I don't want your money, Mack."

"Please take it." He met my eyes. "You spend so much of your time making my life easier, and I can't give you more of *my* time." He put his wallet away and pushed the bills toward me again. "Take it."

"No," I said stubbornly. "We're friends. And friends don't pay each other for favors." I headed for the back hall, where I put on my boots and zipped up my coat. I was about to put on my gloves and hat when Mack joined me by the door.

"Hey," he whispered, grabbing my arm.

"Hey what?"

With a quick glance over his shoulder, he suddenly pulled me close and slanted his mouth over mine. His tongue swept between my lips. His arms twined around me, his hands roaming over my body. For ten full seconds, he kissed me so deeply I was breathless and dizzy when he broke away.

"We are *not* friends," he said, his voice low and firm. He winked before backing out of the hall and calling the girls to lunch.

In a daze, I made my way to the car, not even feeling the frozen sting of the air on my cheeks.

Later I found the two twenties in my coat pocket and realized what Mack had been doing there at the door. I burst out laughing and stuffed them back in.

Every Sunday evening, my mother made dinner for the family. My parents still lived in what we called "the old part of the house," some of which had been taken over and renovated into rooms for the inn after us kids moved out. But they kept plenty of rooms for themselves, including their kitchen, dining room, library, and family room downstairs, and the master bedroom and bath, and a guest suite on the second floor.

Occasionally one or both of my sisters wouldn't make it, especially if they weren't at the inn already. But tonight they were both there.

Chloe cornered me in the dining room as we set the table. "So," she whispered, glancing toward the kitchen. "Any news?"

I couldn't hide a smile as I placed a fork to the left of each plate. "I saw him last night. And again today."

Her jaw dropped. "Jeez. So it's serious, huh?"

"Today I was only watching the girls. Last night was more of a ..." Then I stopped. What had it been? Not a date, really. "A romantic interlude."

Chloe snorted, setting a wine glass at each place. "What the hell is a *romantic interlude*? Does it involve sex?"

"In this case, yes." I paused, debating whether to go on, then thought *fuck it*. "In the kitchen."

Chloe stopped moving and blinked at me. "Seriously? Kitchen sex? I'm impressed."

"Shhhhh." I glanced behind me to make sure Mom and April were still chattering away in the next room. "It was sort of spontaneous. Winnie was asleep upstairs." I told her about the accident at their aunt's house as I set the rest of the silverware out.

"Oh my God, poor little thing," she said, pulling a corkscrew from the sideboard's top drawer. She worked the cork free from a bottle of wine. "Must be hard raising three girls all on his own."

"It is," I confirmed. "He's worried that he doesn't have enough time for me. But I keep telling him I'm not needy. I just want to be with him."

"Be with who?" April breezed in carrying a platter of broiled salmon and set it on the table.

Chloe and I exchanged a wide-eyed look. "Um," I mumbled.

April folded her arms and looked back and forth between the two of us. "Something is up with you two. Spill."

Twisting my fingers together at my waist, I leaned over and looked past April to make sure our mother was still busy in the kitchen, and she was, bickering with my dad over something. "Okay, if I tell you, you have to promise to keep it quiet."

"Of course. Tell me who he is!"

I grinned. "Mack."

Her mouth fell open and then she looked at Chloe. "I *knew* it! I was right!

"Shhhhh," I hushed. "You were. But it's very new and it's kind of tricky because of all the circumstances. I don't want Mom and Dad to know yet."

"Why not? I think it's great."

"It feels great so far," I said, my face getting warm. "But there are kids involved and—"

"What's this little powwow about?" my mother asked, carrying a bowl of green beans into the dining room.

"Ryan and Stella's wedding," April said quickly. "Frannie is making macarons, and she was just telling me which flavors she's going to make."

I gave her a grateful look. "I'm thinking chocolate, crème brulée, and red velvet."

"Perfect." She gave me a wink and we all went into the kitchen to help bring out the food.

About halfway through dinner, the subject of Ryan and Stella's wedding came up again. While April listed some of the details for Chloe and my mom, my mind wandered a little. I imagined what it would be like to plan my own wedding, what colors I'd choose, how many guests I'd invite, what I'd wear. I'd never really thought about it in great detail before, but now I pictured an intimate outdoor ceremony beside the barn at Cloverleigh and saw myself drifting down the aisle on a gorgeous summer evening to the sounds of classical guitar. Waiting for me under the rustic arch overlooking the vineyard was Mack, and in front of me walked his three girls, strewing rose petals in my path. He looked gorgeous in a charcoal gray suit with a sapphire blue tie that matched his eyes, and when he saw me for the first time, he—

"Frannie," my mother said, as if it wasn't the first time she'd tried to get my attention. "What on earth are you doing? I've asked you three times to pass the potatoes."

"Oh! Sorry." Flustered, I picked up the bowl of roasted potatoes and handed them to her. "I was just thinking about the wedding."

April smiled at me. "When I talked to Emme Pearson yesterday—that's Stella's sister, she's a wedding planner in Detroit," she explained to my parents, "she was *raving* about your macarons and hoping you'd open up your business to shipping downstate."

"That's awesome," Chloe said, kicking me under the table. "But you'd probably need your own space for that, right? A bigger kitchen and maybe a storefront somewhere?"

I took a sip of wine for courage and was setting my glass

down as my mother spoke up.

"We've already settled this. I don't think Frannie has the time or energy for that sort of thing," she said. "She's so busy here at the inn, plus being a nanny to Mack's girls. That's really all she can do. In fact, I think she could use more downtime."

"Well, *I* think we should let Frannie speak for herself," said Chloe.

"Actually," I said, sitting up taller in my chair. "Starting my own business is something I would like to discuss."

"But you don't know the first thing about it, and running a business is *very* stressful." Mom gave Chloe a look like she should know better. "Stress is dangerous for Frannie. John, don't you agree with me?"

My father looked at me thoughtfully as he chewed and swallowed. "What sort of business?"

"A macarons shop," I said, nervously twisting my hands in my lap. "Something small and upscale."

"Frannie, your doctors have made it very clear that you need lots of rest and should avoid unnecessary risks to your heart," my mother went on.

"Mom, they meant risks like smoking and obesity." I looked her in the eye and spoke confidently, so she'd see I wasn't going to back down this time.

"Stress is a risk factor," she insisted, picking up her wine glass. "John, can you help me out here?"

"Stress is a risk factor. I agree." My dad wiped his mouth with his napkin. "Your mother and I aren't saying we wouldn't support you, we just want you to be safe and healthy."

"Frannie's not a baby," April said. "Why can't she decide what's safe and healthy for her? I think it's a great idea. And what if the shop was on the Cloverleigh premises? You could invest in it!"

"I don't want it on the premises." I shook my head. "I want my own thing in my own place. And I don't need anyone else's money to do it."

"Frannie, don't be silly," my mother admonished. "Where on earth would you get the money to open a business?"

"It's called a bank, Mom. I'd get a small business loan."

She waved a hand, dismissing me. "Enough. You're not starting a business. You've got enough going on."

"Stop it! I'm not a child anymore." At my heated tone, the entire table went still and silent. I lowered my voice—I wanted to sound calm and self-assured, not petulant and angry. "I'm an adult, and it's time I started acting like one."

"What does that mean?" My mother looked a bit nervous now.

"It means that maybe I need to move out and start supporting myself." I hadn't planned on threatening to move out, but I wanted them to know I was serious. If that's what it took, I'd do it.

"Move out!" she cried. "Why would you do that? You'd have to pay rent anywhere else."

"That's the point. What other twenty-seven-year-old woman still lives with her parents?" I gestured to April and Chloe. "My sisters all left home and chased their own dreams. And even if those dreams brought them right back here, it was their choice. *I want a choice.*"

"What if we charged you a fair rent?" suggested my dad.

"John, you can't be serious!" My mother looked at him in shock. "We're not charging her rent."

"It's better than seeing her move out," he said reasonably.

"Frannie," my mother appealed to me, "you know I only worry about you because I love you so much."

"I know, Mom. But that love has become a little bit over-bearing. I feel smothered and trapped by it. You've got to let go a little, okay? You've got to trust that I know how to take care of myself. I need some freedom to do my own thing, even if it's a mistake. Even if I fail."

Unable to eat anymore, I stood up, my half-full plate in my hands. "I'm not doing this to hurt you, and I'm grateful for everything you do for me. I love it here. But I need more, and I need it on my own terms." I turned to my father. "Thanks for the offer about the rent, Dad. I'll give it some thought."

And with that, I walked into the kitchen on legs shaking with nerves and exhilaration, put my plate on the counter, and left through the back door.

I hadn't planned on making a declaration of independence at Sunday dinner, but I couldn't help feeling damn good about it.

Later that night, when I was dressed for bed and lying in the sheets I couldn't bring myself to change because they still sort of smelled like him, I pulled out my phone so I could give him a hard time about those twenty-dollar bills he'd stuck in my pocket.

Jerk.

I have no idea what you're talking about.

Of course not. Because you're so innocent. With

your filthy mouth.

Hey, that swear jar money goes to charity. I'm only doing my part.

I didn't know that. What charity?

The girls take turns choosing each month. I think it's Felicity's month. She usually chooses the National Geographic Society.

Of course she does.

I saw the rock you gave her. That was very sweet of you. Thanks.

You're welcome. What organizations do the other ones choose?

Millie usually goes for kids charities. Winnie goes for animals.

I love those girls. Such big hearts.

They love you. They refused to take out their braids in the shower. I think they want to be you.

Aww. Are they asleep?

Yes. Finally. It took Winnie some time. I'm still lying here next to her. She is convinced monsters are under her bed, so I had to promise to sleep here.

I pictured him lying next to little Winnie, and my heart throbbed hard.

Poor baby. What a good Daddy. I guess I won't text you anything dirty then.

Hold on now, I can take a break. What kind of dirty are we talking about? Like mildly unclean? Or full on filthy?

I laughed silently as I texted back.

Full on filthy.

Oh fuck. Hold on. I'm going downstairs.

My pulse had started to race. It had not been my

intention to sext him when I picked up my phone, and I'd never done it before. But I had plenty of fantasies to choose from where he was concerned, and tonight had me feeling audacious and free—like I could do anything. Biting my lip, I turned off my lamp and took off my T-shirt. Then I shimmied out of my panties and slid down deeper into the covers.

If I was going to do this, I was going to do it right.

Eighteen

Mack

I WENT DOWN THE STAIRS SC FAST I STUMBLED AT THE BOTTOM and nearly fell on my face. After making sure both the front and back doors were locked, I hurried into my room, shut the door, and whipped off my shirt.

I'm alone now. Are you there?

I'm here. I wish you were too.

The crotch of my jeans was already tight. I unbuttoned and unzipped them before lying back on my bed. Then I called her.

She was laughing when she answered. "I said I'd *text* you dirty things."

"Fuck that," I said quietly, holding the phone with my left hand and sliding my right hand down my lower abs inside my pants. "If you're gonna talk filthy to me, I want to hear you do it. So talk."

Her laugh turned sultry and feline. "So bossy."

"You know you like it."

"You're right. I do," she whispered.

"Where are you right now?" I took my cock in my fist and let the rising flesh slip through my fingers.

"I'm lying in bed. And I'm not wearing a stitch of clothing."

Closing my eyes, I imagined her naked and warm beneath the covers. "Why not?"

"Because every night when I go to bed, I pretend you're next to me. And you like to get your hands on my bare skin."

"That's not all I like on your bare skin."

She laughed again, low and lilting. "No. You like your mouth on me too. I lie here and touch all the places on my body where I want to feel your tongue."

"Do it now," I demanded, my hand moving quicker now. "Touch yourself."

"Where?" she whispered. "Tell me."

"Your tits. Your stomach. Your thighs. Your pussy." I kept my voice low as I imagined her hands running over her body.

She moaned, and my dick grew thicker and harder in my fist. "It feels so good," she sighed. "And just hearing your voice makes me so hot."

"Are you wet?"

"You know I am. Because you're fucking me with your tongue."

Sweet Jesus, I could taste her. I could feel her silky, swollen skin against my tongue. I could hear her breath coming quicker and harder. I could feel her body tense and tremble. "Tell me to make you come."

"Mack," she panted. "Make me come. Oh God, just like that. I love when you do it soft at first, so slow and sweet, like you can't get enough."

"Fuck yes." I fought back against my own orgasm, which threatened to escape my control at any moment.

"And then you do it faster, and harder, and my hands are

in your hair and I'm going to come so hard for you …" Her words changed into soft, pleading little sounds that built in volume and intensity, and I pictured her lying there with her hand between her thighs and her legs open and her body rippling with pleasure as she said my name again and again and again.

My lower body tightened and I thrust into my hand, which was slick with warmth. "I need to fuck you," I told her. "Now."

"Yes. Do it," she said breathlessly. "And don't stop."

"God, my cock is so hard for you. And you're so wet, and so tight, and you take it so deep …"

"I can feel you," she whispered. "I love the way you move, the way you fill me up, the way your body is so heavy on mine. I love your big, hard cock inside me, so deep I want to scream."

"Keep talking." My body was on the edge, my skin humming, my muscles tight. I listened to her voice in my ear and let her words and her breath and the memory of her sweet little pussy tightening around my cock drive me closer to release.

"I love it when you're rough with me. When you tell me what to do. When you take control and make me feel like I'm powerless against you. When you fuck me so hard I can't even breathe, and all I want to do is feel you come. I want every last drop. Give it to me," she urged, and hearing her get greedy and demanding was so fucking hot, I couldn't take it.

Growling a chain of curses that would make any Marine proud, I exploded all over my bare chest and stomach in thick, hot, pulsing ribbons.

Afterward, I heard her breathless laughter. "Are you still there?"

"I think so." My stomach muscles refused to unclench. "Fuck. That was so hot."

"It was. But I still wish you were really here."

"I know. Me too." Something thumped upstairs. I paused and listened. "Shit. I hope I wasn't too loud."

She gasped. "Me too."

"Give me a minute. I'll call you right back."

"Okay."

Tossing my phone onto the bed, I went into the bathroom and cleaned myself up, then did up my jeans, threw my T-shirt back on, and went upstairs to check on the kids.

All three were sleeping soundly, but Millie had evidently moved around enough to knock a book off her nightstand. I must have heard it hitting the floor. After replacing it, I quietly left her room and went back down to mine.

I called Frannie back. "Hey, sorry. Just wanted to check on the kids."

"That's okay. Are they all right?"

"They're fine." I sat down on my bed and exhaled. "But I should take a quick shower and go up to Winnie's room, although I'll probably end up sleeping on the floor in there because her bed is so small."

She laughed sympathetically. "Poor thing. I'd tell you I've got plenty of room in my bed, but that probably wouldn't help."

I groaned. "No, it doesn't."

"Well, the spot next to me is yours any time you can get away."

"Thanks. I wish I knew when that would be."

"What about the night of the wedding?" she asked hopefully.

"Yeah, my folks will be here then. That's a possibility."

"Don't worry, I won't get my hopes up," she said quickly. "It's just an idea."

"I like it." I exhaled. "Let me see what I can do."

"Okay." She yawned, then giggled. "You tired me out from clear across town."

"Here's where I make a joke about how big my dick is."

"It's no joke," she said. "And I'll be thinking about it every night about this time until I can have you to myself again."

"You really do want to torture me, don't you?"

"Yes." She laughed softly. "And no. I just want to be with you, that's all. I know this is brand new, but it feels really good."

"It does."

"So forgive me if I get a little carried away. I've had these feelings for you for so long, I hardly remember a time when you didn't make my heart pound."

"Really?"

"Really. But I was convinced you only saw me as a kid."

I snorted. "Nope. I mean, I thought you were too young and way off limits, but I remember last year at the Christmas party wanting to throw you over my shoulder, take you back to my office, and fuck you on my desk."

"What?" she screeched. "You never said anything!"

"What the hell would I have said?" I asked, laughing. "Your parents were in the room. And my kids. And everyone we work with."

"I guess. But jeez. I wish I would have known. You hid it well."

"I had to. I told myself it was wrong to want you that way."

"Have you changed your mind yet?" she asked softly.

"That's a good question." I decided to be honest. "Yes

and no. I'm still worried about what your parents will think. And I worry about what will happen when you realize I'm not worth all the shit you have to put up with."

"What do you think will happen?" she asked.

"You'll move on because you know you deserve better," I said simply. "And I'll let you, because I'll know it too." *I know it already*, I thought.

"If that's what you think, then you don't know *me* very well, Declan MacAllister. So I guess it's up to me to prove you wrong."

I smiled, picturing that stubborn tilt of her chin. "Okay."

"I'll see you tomorrow." She blew a kiss. "Goodnight."

"Goodnight."

While I was in the shower, I wondered what it was going to be like seeing her at work this week. Actually, not only this week but from now on. Would it be obvious to everyone that we were … *involved*?

Maybe it was stupid of me to think we had to hide it. Maybe this uneasy feeling was due to exhaustion and worry rather than any real reason to think things wouldn't be okay. Maybe I was letting my failed romantic past and divorced dad guilt overshadow the possibility of this new relationship. After all, I was still human. I still needed companionship now and then. I still craved human—*adult* human—connection from time to time. Frannie was sexy and fun and easygoing, she fit seamlessly into our lives, and she was reconnecting me to a piece of myself I'd lost—the part that wasn't anyone's father. I loved the way I felt when I was with her.

But deep down, I knew it couldn't last.

The next morning when I walked into the inn, she looked up from where she was helping guests at the desk and grinned at me. Not a casual grin, either—a *we're secretly fucking* grin, accompanied by a mischievous gleam in her eye.

And I gave it right back to her. I couldn't help it. But I bid her and the guests a very formal "good morning," which she returned just as formally, as if she hadn't been whispering dirty things to me on the phone while I jerked off last night. I felt like a teenager sneaking out of her bedroom without getting caught as I headed down the hall toward my office.

Over the next couple days, we exchanged that grin often but behaved ourselves pretty well. When we passed each other in the hallway or lobby at work, we did our best to keep straight faces, but sometimes I'd squeeze her hand or sneak a kiss if no one was watching. Each night we'd text or chat once I got the kids in bed.

Late in the afternoon on Wednesday, there was a knock on my open office door. When I looked up and saw her, my heart began to race. "Hey, you. How's your day?"

"Great," she said, hugging some papers to her chest. "Got a minute?"

"Of course." I stood up from my chair and walked around my desk toward her. "Come on in. Take a seat."

She entered my office and I shut the door. Then, before she was out of reach, I grabbed her arm, tugged her back, and pushed her up against the door. "But first."

Caging her in, I slanted my lips over hers and kissed her like I wished I could have done last night, tasting her, teasing her tongue with mine, pressing my body against hers. Whatever she'd been carrying dropped to our feet and she slid her hands up my chest. Into my hair. Around my neck.

When the kiss threatened to get out of control and I

found myself groping her over her work clothes, I pushed back. "We better stop."

"Right," she said, breathing hard, bending to gather the papers she'd dropped.

I went around my desk again, adjusted my pants to accommodate my unhappy erection, and sat down. "What can I do for you?"

Her face lit up as she came forward and set the papers in front of me. "Mrs. Radley, the bride who said she was interested in helping me start a business, just dropped this off. She was in a hurry, but look."

On top of the stack was a handwritten note. It read:

Dear Frannie,

Thank you again for rescuing me before the first dance. I haven't forgotten you! After hearing our guests rave about your macarons at the reception, I was more convinced than ever that this is what you need to do! And then first thing this morning when I got back in the office, I got a message from someone looking to sell a little café right in downtown Traverse City. It's a sign! I've enclosed the info here along with my business card and a few other options for spaces to rent or buy. Call me!

Maxima Radley

After thumbing through the other pages, which were all real estate listings for commercial spaces, I looked up at Frannie, whose eyes were bright. "This is awesome. You have to call her."

"You think?" She twisted her hands together. "I want to—I'm just nervous. I haven't gotten a chance to tell you this yet, but I told my parents what I want to do Sunday night at dinner."

"Good for you. What did they say?"

She flipped her hands. "They gave me a bunch of shit

about it, especially my mother. But I didn't back down. I told them it's what I want to do, and it's time I start making decisions based on what I think I'm capable of, not them."

I sat back in my chair and assessed her. "I'm impressed. How'd they take it?"

She squirmed a little. "Not awesome. I threatened to move out too, which I hadn't planned on doing, but I was getting pretty fired up about wanting my independence. My dad suggested I start paying rent."

I raised my eyebrows. "What did you say?"

"I said thanks but no thanks. Not that I wouldn't pay rent, of course, and I will, but that that's not what I meant. All my sisters got the chance to go to school, travel, accomplish their goals. They weren't held back, and I don't want to be held back either anymore. If I fail, I fail, but I've got to try."

"As a father, you're scaring the piss out of me right now. As someone who wants to see you kick ass out in the world, I'm happy as fuck and I want you to go call this woman."

She grinned. "Thanks. I'm going to."

I gathered up the papers for her and paper-clipped the woman's card to her note. "Let me know how it goes."

"I'm nervous," she said, flattening her hands on her stomach. "What if she asks questions I have no answers to?"

"Hey. Listen to me." Leaving the listings on my desk, I came around and took her by the shoulders. "You are smart, talented, and persistent. If you don't know the answer to something, you'll find it. And you're not alone."

"No?"

I shook my head. "You've got your sisters, you've got an ally in this Radley woman, and you have me. I'll be here for you every step of the way."

Her lips tipped up. "You will?"

"Yes."

She slipped her arms around my waist and looked up at me with adorably huge eyes. "Tell me again that I have you."

"You have me."

Rising on tiptoe, she touched her lips to mine. "That's all I want."

The kiss was probably supposed to be short and sweet, but once she was that close, I couldn't resist gathering her into my arms and opening my mouth over hers. Once again, the kiss grew reckless quickly, and suddenly I was pulling her work shirt from her pants and sliding my hands up her ribs as I walked her backward toward my desk. She moved a hand between my legs and rubbed her palm over my dick, whose hopes rose again like a helium balloon. I was about to lift her up when someone knocked on my office door.

Frannie and I sprang apart fast.

I cleared my throat. "Come in."

Chloe entered the office, looking at something on her phone. "Hey, what do you think of this ad copy for—" Then she looked up and stopped. Her eyes roved from Frannie, who was trying to look casual, although her shirt was untucked and she was breathing kind of heavy, to me. Remembering the tent in my pants, I quickly moved around my desk and sat down. Smoothed my hair.

"Am I interrupting something?" Chloe asked, clearly amused.

"No," we both said at once.

She laughed. "You guys are horrible liars."

"I was just going," Frannie said, her cheeks turning a gorgeous shade of pink. She scooped up the stack of papers on my desk and hurried for the door. "I'll talk to you later."

"Okay," Chloe and I both said at once. Then we looked at each other.

"Well," she said.

"It's not what it looks like," I blurted. Then I shook my head. "Actually, it's exactly what it looks like."

Chloe burst out laughing. "Don't look so scared, Mack. I think it's fantastic. Frannie needs somebody like you. It's good for her."

I rubbed my face with both hands. "I don't know about that. I keep thinking your dad is going to come after me with a shotgun."

She dismissed that idea with a wave of her hand. "Nah. It'll take him all of two seconds to see how crazy Frannie is about you. And what Frannie wants, Frannie gets. All she has to do is turn those big green eyes at him, and he's a goner."

All I could do was sigh. "Yeah. I know the feeling."

Nineteen

Frannie

O N MY WAY UP TO MY APARTMENT, I DID MY BEST TO work up my nerve. *You can do this. Chin up. People believe in you.*

Sitting at my kitchen counter, I went over all the notes I'd taken over the last week, the lists of needs and wants I'd made, the approximate cost of equipment, ingredients, and employee time. I'd need at least one helper to start, but I wouldn't be able to pay anyone full-time. I'd been thinking maybe I could find a college student, or even a high school student who was interested in baking and had time on the weekends.

Finally, I called the number on Maxima Radley's card.

"Hello?" She sounded like she was in the car.

"Hi, Mrs. Radley, this is Frannie Sawyer from—"

"Frannie Sawyer, how *are* you? You got my note?"

"Yes. I'm—I was really glad you came in."

"Well, I'm telling you, Frannie, this is meant. To. Be. My entire honeymoon, I kept thinking of what I could do for you, and then the very morning I get back to the office, I got a phone call from the daughter of a friend of my mother's.

They were in pageants together or something." She laughed. "Anyway, this girl, her name is Natalie Haas, has owned this little coffee shop downtown for years and it's doing really well, but she's got a two-year-old son and she's pregnant again, and apparently she runs another restaurant as well, so she needs to cut back."

"What's the name of it?" I asked, wondering if I'd ever been there.

"Coffee Darling."

"Oh, I know that place!" I exclaimed. "It's adorable. That's the shop for sale?"

"Well, she's not sure if she should sell the building, which she does own, or try to find a reliable tenant. She was looking for advice. Her dream scenario, actually, is to find someone to partner with. I thought of you immediately."

My heart had started to race. "Did you tell her about me?"

"Not yet. But I just couldn't help thinking that with her experience, and all the equipment in place, plus a built-in clientele, and your fresh new ideas and youth and energy—I see a home run."

"I'd love to meet her," I said breathlessly.

"Great! I'll set up a meeting. In the meantime, why don't you see if you can get down there and check out the spot? Look at it with your vision in mind and see what you think."

I sat up taller. "I'll definitely do that."

"Perfect. I have to run, dear, but I'll be in touch as soon as I connect with Natalie again."

"Thank you so much," I said.

We hung up, and I set the phone down and sat there for a moment, my stomach a tangled but excited mess of knots. For the first time, I felt like this thing really might happen.

I jumped off the stool and hummed a tune as I went into my room and changed into sweatpants and a hoodie. All this nervous energy inside me needed to burn off, and I could use some time to think as well. A walk outside in the brisk cold evening air would be perfect. The farm was beautiful in the summer, but I loved it in the winter too—the rolling hills blanketed with snow, the evergreens tall and majestic, the sky full of stars you couldn't see in town because of all the lights. Everyone complained about the frigid northern Michigan weather—myself included—but I loved the seasons up here so much, I could never leave. And what was better than hot chocolate or Irish coffee or whiskey by the fire after you came in out of the cold?

For a moment, I wished Mack was around to walk and talk with me, but I knew he was probably already on his way home, and if I wasn't mistaken, it was a Therapy Wednesday. But I texted him quickly.

Great news! Call when you can.

Then I stuck my phone and earbuds in my coat pocket, pulled on my mittens, and went out the door.

After my walk, I was sweaty beneath my winter layers, bursting with ideas to write down, and hungry for dinner, but decided to try again with my mom and dad. I was excited and needed to share my news with someone, and since April and Chloe were already gone for the day—their cars were not in the lot when I got back—my parents were my only option.

My mother had worked with me this week, but she hadn't mentioned the scene at Sunday night's dinner. She hadn't spoken to me much at all, really, and she'd pointedly ignored the envelope Maxima Radley dropped off. It was strange for so much tension to exist between my mother and me—we'd always been close, and I didn't like feeling as if we were on opposite sides of a divide.

But I wasn't going to back down, and she needed to know it.

After pulling off my hat and mittens, I knocked on the door that led to their living room. My father answered, looking surprised to see me. "Hey, peanut. Come on in."

"Hi, Dad. Mom around?"

"Yeah. She's in the kitchen harassing me about retirement again."

I followed him through the dining room into the kitchen, where my mother was stirring roasted Brussels sprouts in a dented old pan. "Hey, Mom," I said, unzipping my coat. "Smells good."

"I made chicken and rice," she said. "Do you want to eat with us?"

"Sure." I slid onto a seat at their kitchen table, where I'd grown up eating breakfast, lunch, and dinner almost every day of my life. Hot, healthy, homemade meals for seven people that I probably didn't appreciate then, but realized now took a lot of time and effort and taught me to value real food, fresh ingredients, and time with family. It was something I wanted to pass on to my own children someday. I told myself to go easy on her.

"I thought we might talk again about my opening a pastry shop," I said. "I have some news."

My phone hummed with a call just as I was climbing into bed. It was Mack.

"Hello?"

"Hey. Sorry it took so long for me to call back."

"That's okay." I hopped into bed and pulled the covers over my legs. "How was your night?"

"It was fine." But he sounded tired. "I took them to therapy, then out for some dinner, but Winnie is still struggling to eat."

"Poor thing."

"Then Felicity freaked out that she didn't have enough valentines for her entire class, so I had to run out to the drugstore. And Millie's eye-rolling is out of control, but all in all, not a terrible night."

I laughed. "Don't take it to heart. She's at that age. Eye-rolling is sort of an automatic reaction to anything your dad says."

That prompted a groan. "I'm not looking forward to the teenage years."

"Maybe it won't be so bad. I wasn't a sassy teenager."

"No?"

"No, but that might have been a reaction to Chloe. She was as sassy as they come, and I saw how my parents struggled. I think I was trying to be the anti-Chloe." I sighed. "I was a pleaser."

"You still are."

I smiled. "But guess what?"

"What?"

"I talked to Maxima Radley, and it went really well. Then I went down to tell my parents about it."

"And?"

"And I convinced them that if they really loved me, they

would support me in this. I told them that I was doing this with or without their support, but I'd much prefer to have it."

"What did they say?"

"My dad asked me some practical questions. My mother mostly gave me the silent treatment. But in the end, it was my father who talked her into easing up on me."

"Really? How?"

"It was pretty incredible. He said he'd been thinking about it all last night and all day today. He reminded her of how her family—which was wealthy and old money—had treated her when she announced she wanted to marry a guy she'd met at college who ran a family farm up north. And how they told her it was beneath her to run an inn. And how *everyone* told them they were crazy to buy more land and plant a vineyard." I felt my throat getting tight as I described the next part. "Then he took her hand and reminded her how they'd always agreed that raising children was the hardest, most important job they'd ever do ... but that the job was over. That even though they're still parents, their children were all grown, and they had to trust that they'd raised smart, kind, responsible people unafraid to face the world and chase their dreams. Otherwise, he said, they'd have failed."

"Wow. How'd she take it?"

"She shed a few tears. But in the end, she came around. She admitted that maybe her clinging to me had more to do with herself than with me. Her identity for so many years has been wrapped up in being an overprotective mother. Once that's gone, she fears feeling lost. She doesn't know what the next phase of her life is supposed to look like."

He was silent a moment. "I can relate to that."

"My dad told her it can look like anything she wants it to. He said maybe they should stop talking about traveling more and do it. Enjoy the years they've got left while they still feel young enough."

"What did she say?"

I laughed. "She said three things. One, she'd love to travel more, especially to see her grandchildren. Two, she said it only works if he agrees to step back from work a bit, so he should really get a plan in place for his retirement. And three, she said she wants *more* grandchildren in her life. Then she gave me a look."

"A look? What kind of look?"

"A look that says, *Is there any hope of you giving me a grandchild in the future?*"

He coughed. "You've got three other sisters. How come the pressure's all on you?"

"I don't know. Maybe she figures April would have started a family if she'd wanted one by now? Or that Meg is too much of a career woman? Or that Chloe can't be trusted to raise kids that aren't little hellions like she was?"

"Do you even want kids?"

"Oh, definitely," I said. "I've always wanted them. And I've asked the doctor if there's any reason I might have a difficult time because of my heart, and he said no. I can absolutely have kids."

"That's … that's good."

I smiled, because I could hear the anxiety in his voice. "Don't worry. I'm not in a rush."

He laughed. "That's even better."

I filled him in on the details of my conversation with Maxima, and told him that I was waiting on her to get back to me about meeting Natalie Haas, owner of Coffee Darling.

"Oh yeah, I know that place. I think she was a Nixon. Sylvia and I graduated with her older sister, Jillian."

"Really? Cool, I'll mention that when I meet her." I took a deep breath and wiggled my toes beneath the covers. "I don't want to jinx myself, but I have such a good feeling about this."

"Good."

"I'm going to go check out the space as soon as I can."

"I'm really happy for you, Frannie."

"Thanks. I'm happy for myself."

"Oh, shit. Hold on a sec." There were muffled voices in the background, and then he came back. "I'm sorry, I have to go. Winnie is up. She heard something under her bed, so I have to go check for monsters."

"That's okay. Give her a hug from me. I'll see you tomorrow."

"See you tomorrow."

I set my alarm and put my phone back on the nightstand, switched off my lamp and buried myself in the covers. It was probably way too premature to feel so positive about things, but I couldn't help it.

My own business, more independence, Mack ... all the things I wanted most in life were right within my grasp.

Twenty

Mack

I GOT WINNIE BACK TO SLEEP PRETTY QUICKLY AND RETURNED to my bedroom, leaving the door open in case she called out again. I undressed, brushed my teeth, and got into bed, where I lay awake with my eyes closed, hands behind my head.

But I felt weird about something, and I couldn't relax.

She wanted kids. Of course she did. Look how awesome she was with mine, why wouldn't she want her own? But it was out of the question for me. There was no way in hell I was having any more kids. Jesus fucking Christ, I'd go insane. Talk about sleepless nights—I'd have eye-rolling, rule-bucking teenagers on one end of the spectrum, dirty-diapered screaming infants and tantrum-throwing toddlers on the other, not to mention the kids needing attention in between. I couldn't do it. There wasn't enough of me to go around. Did I have to make sure she knew that *that* kind of future with me was not a possibility?

Or was that fucking stupid? Just because she wanted a family somewhere down the line didn't mean she was thinking about a family with *me*, did it? She said she wasn't in a rush. Christ, we'd only been fooling around for a couple weeks.

Flopping over onto my stomach, I shoved the pillow over my head and forced myself to stop thinking about it and go to sleep.

She came over Thursday to watch the girls, and I was late getting home because a meeting ran long. When I arrived, the house smelled delicious and they were all in the living room. Felicity and Winnie were sorting valentines on the couch, and Frannie and Millie were doing something on the living room floor with white T-shirts, glue, and glitter. I recognized one of the shirts as mine.

"Is that fucking glitter?" I demanded, watching in horror as Millie tossed handfuls of pink and red sparkly shit over glue lines on my shirt.

"Yes, but don't worry. When we shake it off, there won't be so much."

At that, Frannie burst out laughing so hard she rocked onto her back and stayed there, cracking up.

"And what are you laughing at, huh?" I gave Frannie's leg a nudge with my foot. "Maybe I will take you up on that offer to be in this show instead of me."

"No way," she said. "You made a promise."

"That's right." Millie picked up the bottle of glue and gave me a smug look. "And it was your idea."

"I need a beer," I said.

"I made dinner for you," Frannie said, getting to her feet. "It's in the oven keeping warm."

"Is that what smells so good? You didn't have to do that."

She smiled. "It's just a casserole. Not a big deal."

"It is. And I appreciate it. Have the girls eaten?"

"Yes, so I'll get going. Bye, girls. Happy Valentine's Day!"

"Happy Valentine's Day!" they shouted.

Fuck, I'd forgotten. All day long I kept telling myself not to forget to stop and pick up a little something for her, but it had gotten hectic at work and then I was running late … God, I was shitty at this.

I followed her to the kitchen. Glancing behind me to make sure the girls weren't watching, I tugged her into the back hall, opened the closet door, and pulled her in there with me. She giggled as I shut the door, closing us in pitch black dark.

"What are you doing?" she whispered, her voice muffled by all the coats.

"I'm stealing thirty seconds alone with you for Valentine's Day." I wound my arms around her. "This is what it's like to be my valentine. Isn't it romantic?"

She giggled. "Totally."

"I wish we had some time alone. And I should have gotten something for you. Flowers or chocolate or something."

"I don't want gifts, Mack. I just want you."

"But I can't even give you that. Not the way I want to, anyway."

She put her hands on my chest. "Shut up and kiss me."

I tried, but it was so dark in there I missed her lips the first time and ended up licking her chin. We were laughing and kissing when the door swung open and Winifred stood there staring at us.

"What are you doing in there?" she asked.

"I was … changing a lightbulb," I blurted, reaching up

and pulling the string hanging from the bare bulb. The light clicked on. "Oh good. It works now."

"What was Frannie doing?" Winnie asked, eyeballing us both as we came out of the closet.

"I was helping," Frannie said, grabbing her jacket off a hook and trying not to laugh.

"Can you help him make dessert?" Winnie wondered hopefully.

"No, she's got things to do, Winn." I grabbed my youngest and got her in a loving chokehold. "We'll see her tomorrow."

"Bye." Frannie zipped up and opened the door. Her cheeks were scarlet and she couldn't stop grinning. "See you tomorrow."

The next morning, I still felt guilty that I hadn't gotten her even a small gift for Valentine's Day after she'd stayed late at the house and even made dinner. I could pay her more, and I would, but I also still wanted to do something nice for her. Could I bring something to work for her? Coffee? A muffin? A card? On a whim, I turned into the parking lot of a drugstore and ran inside.

In the greeting card aisle, I found the picked-over remains of the Valentine options. It was a fucking mess. Overwhelmed, I moved over to the I'm Sorry section and looked for one that might be appropriate.

There were cards with roses and fancy cursive apologies, cards with kittens and cutesy script, cards with illustrations and funny quotes and inspirational sayings and promises to do better. I read about a thousand of them, getting more agitated with each passing second. Part of me sort of felt like buying the whole rack—I'd probably need them all sooner or later.

In the end, I grabbed one with a drawing of a lollipop on it that said I SUCK. (SORRY.)

I paid for it and ran back to my car, where I quickly scribbled a note on the blank inside.

Sorry yesterday wasn't more romantic. I'll make it up to you.
Mack

I shoved it in the envelope, wrote *Frannie* on the front, and tucked it into my jacket.

My next stop was the florist, where I bought a dozen red roses. Back in the car, I tucked the card between the stems and drove to work. I realized that if anyone else was at the desk, it would probably be pretty fucking obvious what was going on, but I decided I didn't care.

But she wasn't at the desk when I got to the inn—her mother was. That's when I remembered that she didn't work there on Fridays.

"Well, good morning," Daphne Sawyer said, smiling at me as I approached carrying the roses. "And who's the lucky lady?"

My stomach lurched, but I told the truth. "Um, they're for Frannie, actually. She's been so great with the kids, and she stayed late and made dinner yesterday ... I just wanted to let her know I appreciate her."

The smile widened. "How nice. She's not working this morning, but she's at home as far as I know. Why don't you bring them to her?"

"Maybe I will, thanks." I went back to my office, glad that Daphne didn't seem upset or even all that surprised by the fact that I'd bought flowers for her daughter. Maybe Frannie was right, and her parents weren't going to be shocked or angry about us.

When I got back to my office, I texted her.

Morning, beautiful. What are you up to?

My elbows in batter LOL. I have a lot of baking to do. Busy weekend. Events booked all three nights.

That's right, it's Presidents Weekend.

Inn sold out?

Yes.

Which meant she was totally busy and probably didn't have time to fuck around with me, but I was dying to give her the roses and grab at least a few minutes alone with her. I decided I'd sneak up there at lunchtime.

However, I only made it until about nine-thirty before I couldn't wait any longer and stealthily crept up the stairs to her apartment, hiding the bouquet behind my back.

When she answered the door, she looked surprised but happy. And fucking adorable—her hair was all piled on the top of her head in a big sloppy mess and she had a smudge of pink batter on her cheek.

"Hey," she said, her smile bright. "What are you doing up here?"

"I brought you something." I held out the flowers.

She gasped. "What's this for?"

"For Valentine's Day. For everything you do." Unable to resist, I caught her around the waist and kissed her lips. She tasted sweet—like strawberries and cream.

"You didn't have to do that. But thank you." She glanced down at her T-shirt and sweatpants. "I wish I'd have known you were coming. I'm a mess."

"You're perfect." I looked at her hair. "But I do think even I could do a better bun than that."

Laughing, she swatted me on the chest. "Now you're just getting cocky."

"Oh, I've always been that."

"Want to come in?" she asked. "Or do you have to get back to work?"

"I should get back," I said reluctantly.

"Just for a few minutes?" She rose up on tiptoe.

Fuck, she was so cute. "Okay. A few minutes, but that's really all I have. I'm meeting with your dad and DeSantis in half an hour."

"I promise to kick you out by then." Grinning, she stepped back and I entered her apartment, which smelled as good as she tasted.

"Let me grab a vase for these." She set the flowers on the counter and pulled out the card. As she read it, her lips curved into a smile. "Awww. Thank you."

"You're welcome. It's not much, but I wanted you to know I was thinking of you. And how lucky I am to have you in my life."

"I feel the same."

"Your mom saw me with the flowers and asked who they were for."

Frannie's jaw dropped. "What did you tell her?"

"The truth, actually." And suddenly, I felt really good about it.

"You did?" She set the card down and threw her arms around my neck, hugging me tight. "That makes me so happy!"

I wrapped my arms around her and held her close, lifting her right off her feet. "I'm glad."

"Was my mother surprised?" Frannie asked.

"Not as much as I thought she would be. She seemed fine with it."

"I told you." Then she inhaled deeply. "Mmm. You smell good."

"You smell good too. I could eat you right now." Just for fun, I sank my teeth lightly into her throat.

Squealing, she tried to wiggle out of my arms, but I held on tight. I kept my mouth on her neck, licking and sucking and kissing her sweet-tasting skin, and then before I knew it, I was walking her backward into her bedroom, stripping off her clothes, and letting her pull at mine. Within minutes, I was buried inside her, her body pinned beneath mine on top of her quilt, her hands braced on the headboard so her head didn't bang against it. It ended as quickly as it began, with both of us breathless and frantic, our bodies pulsing together in short, ecstatic bursts just as the oven timer went off in the kitchen.

Laughing as we recovered our senses, Frannie looked up at me. "Good timing."

"Does that mean you have to get out of this bed?"

"Yes, unfortunately."

"I don't want you to."

"I'll come right back."

Reluctantly, I let her slide out from underneath me. She hurried into the bathroom first, and then out to the kitchen, and a moment later the timer stopped beeping. I heard her open and shut the oven door, and then she darted back into her bedroom.

"I only have a few minutes," she said, hopping back into the bed. "And so do you. What time is your meeting?"

I sat up. "Fuck! I forgot about that. What time is it now?"

"A few minutes to ten."

"Shit!" I jumped out of bed and looked around for my pants. "My meeting is at ten."

Frannie laughed as I frantically pulled my clothes on. "Sorry. I guess I was supposed to boot you out sooner."

I gave her a dirty look as I struggled to get my second leg into my pants, hopping on one foot. "Yes. This is all your fault. If you hadn't smelled so good or been so fucking cute when you answered the door, I'd have been on time for my meeting."

She threw a pillow at me.

I zipped up my pants and tackled her, throwing her back onto the bed. "You're asking for it."

Giggling, she looped her arms and legs around me. "Hard and often."

I groaned, giving her a quick kiss before detaching myself from her limbs. "Fuck, I have to go. I wish I didn't."

"Me too." She sighed and sat up, watching me throw my shirt on. "It's so nice to be alone with you again."

"I'm sorry. I feel bad we can't be like normal people and do this during non-working hours."

"It's okay." She smiled. "It's kind of fun to sneak around."

"Except I'm late for a meeting with your *dad* right now," I said, frowning at my freshly-fucked hair in the mirror over her dresser. "And I look like I just got out of bed."

A couple minutes later, I raced out of her apartment with my boots untied, leaving her at the door in a fuzzy pink robe. "I'll see you at home tonight," she called, laughing as I stumbled down the first few stairs. "Thanks again for the flowers!"

"You're welcome!" I shouted back, skipping the final few steps and jumping down to the landing. As I hurried back to my office, her words stuck in my head. *I'll see you at home tonight.*

I liked them.

Twenty-One

Mack

THAT NIGHT WHEN I GOT HOME, WE ORDERED PIZZA AND Frannie stayed to watch a movie with us. We sat next to each other on the couch and copped a few PG-13 feels beneath the blanket, but that was about it. I couldn't even kiss her goodbye because I felt like the kids were watching us so closely. Maybe it was in my head, but Millie especially seemed to be looking at us a lot that night.

On Saturday, I didn't see her at all, and I hardly heard from her—just a short text in the morning saying they were swamped at the inn and wishing me a good day, accompanied by a little red heart. And it *was* a pretty good day—I got Millie to ballet on time for once, grocery shopped, cleaned the house, caught up on some work, and washed everyone's sheets and towels. But I thought of her non-stop, and I realized as the day went on how much I missed her. Like *physically* missed her. I had Monday off, and knowing that I wouldn't see her until Tuesday put a dull ache in my chest.

That night, I took the kids out for dinner. We had just been seated at the table when Felicity said out of nowhere, "I miss Frannie."

"Me too," said Winnie. "I wish she was here."

"Can we call her, Dad?" Millie asked.

I cleared my throat. "No, she's working tonight. We'll see her next week."

"Maybe she could come over tomorrow and do braids again," Winnie said.

"And help me with my shirts," added Millie, reaching into her coat pocket for her phone. "I'll text her."

"No, don't do that." I put a hand on Millie's arm to stop her, as if I wasn't dying to see Frannie myself. "Let's let her have the weekend to herself, okay? She's probably tired of us."

I didn't really think she was, but even if she wasn't busy tomorrow, it was getting too hard to keep our feelings a secret from the girls when we were together. I couldn't fucking keep my hands to myself. And I just wasn't ready to tell them yet—it was too soon. Plus, it was making me kind of uneasy that I missed her this way. I didn't want to miss her. The whole point of this thing was to have some fun, to feel like my old self again, at least for a little while. Right?

But later, as I lay in bed that night, I couldn't resist calling her. She didn't answer, and I didn't leave a message.

A few minutes later, she called me back. "Hi. Sorry I missed you. Chloe needed help tonight, so I'm pouring wine at this stupid corporate thing in the tasting room."

"Guess that means you're not going to talk dirty to me."

She laughed. "Probably not. Might be awkward. How was your day?"

"Good. Nothing too exciting." I filled her in on the details. "The girls missed you at dinner. They wanted to call you."

"Awww. I'm sorry. This weekend is crazy here."

"I know. I told them you had to work." I hesitated, torn between admitting I missed her too and not wanting to say the words out loud, as if leaving them unsaid would make them less true. "I should let you go."

"Okay. Give me a call tomorrow if you can?"

"I will," I said.

But I didn't.

My mother called on Sunday night. Felicity answered the kitchen phone, and from where I was standing at the dining room table folding laundry, I heard her excitedly retelling the story of Winnie's tumble down Aunt Jodie's basement stairs last weekend. This infuriated Winnie, who could hear her sister from where she sat at the counter having a snack.

Eventually, each granddaughter took her turn talking to Grandma, and I managed to finish folding their laundry, put it away upstairs, and get the dishwasher started. Millie was the last to chat, and I heard her telling my mom about the fashion show.

"Yeah, it's supposed to be mother-daughter, but they said Daddy can participate." Then she laughed. "We have to make our own outfits. Frannie is helping me."

Inwardly groaning at the thought of having to wear that fucking glittery T-shirt in public, I wiped off the counters and swept the kitchen floor.

"Okay. I love you too. Bye." Millie handed the phone to me. "Can I have a little screen time?" she asked.

"Shower first."

She nodded. "Got it."

I tugged one of her braids and put the phone to my ear.

"Hi, Mom."

"Hi, sweetie. How are you?"

"Good. Busy. You?"

"Great. We're excited for our visit."

"We are too." It wasn't a total lie, although my mother could be a bit overbearing at times. And there was no situation where she didn't feel compelled to voice her opinion. I leaned back against the counter. "You arrive tomorrow?"

"Yes. We'll stay at Jodie's for two nights, then we'll drive down to you for three. Does that still work?"

"Yeah, that's perfect. The wedding isn't until Saturday, but I have the rehearsal Friday, and I'm supposed to spend some time with Woods on Thursday night."

"And who's the bride? Do I know her?"

"She's Ruth Gardner's granddaughter. Lives in Detroit."

My mother clucked her tongue. "Oh, I just love Ruthie Gardner. How is she?"

"She's fine."

"And what about you? The girls told me it was quite a week. Poor Winnie!"

I sighed. "Yeah."

"They all talked a lot about Frannie."

At the mention of her name, my stomach flipped over. "Yes. She's been helping out a lot. She's great with them."

"Sounds like they adore her."

"They do."

"And it seems like she spends a lot of time with them."

Was I imagining it, or was there a note of suspicion in my mother's tone? It made me feel a little defensive. "Well, Miriam Ingersoll broke her leg a couple weeks ago, so Frannie had to fill in. They saw a little more of her than usual."

My mother gasped. "Oh, no! Poor Miriam. Thank goodness you had extra help." Her voice grew curious again. "I hear Frannie is doing more than just babysitting at your house."

I almost choked. "What? Who said that?"

"Felicity said she's been cooking dinner."

"Oh." I relaxed a little. "Yeah. Sometimes, if I work late."

"That's awfully nice of her."

"She likes to cook for people," I said, feeling defensive again. "And she lives alone, so she doesn't get to do it very often."

"How old is Frannie now? Last time I saw her, she was probably close to Millie's age."

"Twenty-seven."

"And you said she lives alone?"

"Yes." Suddenly I knew where this was going.

"Is she attractive?"

"*Mom.*"

"What? I'm just trying to picture her," she said innocently.

I exhaled. Counted to three. "Yes. She's a pretty girl."

"Is there something going on between you two?"

"Jesus, Mom!"

"I'm only asking because I think you need to be very careful. The girls have been through so much and it could be confusing and hurtful for them to see you with another woman so soon."

"I *know.*"

"I'm not saying you have to be alone for the rest of your life, but they're just so young, and they've still got to be traumatized about their mom running off with another man.

Deep down they're probably afraid of losing you that way too. You want them to feel one hundred and ten percent certain they are the most important people in your life."

"They do," I snapped. "I don't need to be told this."

"And maybe it would be best not to take up with their beloved nanny," she went on. "I mean, what happens if you two have a fight and she quits? Then the girls lose her too."

"And it would be my fault. I get it."

"I'm not blaming you for anything, darling. I know how hard this has been for you, and I feel awful we're not there more often to help you out. But the extreme cold is bad for Daddy's blood pressure."

"We're fine, Mom. I'm managing."

"Of course you are. You're a wonderful father, and I know you love those girls to pieces. But I also know you must be lonely too, and with a pretty young girl around so much, I can see how tempting it would be to … take advantage of the situation."

"I'm not taking advantage of anything!" I yelled.

"Okay, okay. I didn't mean to upset you, I just want to make certain the kids are protected."

I closed my eyes, my jaw clenched hard. I knew she meant well, but I was about to lose my shit. Did she think I didn't understand the gravity of the situation? Did she think I took this lightly? "The kids are my number one priority, Mom. They always have been. And they'll stay that way no matter what."

"Good. Well, I'll see you Thursday then, dear."

"Have a safe trip." I hung up and stood there fuming for a moment, wishing I had a heavy punching bag in the house so I could hit something as hard as I wanted to. I wished I had a motorcycle I could take off on for days. I wished

I could down half a bottle of whiskey and drown out my feelings.

But I couldn't do any of those things, because the kids were upstairs waiting for me to put them to bed, and that's the guy I had to be.

Every. Single. Night.

Later I was lying in bed, my mother's words weighing heavily on me, when my phone buzzed again. It was fucking Carla. I should have ignored it, but I sort of felt like punishing myself.

"Hello?"

"Who's Frannie?"

"What?"

"Frannie. Millie texted me all weekend about Frannie this and Frannie that. Who is she?" From the way Carla was slurring her words, I knew she'd been drinking.

"Frannie Sawyer. From Cloverleigh. She babysits for them."

"Is she my replacement?"

"I'm hanging up, Carla. You're drunk."

"Are you fucking her?"

"That's none of your business."

"The hell it isn't. I'm their mother. How dare you bring some little slut into the house? How old is she, twenty-two?"

"Twenty-seven," I said before I could help it.

She squawked with laughter. "Well, I get why you're chasing *her* around, but what the hell does she want with you? Does she think you have money or something?"

My jaw clenched. "She knows who I am."

"Oh, so she's a mind reader? Because you never told me

who you were. And why does Millie think she's so great?"

"Because she's *here*," I said angrily. "And she *cares* about them. She gives them love and attention, which is more than they get from you."

"I'm their mother. They're supposed to love me no matter what."

"You *left*."

"Because you forced me to!" she shouted. "If you would have been a better husband, I wouldn't have felt so alone! It's your fault I had to leave."

"Carla."

"Just admit it—you didn't want to marry me in the first place."

"You're right. I didn't want to get married that soon. We'd only known each other for a few months. We were young. I was about to deploy for Iraq. But I did what I thought was right."

"I never wanted to be your charity case!" she cried.

"It wasn't like that, and you know it. I tried hard to be a good husband and father."

"You didn't try hard enough."

"You wanted too much from me, Carla. No matter what I did, it was never enough."

"I only wanted you to pay attention to me. I wanted you to *love* me."

"I did, Carla." I lowered my voice. "But you were always sulking and pouting. Punishing me for things I had no control over."

"Like leaving us all the time?"

"I had no choice about my deployments, Carla. You know that."

"And when you got back, you were always so happy to

see the kids but not me."

"That isn't true."

"Well, that's what it felt like. You were cold and distant."

"I needed time to readjust. Life at home was a shock to me. You never understood that. You never let me talk about it."

"Because I wanted you to just forget it and be the husband I'd dreamed about. The husband I deserved. I'd waited and waited and waited for you, and then you came home and disappointed me."

"I'm sorry," I said grimly, feeling that sense of failure all over again.

"That's why I had to spend all that money on *things*," she went on. "That's why I drank. I was trying to fill the void you left in my life."

I took a steadying breath. "I hope you're happier now."

"I am!" she snapped. "And since you're all doing so well without me, maybe I'll *never* come back."

"You do what you want, Carla. You always have."

She hung up on me, and I tossed my phone aside. Great. Now she'd have even more reason to blame me for ruining the kids' lives. And she'd aim at them to get back at me. She knew that was the only way to actually hurt me. Tomorrow she'd probably tell Millie that I'd forbidden her mother from coming to visit, that I didn't want them to see her ever again, and maybe even that I was screwing the nanny. I flung my arms over my eyes.

Somehow I'd fucked that up without even trying.

What else was new?

I didn't talk to Frannie again until Monday night. She called at about quarter to ten, as I was catching up on some work emails at the dining room table. It had been hard not to call or text her for two days, but every time I thought about doing it, I remembered what my mother had said and felt guilty.

"Hello?"

"Hey, guess what?

"What?"

"I just talked to Maxima. She said Natalie from Coffee Darling is really excited, and we set up a meeting for four o'clock tomorrow."

"That's great."

"I know it's a lot to ask, and it's probably impossible with your schedule, so don't feel bad if you can't, but if there's any way at all—"

"For fuck's sake, Frannie. I'm getting old here."

She giggled nervously. "Sorry. I was just wondering if maybe you'd want to go with me."

Of course I wanted to. I wanted to do all kinds of things for her, and in a perfect world, I'd be able to. But we didn't have perfection—not even close. And this felt like something I could manage that didn't look overly romantic. "I'll make it work, although I might have to meet you there. I told DeSantis I'd go look at some bottling equipment they've got over at Abelard Vineyards on Old Mission. But I should be done by that time."

"Okay. Great. I'm so excited, Mack. Like really prematurely excited. But something about this just feels so right. I mean, this is so silly, but I keep thinking, what if that strap on Maxima Radley's wedding dress hadn't broken? What if I hadn't been filling in at the desk that night? What if I hadn't noticed the toilet paper stuck to her shoe?"

I smiled at her breathless enthusiasm. "So it's fate, huh? With a little help from Charmin?"

She laughed, and the sound made my chest tighten. "Yes. Exactly. But fate isn't enough—I still have to be the one to go after what fate puts in front of me. Know what I mean?"

"Sure."

"And look at us. I mean, what if Mrs. Ingersoll hadn't broken her leg? What if it hadn't snowed so much that night? What if you could actually get a pillowcase on a pillow in less than five minutes?"

I grimaced. "That's not fate, that's just incompetence."

"Either way—I was there, but you still had to go after what you wanted." Her voice quieted. "And I'm really glad you did."

"Me too," I said, and it wasn't a lie. I *was* glad I'd gone after her. But the more time I spent with her, the more I wanted with her. And not just sneaking-around time, either—*real* time, where we didn't have to hide or rush or worry about being caught. That was impossible without telling the kids, and it was too soon to do that. I supposed I could hire another babysitter and spend time with her apart from the kids, but that would take away from time with my girls, which would make me feel selfish and guilty, and it would give their mother even more ammunition.

I couldn't win.

Twenty-Two

Frannie

O N TUESDAY I PARKED ON THE STREET ABOUT A BLOCK and a half down from Coffee Darling, and walked to the shop with butterflies in my belly, my boots crunching in the snow on the sidewalk. Mack had texted about half an hour ago that he was running late but he'd be here as fast as he could.

The shop had closed earlier in the day—at 2:00 P.M., the hours on the window said—so the glass door was locked when I tried to pull it open at quarter to four.

I peered inside, my pulse racing. The space was narrow and deep, with a counter and a few glass cases over to the left, and tables lining the wall on the right. I knocked on the glass and a few seconds later, I saw a woman come from what I assumed was the kitchen and hurry around the counter toward the door. She unlocked it and pushed it open.

"You must be Frannie," she said with a warm smile. "Please come in. It's freezing out there."

"Thanks." I entered the shop and she locked the door behind me. She had medium-length dark hair pulled into a ponytail and was clearly pregnant, although she didn't have that about-to-pop look about her.

"Welcome." She held out her hand. "I'm Natalie, and …" She shrugged, laughing. "This is the place."

I laughed too as I shook her hand. "I'm Frannie, and I love the place. I've been in here several times and have always thought it was so cute."

Natalie beamed. "Thank you. It's been a great location for me. I opened it five years ago and I swear, we're busier every year, even in the off season."

"Really? That's amazing."

She nodded. "Of course, we get a lot more people in the summer because of tourism, but we've got a lot of loyal locals now too. Would you like to see the kitchen? Maxima should be here shortly, but we can go on back."

"Thanks. I asked a friend to meet me here too." I tucked my hair behind my ears. "I hope that's okay."

"Of course!"

"Actually, he knows you—sort of. He said he went to school with your sister, Jillian?"

"What's his name?"

"Declan MacAllister, but he goes by Mack."

"That sounds familiar, actually."

"You might have known my sister too—she graduated that same year. Sylvia Sawyer?"

She nodded. "That definitely sounds familiar. Small world up here, isn't it?"

I laughed. "Yes."

"But I like small town connections." She smiled at me over her shoulder. "Follow me."

She showed me the kitchen, which wasn't huge but was clean, well-organized, and full of shiny new equipment. My eyes popped as I looked everything over—the marble and wood counters, the rolling racks of pots and pans, the mixers lined up like soldiers, the massive stainless appliances. It wasn't as big as the kitchen at the inn, but it was better suited to baking and seemed neater.

"It's beautiful," I said, running my hand along the cool marble.

"Thanks. Let me show you around."

By the time she was done showing me the kitchen and tiny office, Maxima had arrived. She asked some questions as Natalie finished the tour out front. Mack still hadn't arrived, and I looked at my phone again. I'd missed a call from him a few minutes ago and he'd left a voicemail. Feeling like it would have been impolite to listen to it now, I tucked my phone back into my bag, hoped everything was okay, and crossed my fingers that he could still make it. I really wanted his opinion.

But he never showed.

Natalie poured us each a cup of coffee and she, Maxima, and I sat down at one of the tables along the wall. From my bag I pulled out a white box of macarons I'd baked last night—pink-hued rosewater cream and violet-colored orange lavender.

Natalie gasped. "They're beautiful!"

"Wait 'til you taste them," said Maxima.

"Can I?"

"Of course," I said, pride warming my insides. "I brought them for you."

She picked out a lavender macaron and took a bite. "Oh my God," she mumbled. "It's exquisite."

I smiled. "Thank you."

We sipped coffee and nibbled macarons as we went

over the options. Natalie said she'd sell the building if she found the right buyer, but she was emotionally invested in the place and would really prefer to take on a partner. "I know it sounds silly," she said, her eyes welling as she looked around, "but this shop is like part of me. I opened it when I was just twenty-three and had no idea what I was doing. I got engaged right outside the door. I have more memories in this shop—of family and friends and people in my life—than I do at my own house. I've been here longer. Sorry." She grabbed a napkin and dabbed at her eyes. "I'm always more emotional when I'm pregnant."

"It's okay," I said softly. "I understand. I feel attached to Cloverleigh that way too. I was thinking recently that I don't know if I could ever move too far away, because it's so much a part of me. I grew up there. My roots are there. My heart is there." I took a breath. "But if I don't try to branch out a little, do something more just for me, I'll always wonder what if."

Natalie put a hand over mine. "I know exactly what you mean. And even if this place isn't what you had in mind, I think you should go for it." She gestured toward the empty macarons box. "You're so talented. I'd carry these in my shop every day of the week."

"Thank you." I glanced at the door, wishing I had Mack here for confidence. "I think this place is perfect. What I'm looking for is kitchen space to bake in and counter space to sell in. I also need time to bake extra for weekend events like weddings. The busier I get, the tougher it is to use my own little kitchen, especially if I do events outside Cloverleigh."

"Are you an early riser?" Natalie asked. "Bakeries are not for night owls."

"I'd definitely say I'm more of an early riser," I told her.

"I like schedules and routine, and I'm good with deadlines. I'm organized, outgoing, and easy to work with." Then I paused. "But I'll be honest and say the thought of running my own business leaves me weak in the knees."

"Are you willing to learn?" Maxima asked.

"Totally."

"And I'm willing to teach," Natalie said, placing her hands on her stomach. "At least until I pop this one out in May."

"Do you know what you're having?" asked Maxima.

"A girl." Natalie blushed and smiled. "I'd have been happy either way, of course. We already have one of each, but I've got sisters and there's something so special about that bond."

"I agree," I said. "I've got sisters too."

"Any kids?" she asked, glancing at my left hand.

"No. Not yet." I smiled and shrugged. "Hopefully someday."

"Well, you'll be pretty busy with a new business for a while, so no need to rush." Natalie looked at Maxima. "Okay, so what's the next step?"

Maxima said that since it wouldn't involve the sale or rent of the building, this was a little outside her area of expertise, but she had business experience and gave us her advice. She also said again that she'd be glad to invest in me if I needed money to buy in.

About an hour later, Natalie and I parted with an impulsive hug and a promise to meet again soon. Maxima had recommended forming an LLC for the partnership if we decided to go through with it, but I wanted to talk to Mack or my dad first. My head was spinning.

On the walk to my car, I pulled out my phone and

listened to Mack's message. "Hey, I'm so sorry, but I can't meet you today. Mrs. Ingersoll called, and said Felicity came home with a bad fever. I'm running home to take her into the doctor. I feel horrible, and I won't blame you for being mad. I'll call you as soon as I can. I want to hear how it went."

I reached my car and jumped in so I could start the heat. While the engine warmed up, I texted him back.

Poor Felicity. I hope she's okay and please tell her I said to feel better. Everything went great here. I can't wait to tell you about it. And I'm not mad!

On the contrary, I wasn't sure anything could take away from my excitement. I was disappointed that he hadn't been able to make it, but I understood. Mostly I was just dying to tell someone about the meeting. I called Chloe on the way home and filled her in, and she was thrilled for me.

"That's awesome, Frannie," she said. "I know exactly the place you're talking about and I think it's perfect."

I called April too, but she didn't answer. I left her a message as I was pulling into the garage at home, and went up to my apartment, unable to stop smiling. While I was unzipping my coat, my phone buzzed—it was Mack.

"Hey, how's Felicity?"

"She's okay. Just a virus. I gave her some Motrin and put her to bed. Mrs. Ingersoll just left. Now I've got to feed these other two monkeys and make sure they get their homework done."

"You sound exhausted."

"I didn't sleep well last night, and this week is nuts. I have to get the house in shape for my parents' visit, I have Best Man shit to take care of, and I have to cram five days of work into three since I'm taking Thursday and Friday off—mostly to spend some time with my parents since the weekend will be full of wedding shit."

"Why don't you let me come over and help? I can be there in fifteen minutes, and you can deal with the homework and the house while I make dinner. That way you're not trying to do everything on your own."

"That's okay. I'm used to it. And you don't owe me any favors right now, that's for sure."

"Mack! Stop it. What are you going to feed them, anyway?"

"I don't know. Chicken nuggets."

Glancing at my kitchen, I remembered the stuffed shells I had in the freezer. "I could bring the stuffed shells I made last Saturday night ..." I teased.

He groaned. "That sounds so good. But I don't want you to think you have to rescue me all the time. I can handle things on my own."

"I know you can. But why do it alone when you don't have to? I'm standing here alone in an empty apartment, Mack. I'd much rather be at your house. Besides, that way I can tell you about the meeting."

Exhaling, he said, "Okay. If you're coming because you want to, I guess it's fine."

"I *want* to. I'll be there soon."

Twenty-Three

Mack

SHE CAME OVER THAT NIGHT WITH STUFFED SHELLS AND TOLD me all about the meeting while she reheated them. When dinner was done, she and Millie loaded the dishwasher, singing and giggling like friends while I got Winnie in the shower and tended to a miserable Felicity. When I came back down after getting Winnie in bed, Millie was in the shower and Frannie was putting on her coat in the kitchen.

"I'll get out of your way," she said, zipping up. "I know it's been a long day."

I took her in my arms for the first time that day and kissed her forehead. "Thank you for everything. I don't deserve you or your shells."

Laughing, she squeezed my torso. "Thanks for listening to me babble on about the coffee shop."

"I loved hearing you so excited. I think it's a great plan. Less risk than if you were going it alone, and you get the benefit of her experience and loyal customers."

She sighed. "I can't decide if I should ask my dad for the money to buy in or take Maxima Radley up on her offer for a loan."

"Both have positives and negatives. Your dad would probably give you a better interest rate—if he made you pay it back at all—but taking money from family members can be fraught with problems. Now, your dad doesn't seem like the kind of guy to hold it over your head, but it's still a risk. Talk to him."

"Okay."

"I know if it were me," I went on, "I'd want to be the one to help my daughter if I could. And I'd hope that she came to me to ask."

She kissed my cheek. "Thank you. I'll see you tomorrow."

"Dad?"

Frannie and I jumped apart so fast, her tailbone hit the island and she winced, rubbing it. Millie stood in the dining room blinking at us.

"I thought you were in the shower," I said, my heart pounding. "The water is running."

"I just turned it on and remembered that I forgot to tell you I need the twenty dollars for the fashion show tomorrow."

"Wait a minute, we have to *pay* to be in this thing?"

"It's for charity, Dad. Everybody has to pay." Then she looked at Frannie. "Will you come to the show? It's a week from Saturday."

"Of course I will. I wouldn't miss your dad in a pink glittery shirt for anything."

I groaned, turning Millie around by the shoulders and giving her a gentle shove toward the stairs. "Get back up there and get in the shower, or I'll have no hot water left."

When she was gone, Frannie and I exchanged a wide-eyed look. "Do you think she saw?" I asked.

219

"Maybe not," she said, but I could tell she didn't mean it. "But we should definitely be more careful."

I watched her leave, feeling that ache in my chest again, and I wished there was a way I could've asked her to stay. I was tired of being careful, tired of missing her at night, tired of feeling bad for wanting her, tired of feeling like I was one person with her, and a different person with the kids. Neither version of me was complete.

I wanted to be both at once.

Was it impossible?

On Wednesday, Mrs. Ingersoll said she'd take care of feeding the kids if I needed more time at work, so I was still in my office at seven when I heard a knock.

"Come in."

The door swung open, and Frannie peeked around it. "Hi."

"Hey." I closed my laptop, glad to see her face. "How's it going?"

"Good. I just had an awesome conversation with my dad."

"Oh yeah? Come on in. Tell me about it." I gestured at one of the two chairs in front of my desk. "I haven't seen you all day."

She shut the door and leaned back against it, her expression wary. "You're not too busy? I don't want to bother you. I know you're short on time this week."

"I could use a break."

"Well, I won't take up too much time, I just wanted to tell you that I went over the numbers Natalie gave me with my dad, and he said he'd give me what I'll need to buy in."

"He's *giving* it to you?"

She nodded, her smile radiant. "Uh huh. He said it's about equal to what my sisters' educations cost, and since I never went away to school, I can have it to invest in my business."

"Frannie, that's amazing." Her eyes were bright and her skin was flushed with happiness. She looked beautiful and sexy and I was dying to touch her.

"I know! I'm so excited, I don't even know what to do with myself." She pushed off the door and bounced around a little.

"I've got an idea. Come sit on my lap."

She waved a hand at me. "No, you've got work to do. I should go."

"Don't make me come over there and get you." I stared hard at her, my face stony. "Lock the door."

She did as I asked, a smile on her face. "Want me to turn out the lights?"

"Fuck no. I want to watch you."

"Watch me what?" she questioned coyly, one eyebrow arched.

I'm going to hell, I thought. But I said it anyway. "Watch you get on your knees and take my cock in your mouth."

Her jaw fell open, and for a fraction of a second, I thought I'd gone too far. And then the little vixen dropped to the floor and fucking *crawled* to me, her back arched, her eyes hooded, her hair dangling seductively.

I turned my chair to face her as she slinked slowly around my desk. When she reached my feet, she put her hands on my knees. I unbuckled my belt and she watched as I took my cock in my hand, working it slowly up and down the thickening shaft. Her eyes were wide.

"Are you nervous?" I asked.

She shook her head. She licked her lips. She slid her hands up my thighs and took my dick from my grasp, wrapping her fingers around it.

Then she lowered her head over my lap and teased me with her tongue, slow swirling strokes over the crown that made my stomach muscles tighten and my legs tense. With my other hand, I reach for her hair, lifting it off her face. My breath caught as I watched her head dip lower to leisurely lick her way from the bottom to the top, where she circled the sensitive tip. Three fucking times she tortured me that way, and on the third time, her eyes met mine. She kept looking at me while she took only the head between her wet lips and sucked gently.

"More," I growled.

Lowering her eyes and her mouth, she took me in a little deeper and moaned. It felt so good I nearly lost my patience and found my hand fisting in her hair. I must have pulled a little too hard because she gasped and took her mouth off me.

I loosened my grip and frowned. There was a reason this activity had been verboten during my marriage. "Sorry."

"Don't be," she panted, looking up at me again, that wicked spark in her eye. "I told you I like it when you get rough. I meant it."

My dick throbbed in her hand, and I tightened my fist again in her hair. "In that case ..."

She made a noise somewhere between a laugh and a moan, and put her mouth on me again. This time, she took me all the way to the back of her throat, and I watched in ecstatic disbelief as her lips and tongue moved up and down my cock. But it wasn't long before watching wasn't enough—the restless, fiery tension building up in my body demanded I move. With my hands on her head, I leaned back and began to thrust up—quick, hard jabs that forced her to take me in deeper. She gasped and grunted and struggled to breathe, but she never pushed me away. Her hands moved to my hips and she dug her fingers into my flesh as I fucked her hot little mouth faster and faster, my blood running hotter and hotter until suddenly the orgasm erupted within me and I poured into her without even giving a warning.

A nicer guy probably would have pulled out instead of pulling her closer, but at that moment I was content to be the biggest asshole on the planet as long as I got to come with my cock hitting the back of her throat. It was selfish as fuck, but it was pure ecstasy. Not only the orgasm, but the awareness that she wanted *all* of me. Accepted all of me. Even *craved* all of me. I forgot where we were, what day it was, what I was supposed to be doing—it's possible I even forgot my own fucking name.

When I finally let go of her head and she sat back onto her heels, looking up at me like she'd just won a million fucking dollars, my head was spinning, my heart was throbbing, and I could hardly breathe. It was like nothing I'd ever felt before.

I looked at her on the floor at my feet and thought, *Either I'm about to die and that was life's final parting gift, or I'm in love with her.*

I wasn't sure which one was worse.

Twenty-Four

Frannie

"**J**ESUS," HE WHISPERED, LOOKING ALMOST FRIGHTENED. "That was so fucking intense."

I smiled and wiped my lower lip with the back of one wrist.

Suddenly he reached down, grabbed me beneath the arms and hoisted me onto the desk in front of him. "Are you okay?"

"More than okay. I loved it. I'm all hot and bothered right now."

His jaw dropped for a second. "You're telling me doing that turned you on?"

I shrugged, giving him a shy smile. "Yes. I like hearing you. And feeling you. And being able to give you all of my attention without any distractions. Usually when you come, I do too, and I'm too carried away to focus on you."

"I happen to like when you get carried away," he said, reaching for the button on my pants. "So now I think it's my turn to give you all of my attention without any distractions."

"Mack, no! You're supposed to be catching up on work." I tried to push his hands away, but instead he succeeded in tipping me backward by the shoulders so I was on my back, legs dangling off the desk.

"Fuck work." He removed my shoes, and grabbed my pants, yanking them all the way off, along with my underwear.

I propped myself up on my elbows. "And it's late. Won't Mrs. Ingersoll be expecting you?"

"Fuck Mrs. Ingersoll." He dropped to his knees and threw my legs over his shoulders.

"But … what about … the kids …" And then I couldn't talk anymore, because his tongue was doing things that took away my ability to form coherent thoughts.

After a few long, slow strokes up my center and several seconds of soft, swirling circles over my clit, he picked up his head. "I'm not thinking about the kids right now. And I don't want to. I spend all day every day doing things for them, and I will for the rest of my life. But right now, it's about what *I* want. And that is to bury my face in your pussy and make you come with my tongue. Then I'd like to fuck you on my desk. Does that work for you?"

"Uh. Yes," I said, my body already wet and aching for him.

"Good. After that, I will go back to being a responsible person." He returned to what he'd been doing before, but this time, he slid one long finger inside me as well.

"You will?" I asked weakly, my eyes popping at the sight of his dark hair between my thighs.

"Maybe." He looked up and pushed two fingers in this time, his breath hot and quick on my tingling skin. "I'm not too good at keeping promises."

After checking that the coast was clear, he walked me up to my apartment—the back way, so we didn't have to go through the lobby. My mother was still at the desk, and he wanted to avoid her.

"I'm telling you, she is *fine* with us," I said as we climbed the stairs. "She asked me over the weekend if there was something going on."

"What did you say?"

"I said we were taking it slow for the sake of the kids, but that we've been getting to know each other better. She said that was smart."

He tucked his hands in his pockets. "My mother reacted a little differently."

I stopped halfway up the staircase. "You told her?"

"No, but when she called on Sunday night, she sort of suspected, based on how much the girls talked about you. Then she asked a bunch of questions, and my answers must have made it even more obvious."

Moving slowly, I resumed going up the steps. "So what did she say?"

"Just a bunch of things that I already knew."

"Like what?"

He shrugged as we reached the landing. "Mostly that I need to be careful."

I felt like there was a lot more he wasn't saying, but I didn't want to push. From the look on his face, it was clear he wasn't happy about the conversation. "Well, I definitely think you're being careful." Then I winced. "Although Winnie *did* catch us in the closet. And Millie *might* have seen us in the kitchen."

His frown deepened. "Yeah."

"We've probably gotten a little careless. We can do better."

"I wish we didn't have to worry about it. But that

conversation with her has been eating at me this week. She made me feel guilty—well, guilti*er*—about what we're doing."

"Moms are good at that. They know exactly how to push our buttons."

"It's not fair to you." He shook his head. "What the fuck are you doing with me? You've got so much to give and I've got nothing."

He looked so upset, I grabbed him in a hug. "Hey. That's not true. We knew this would be tricky at the start, but we're making it work."

"My ex called on Sunday too."

I stiffened. "She did?"

"Yeah. She knows about us too."

"You told her?" Surprised, I released him and stepped back.

He shook his head. "No. She made the accusation based on how much Millie was texting about you. I didn't deny it."

"You didn't?" I wasn't sure whether to be happy or not. It seemed like a step in the right direction, but he looked upset about it.

"No. But maybe I should have. I don't know." He rubbed his face with both hands.

I swallowed hard. "Well … what did she say?"

"A lot of ugly shit about me, which I don't care about, but then she threatened never to visit the kids again. Which would be fine with me, but she'll find a way to twist everything so it's my fault the kids don't have a relationship with their mother."

"Oh, Mack." I twisted my fingers together at my waist. Clearly this had been weighing on him for days. "I'm sorry. Why didn't you tell me?"

He shrugged. "Because this isn't your problem. I don't want you to have to deal with my hostile ex-wife. Hell, *I* don't want to deal with her. But I have to. I'll always have to, because she's my kids' mom. That will never change. And neither will she."

I could see him getting more and more worked up, and I put my arms around him again. "Hey. It's okay."

"It's not. And it's just one more reason why you should walk away from me and find someone easier to be with."

"I'm not going anywhere, Mack. You know that, right?"

His arms came around me, warm and tight and strong, which was reassuring.

But he said nothing, which was not.

On Thursday, April came by the desk during my morning shift. "Hey, I'm meeting with Stella Devine tonight at six to go over some details. Want to join us?"

"Sure. Your office?"

"Bar, actually."

I nodded. "I'll meet you there."

My shift ended at five, and I ran upstairs to change out of my work clothes and grab a bite to eat. At six, I went down to the bar, where April, Stella, and her sister Emme were sitting at a rectangular high-top table. Stella and Emme both had glasses of sparkling wine, and their faces were glowing after their day at the spa.

We went over the details and timing from the rehearsal dinner all the way through the late-night pizza buffet at the reception. Stella was an easygoing bride, and between Emme and April, the plans were so well organized that it seemed impossible anything could go wrong. At quarter to seven, they went up to change for their girls' night out, and April and I lingered at the table.

"Whew, we're off duty for the night," my sister said. "Want a glass of wine?"

I nodded. "I'd love one."

We moved to the bar so we weren't taking up a table for four and ordered two glasses of pinot noir.

"So how are things?" she asked with a smile. "I've been getting an earful from Mom about your big plans, but we haven't had a chance to talk."

"Things with that are great, actually." I filled her in on all the details. "Dad and I are going to meet with Natalie Haas next week about the financing, and I pretty much gave Mom my notice. Week after next, I'll be at Coffee Darling full time."

"That's so awesome. I remember Natalie Nixon from school, although she's a little younger than me. That whole family is nice."

"Mack said he went to school with her sister Jillian."

April nodded. "I graduated with the middle sister, Skylar. She works at Abelard Vineyards now, and I think Chloe knows her pretty well." She sipped her wine. "Speaking of Mack, how are things with you two?"

"Pretty good, I guess."

"You guess?"

"Well, it's kind of hard to tell. When we're alone, it's amazing. Actually, even when the kids are around, it's amazing. He's sweet and funny and he's so flipping hot, I can't stand it. The sex is unreal."

"But …" she prompted.

I took a breath. "But it's difficult. I feel bad for even

saying this out loud, but trying to date a full-time single dad with three kids and keep it from them is tough—especially when you're the nanny. Twice now the kids have walked in on us kissing in the house."

April gasped. "What did they say?"

I had to laugh a little, remembering the looks on their faces. "Nothing really, but it's obvious they're confused. Kids are smart. They have to sense something is up."

"Why doesn't he want to tell them?"

"Well, when it first started, we agreed to keep it to ourselves because it was so new. But I don't think we realized how quickly things were going to progress—I know I didn't. I just hope he feels what I feel. I'm nervous he doesn't."

"Because he won't tell the kids?"

"No, I get that, but the other night he said this thing that I can't get out of my head. He said he worries about what will happen when I realize he's not worth the shit I'll have to put up with. He said, 'You'll leave, because you know you deserve better. And I'll have to let you, because I'll know it too.'"

April's eyebrows rose. "Damn. What did you say?"

"I told him I'd prove him wrong." I sighed despairingly. "And I hope he gives me time to do that, but what if he decides *I'm* not worth all the sneaking around and feeling bad? He told me last night that his mother was suspicious something was going on with us and lectured him about it." I shook my head. "He warned me this was going to be tough, and he was right … but he's worth it, April. I feel this down deep. I don't want to give up."

She reached over and rubbed my arm. "You want my advice? Just give it time. It's only been a few weeks, and he's probably still got a bad taste in his mouth about relationships because of his history. Divorce is really hard—it messes with your head. He's trying to protect his kids, maybe even himself."

"Himself?"

She shrugged. "Sure. Love is scary. You have to wear your heart outside your chest. He did that once and got burned."

I closed my eyes. "God, that's exactly it. It does feel like I'm wearing my heart outside my chest with him. Like my chest isn't even big enough to hold it. But even though it feels huge, it feels fragile too."

Her lips curved into a smile. "Congratulations, little sister. You're in love."

Twenty-Five

Mack

MY FOLKS ARRIVED ON THURSDAY, AND THAT NIGHT I met up with Woods at Hop Lot Brewing Co., one of our old favorite places for food and drinks after work. I was looking forward to it, not just because I hadn't seen Woods in a long time and he was like a brother to me, but because I'd had this fucking knot in the pit of my stomach all day long, growing tighter and tighter every time I thought about Frannie.

I'd lain awake all night long hearing her voice in my head. *I'm not going anywhere. You know that, right?* And then I'd picture her the way she'd looked kneeling at my feet, so sweet and sexy and happy, and my heart felt like it was going to explode. It was too much. Things had moved too fast, and my feelings for her were running too deep. She was all I wanted, and I wanted her *all* the time.

How had I let this happen?

Sitting at the bar, Woods and I caught up over local IPAs, wings, burgers, and fries. He told me how things were going for him downstate, about his job as groundskeeper for a country club, and the work he was doing on their house.

He also grumbled a fair amount about the cost and planning of the wedding and said he'd be glad when it was all over. "I can't fucking look at another flower, cake, or seating arrangement," he said. "Seriously, just shoot me first."

"Is it that bad?"

"Yes. I have absolutely no opinions on that shit and she doesn't seem to understand that. It's like she takes it personally. I tell her all I care about is that we walk out of there married. She could wear a paper bag for all I care."

"Oh, Jesus." I shook my head. "You did not say that to her."

"I did. She was not pleased with me." He took another sip of his beer and set the glass down. "So when are you gonna tell me what's up with you?"

I picked up my beer and frowned into it. There was no use pretending with Woods. We knew each other too well. "I think I fucked up."

"I'm sure you did."

I tried to smile, but couldn't.

"Shit. You're serious. Is it one of the kids?"

"No." I took a few swallows and set the glass down. "It's Frannie Sawyer."

"Frannie Sawyer? What about her?"

I looked over at him. Met his eyes but said nothing.

He got it in a heartbeat. "Jesus. Did you?"

Lifting my glass again, I nodded. "Yeah. I did. Multiple times. It's sort of an ongoing fuck-up."

"Shit." He rubbed a hand over his jaw. "How old is she?"

"Twenty-seven."

"Oh. Well, that's not bad. Are you worried about Sawyer?"

"I'm worried about a lot of things." I shook my head. "I

233

don't know what the fuck I was thinking, starting something with her. I don't have time for a girlfriend. I barely have time to piss with the bathroom door shut."

Woods laughed. "I bet."

"It's impossible to be alone with her. The kids are always around."

Woods ran a hand through his hair. "She's probably great with the kids, though."

"Yeah," I said dully. "They're crazy about her."

"Do they know about the two of you?"

I shook my head. "Not yet. It's only been a few weeks. But it's getting harder and harder to keep it from them, especially since she's at the house a few days a week. And I know she wants to tell them."

"You don't?"

"No. I don't want them to feel like they're getting less of me, I don't want to throw a major wrench into their lives when we're finally doing okay, and I don't want them to get attached to the idea that she's going to be around forever," I said, getting worked up. "Because she's not."

"How do you know?"

"Why would she be? I can't give her what she wants."

He sipped his beer again. "What does she want that you can't give her?"

"Time. Attention. A future. I know for a fact she wants a husband and kids. I can't be that guy. I'm never getting married again."

"Have you told her that?"

"No."

"Why not?"

"Because I'm an asshole."

"Well, sure, but …"

I couldn't even laugh. "Because I don't want to give her up. It's so wrong on so many levels, I know it is, but it's also *so fucking good*. Not just the sex, either, although that part is unbelievable. She's all young and hot and"—I struggled for the right word—"enthusiastic."

Woods burst out laughing. "You definitely don't want unenthusiastic sex."

"But that's what I was used to. Uninspiring, unexciting, unenthusiastic, obligatory sex with someone who didn't actually give a shit about me. She never even knew me."

"No?"

I shook my head. "No, everything spun out of control so fast when Carla got pregnant, and I did three tours practically back to back, and suddenly we had three kids, a mortgage, and a stockpile of weapons to use against each other."

"That's tough."

I took another drink of my beer. "It was always all about Carla—what she wanted, what she wasn't getting, what I was doing wrong as a husband. With Frannie, it's so different. She wants to *know* me. She's so easy to be with. She loves the girls. She puts up with a lot of shit that no one else would. And ..." I took a deep breath. "She cooks. She fucking comes over and cooks for us because I'm too clueless and exhausted to figure out how to feed my kids healthy food at the end of the day."

"Sounds like maybe you should keep her around."

I shook my head. "I can't keep letting her waste all this time on me. There are too many complications, between the kids and Carla making things difficult at every turn, and what people will say and what she wants for the future."

"What will people say?" Woods asked.

"You know. They'll just gossip." I ran a hand through my

hair. "They'll say I'm fucking the nanny, and she's so much younger, and my divorce is barely final, and it's not fair to the kids, and I'm just taking advantage of her, and—"

"Fuck that," Woods stated emphatically. "Anyone who knows you will know that's complete bullshit. And since when have you ever cared what people say?"

"I can't take that attitude where the kids and Frannie are concerned. This isn't just about me."

Woods exhaled and lifted his glass to his mouth. After a long drink, he set it down and looked at me. "Do you remember what you said to me after I broke things off with Stella?"

"That you were being a dipshit?"

"Yeah, and you are too, by the way, but you also said something else that I always remembered."

I sat up taller. "What?"

"You said something like, 'If I had someone I trusted, who understood me and baked pies for me, and the sex was even *marginal*, I'd marry her tomorrow."

Frowning, I slumped over again. "But our situations are not similar at all. I meant I'd do that if I were *you*. I've got kids to think about."

Woods gave me a look that called bullshit, but he didn't say anything. He just picked up his beer and took another drink.

"And I'm thinking of Frannie, too. I'm letting her believe this can go somewhere when I know it can't. And the longer this goes on, the worse it's going to be for everyone involved when it ends. The girls are already too attached to her. It's dangerous to be that attached to someone."

"So what are you gonna do?"

My gut twisted. "I have to break it off. For the kids' sake."

Woods was silent a moment. Then he said, "You do what you've gotta do, Mack. I just want to say one more thing, and then I'll shut up. Because this is probably going to piss you off, but we all need that one asshole in our life who says what needs to be said."

I gave him the side eye. "What?"

"Are you doing this because the *girls* are too attached to her? Or because *you* are?"

I sat up taller. "Fuck off. I'm not doing this for me."

He held up his hands. "Okay, okay. I know you guys have been through a lot, and I'm not a father, so I don't know what that's like. If you're that sure things can never work out with her, go ahead and break it off."

"I'm sure," I said, the knot in my stomach thickening. "I have to break it off."

The moment I saw her at the rehearsal the next day, my heart seized and my breath stopped and my legs didn't want to move. I was standing at the back of the wedding barn, where the ceremony was going to take place, and she came over with a big smile on her face.

"Hey, you," she said. "How was your night out with the guys?"

"It was fine." I could hardly look her in the eye.

"What did you do?"

"Just had a few beers. Some food."

"No strip clubs?" she teased. "Not that there are any within a hundred miles."

I couldn't even smile. "No."

"Did you get in late?"

"Not too late." I hesitated. "Sorry I didn't call. I was tired, I guess." God, this was torture. I didn't know where to look, so I stared at the ground between our feet.

"Did you ask your parents about staying over tomorrow night?" she asked hopefully.

"Oh, uh … not yet." Fuck. What the hell was I going to do about that? How could I stay with her knowing what I was going to do? I already felt like the biggest jerk on the planet. That would just make it worse.

"Is everything okay, Mack?" She sounded confused, and I didn't blame her.

"Yeah. I'm just … you know. Busy." It was bullshit. The rehearsal hadn't even started yet.

"Oh. Okay, well, I won't keep you. Just wanted to say hi."

I nodded, feeling like fucking dirt, and she gave me one last smile before walking away, but it wasn't a happy smile. It was nervous and tentative, and I hated myself for it.

But that was nothing compared to the following night.

Twenty-Six

Mack

THREE PAIRS OF EYES WATCHED ME KNOT THE DEEP BURgundy tie around my neck. My hair was trimmed, my shave was close, my navy suit fit perfectly. On the outside, everything was perfect.

On the inside, I was a mess.

"You look nice, Daddy," said Felicity. All three girls were lying across my bed on their bellies, studying me as I finished getting ready for the wedding.

"Thanks." But my tie was crooked. Frowning, I loosened the knot and tried again.

"I wish we could come to the wedding," said Millie.

"Adults only," I told her.

"I know, but I want to see the bride. Frannie said she'd send me some pictures." She sighed dramatically. "I've never been to a wedding."

My mother appeared in the doorway. "My goodness, don't you look handsome," she said, leaning on the frame with her arms folded.

"Thank you." I dropped my arms to my side. "I guess I'm ready." But I didn't want to leave.

"What time is the ceremony?" she asked.

"Four. Then pictures, then cocktails, then dinner." I recited the bare bones plan that Woods had given to me. By contrast, the women all had three-page, color-coded itineraries for today.

"Better get going," my mother said. "It's nearly two and it's snowing again. Are you staying at the inn tonight?"

I frowned at my reflection and tugged at the knot again. My collar was a little tight. "Maybe. I'll let you know."

"Just do it." She came into the room and turned me to face her, fussing with my tie. "That way you can relax and enjoy yourself without worrying about the roads or having a few drinks or whatever. You can stay and be social. Ask someone to dance. Be charming and make conversation."

The girls giggled, and I gave them the stink eye before pushing my mother's hands away. "Okay, enough. I have to go."

"Bye, Daddy!" All three hopped off the bed and accosted me for hugs as I tried to get out the door. "Have fun!"

I hugged and kissed them, gave my mother a peck on the cheek, waved at my dad, who was on the couch watching football, and hustled out the back door.

On the drive to Cloverleigh, which was shitty because of the snow, I made up my mind that I was not going to spend the night with Frannie. It was too selfish. I'd make up some excuse why I had to go home, and then tomorrow, maybe we could talk.

And then I saw her.

Around quarter to four, she poked her head into the room the groomsmen were using at the inn to wait for the ceremony to begin. "Everybody decent?"

"Come on in," Woods called.

Frannie entered the room, and my knees almost buckled. She wore a black velvet dress that clung to her curves for dear life. It had short sleeves, a deep V neck, and hit her right at the knees. She wore spiky black high heels with an ankle strap and her gold-threaded hair was loose and wavy, flowing over one shoulder. I had to stop myself from rushing over to her and burying my face in it.

"It's time," she said, smiling at us with deep red lips. "I have instructions to come get you guys and take you over to the barn."

"Finally." Woods looked excited to take action. "Got the rings?" he asked me.

I patted my pocket. "Got 'em."

On the walk over to the barn, we had to go outside, and I hung back to fall in step next to Frannie. "You look gorgeous," I told her. "But you must be freezing. Take my coat." I slipped out of my suit coat and draped it over her shoulders.

"Thanks," she said, smiling shyly at me. "You look nice, too."

"How are you?" I asked.

"Fine." She looked up ahead at Woods, who was practically running toward the barn, and laughed. "He's so excited."

"Yeah."

"I'm so happy for him. For both of them." Then she sighed. "And I'm envious too."

"Because you want to get married?"

"Well, yes, eventually. But I guess I'm mostly envious that it seems so easy for them to be together. I wish it was like that for us. Can you stay tonight?" She gave me a hopeful smile.

I frowned and pulled the door to the barn open for her, torn between what I wanted to do and what I should do. But either way, this wasn't the time to deal with that. "I think so."

Her smile widened, and her eyes danced with light. "Good. Okay, take your coat. I'm going to go let April know you're here. Don't move."

I watched her walk away and felt like shit. I stood by my best friend as he married the love of his life and felt like shit. I watched them speak their vows, slide rings on each other's fingers, share their first kiss as husband and wife—and every moment made me feel worse.

Because I knew that Frannie was watching too, and I saw her wide-eyed with wonder, tearful with emotion, smiling with joy. She was probably dreaming of the day she walked down the aisle on her father's arm, radiant with happiness just like Stella was, her future husband waiting to take her hand, to begin a new life, to start a family. I could never give her that. I could never give her anything. I couldn't even kiss her in front of the kids.

As the evening unfolded, I grew more and more ill at ease. I forced a smile in pictures. I barely touched my dinner. I watched stiffly from my place at the head table as the bride and groom danced for the first time, nursing a second glass of scotch.

Frannie was sitting with her family, and I saw her looking at me from across the room throughout the meal, but I never made eye contact. It was killing me to know that I had to break her heart. And I didn't want to do it tonight, but I wasn't sure I could take any more of this. I'd never been someone who put off doing what needed to be done. Why prolong this torture?

After cake was served and the dancing began, she wandered over to where I sat with a glass of champagne in her hand.

"Hey," she said, offering a smile.

"Hey."

"Didn't you like the cake?" She gestured at my dessert plate, which was still full. I hadn't taken a bite.

"I'm not that hungry."

Her eyebrows lifted. "I've never heard you say that before. Are you feeling okay?"

"Actually, not really." I loosened the knot in my tie. "I'm a little warm."

"Well, I was coming over to see if you wanted to dance, but maybe you'd like to get some air instead?"

"Uh, yeah. Air would be good."

She set her champagne down on the table. "Let me grab my coat from the back."

"You can wear mine." I shrugged it from my shoulders and she turned around to slip her arms into the too-long sleeves.

"Thanks." She wrapped her arms around herself. "Mmm. It's nice and warm." She sniffed the collar. "And it smells good."

The queasy feeling in my gut intensified as we walked to the back of the barn and snuck out through the doors leading to the covered patio. In the summertime, wedding guests would have been out here as well, but since it was February, we had it to ourselves.

Frannie breathed in and exhaled, creating a little white cloud in the icy dark. "Whew, it was warm in there."

"Yeah." Sticking my hands in my pockets, I took a few deep breaths too, hoping they'd calm my fraying nerves.

"You're not off the hook, though. I still want to dance with you." She elbowed me gently.

"I'm not sure that's a good idea."

She turned to face me. "Why not?"

"Because …" I forced myself to say words I didn't feel in my heart. "I think we should slow down. Cool off."

She shook her head slightly. "What? Where is this coming from?"

"I've just been thinking we're moving a little too fast."

"Since when?"

I shrugged. "Last week."

"I don't understand. On Wednesday in your office, things were fine. I've hardly seen you since."

"That's part of the problem, Frannie. We can't even see each other. It's too hard with all the sneaking around. And it's not fair to you."

Again, she shook her head, and tears glistened in her eyes. "I've told you a hundred times, I don't mind."

"Well, I do. I can't keep doing it. It's making me feel like shit. I can't be what you deserve and what my kids need. I just can't. I feel like I'm being torn in two."

"But Mack," she said, a tear dripping down her cheek. "I'm in love with you. I can't just walk away."

I felt it like a sledgehammer to the chest. "Don't say that. It'll only make things worse."

"But it's true," she wept. "I've never felt this way about anyone before in my entire life."

"You're so young, Frannie. You'll meet someone else who can be what you want."

"I want *you*, you big jerk," she said, going to wipe her eyes but struggling to get her hand free from the long arms of my coat. Finally she gave up and the tears fell freely while

I stood there helpless and angry. The thought of her with someone else made me want to put my fist through the barn's glass door.

"You think you want me, but you don't," I told her. "Where do you see this going, Frannie? Where does it end? Because it has to end somewhere."

"Why?" she sobbed.

"Because you want things I can't give you."

"Like what?"

"You want a husband. You want children." I shook my head. "I'm never getting married again, and I've already had my children."

"I've never even brought that up," she said, finally fishing a hand from my sleeve and dragging her wrist below her nose.

"But it's true, isn't it? You're envious of Ryan and Stella. You see how easy it could be. You want that promise of a future together, and you should have everything you want. I just can't be part of it, and when you realize that down the road, you'll leave."

"You mean you *won't*."

"What?"

"You *won't* be part of it." She took a step closer to me and looked me right in the eye. "You're choosing to end this now because you'd rather be alone than take a chance on a future with me. You're afraid."

I bristled. "I'm realistic. I know what I am and what I'm not capable of. And the girls are already too attached to you. What happens to them when this falls apart? They'll be devastated. They'll hate me."

"Don't blame this on the girls," she said, sliding my coat from her arms and shoving it at me. "This is all you."

"Frannie, come on. I didn't want it to be like this."

But she spun on her heel, yanked open the door, and disappeared inside the barn.

Hanging my head, I stood there for a moment with my coat in my hands and told myself I'd done the right thing—for my kids, for Frannie, for myself.

But I'd never felt worse.

Somehow I made it through most of the reception, but just after nine I told Woods that I had to get going. I made up a story about one of the kids not feeling well, but I think he knew it was bullshit. He didn't say anything, though, just gave me a hug and said he'd give me a call once he and Stella were back from their honeymoon. I congratulated them both, kissed Stella on the cheek, and left.

I knew what Frannie meant when she'd said she envied them. I did too.

My coat was in my office back at the inn, so I walked across the path and went to retrieve it. While I was there, I dropped into my chair and sat there for a moment, feeling dejected and empty. It didn't seem possible that just a few days before, I'd had Frannie right here on this desk, not a care in the world beyond making her feel amazing. And now look what I'd done.

I should have known better.

Squeezing my eyes shut against the image of her and everything good she brought to my life, I jumped up from my chair, threw my coat over my arm, and took off.

At home, I undressed in the bathroom and crawled into Millie's bottom bunk, where I'd been sleeping since my parents arrived. But there was no way I could sleep tonight. Every time I closed my eyes, I saw those tears running down her cheeks in the dark. I heard her voice telling me she loved me. I felt the unbearable burden of knowing that I'd broken her heart.

I hoped she'd forgive me someday.

Twenty-Seven

Frannie

I KEPT MY HEAD DOWN AS I HURRIED THROUGH THE BARN, WHICH hummed with the happy noise of a wedding reception—the band playing up front, the clink of silverware on glasses, the laughter and chatter of the guests. With tears continuing to fall, I blindly made my way to the back of the room and hunted for April. Spotting her over by the cake table, I headed in that direction.

"Hey," I said, tapping her shoulder.

"Hey." She turned and gasped. "What's wrong?"

"I need to leave. Do you have enough help the rest of the night?"

"Of course. Are you okay?"

I shook my head and tried to choke back the sobs that threatened to erupt. "Mack broke it off."

Another gasp. "Why?"

"He had a lot of reasons, but I don't really want to talk about it right now."

"Okay. I understand." She gave me a hug. "Go cry it out. I'll call you tomorrow."

"Thanks. Make an excuse to Mom and Dad for me, okay?"

"Sure. I'm really sorry, Frannie. I know how you feel about him."

I couldn't even talk anymore, so I just nodded and walked away, my chest aching and my throat tight. After grabbing my coat from the back office, I stuck my hands in my pockets and walked along the pathway from the barn to the inn, crying openly.

When I'd gotten dressed tonight, I'd been so excited. So hopeful. So happy.

How had everything gone so wrong so fast?

The next morning, I woke up to the sound of knocking on my apartment door. I reached for my phone to check the time. To my surprise, it was after ten already. I never slept this late, but then again, I'd barely slept at all.

Dragging myself out of bed, I wrapped my bathrobe around me and stumbled for the door.

"Yes?" I croaked before opening it. My voice was hoarse from crying and my eyes still stung.

"Hey, sweetie. You okay?" The voice was Chloe's.

I opened the door and saw her standing there with two cardboard coffee cups in her hands. "I take it April told you what happened with Mack."

"Yes, but only me. Mom and Dad think you weren't feeling well, which freaked Mom out, of course, but then I told her it was just cramps."

"Thanks. Come on in."

"You look terrible," she said, kicking the door shut.

"I feel worse," I assured her, heading for the couch. I flopped onto it and curled into a ball, wrapping my furry blanket around me.

"So do you want to talk about it?" She sat next to me and set one cup on the table. "That's for you."

"What's to talk about?" I set my chin on my knees. "He doesn't want me."

"No. I don't buy it. I've seen the way he looks at you, I've heard the way he talks about you. The guy adores you."

"Not enough," I said, feeling my throat get tight again. "He said things were moving too fast and it was making him feel bad. He hated all the sneaking around, but he didn't want to tell the kids."

"I don't get that." Chloe frowned and shook her head. "I could see if you were some strange woman he met at a bar somewhere that he wouldn't want to bring you around his kids too soon. But he's known you for years. He's known this family forever. And his kids already love you."

"I think that's part of the problem." I took a shuddery breath. "He's afraid they're too attached to me."

"How is that a problem?"

"It wouldn't be if we wanted the same things in the future. But he claims he's never getting married again and doesn't want more kids."

"Are you okay with that?"

"I don't know. I mean …" I sniffled. "Not really. I *do* want a husband and kids of my own someday. But it's not like I need them tomorrow! Why can't we see where this goes? Why does he have to freak out *now*?"

"Maybe he doesn't want to lead you on. Or lead the kids on." Chloe sipped her coffee and shrugged. "I mean, let's say it goes great for a year, and you start to get dreamy about a diamond ring and a big white dress. Then what?"

"Then we could talk about it," I snapped, annoyed that

my sister would see his side.

"Okay, let's say you talk about it and he stands firm. There will be no second Mrs. Declan MacAllister. Then what?"

I struggled with it. "I don't know. Why can't he just love me enough, goddammit? And why are you on his side?"

"Oh, honey, I'm not. I think he's crazy to give you up. I'm only trying to help you see it's not that he doesn't feel what you do. But he's older and he's been through a lot more. He's not looking at this the same way you are. And he has a lot more baggage."

"I know. Just forget it. It's hopeless." Dissolving into tears again, I tipped sideways in my faux fur cocoon and put my head in Chloe's lap. "It was hopeless from the start."

She stroked my hair and let me cry, but she didn't tell me I was wrong.

Twenty-Eight

Mack

MONDAY MORNING, I USED THE BACK DOOR TO THE INN so I didn't have to walk by the desk. By that afternoon, I was coming out of my skin, so I thought up an excuse to wander out to reception. Frannie's mother was at the desk alone, and I asked her something inconsequential before ducking back down the hall to my office.

The day went on, and I never saw her. I started to get concerned. A few times I pulled out my phone and thought about texting or calling her, just to make sure she was okay, but I couldn't bring myself to do it.

But she wasn't there Tuesday, either, and I couldn't take it anymore. Around ten, I wandered up to the desk and asked Daphne where she was.

"Oh, didn't she tell you? She's working in Traverse City this week at that coffee shop. She thought it would be a good idea to start there as soon as possible, learn the ropes before she started her own thing there." Then she sighed. "I still think this is a crazy idea, and I can't imagine what her father was thinking to encourage her, but ..." She threw up her hands. "I'm just her mother, what do I know?"

"So she's not working here at all anymore?"

Daphne shook her head. "No. On Sunday afternoon she came down and said that she really needed to start there as soon as possible, and could I please do without her starting Monday. I said I could, and I'm looking for a replacement. You don't know anyone who'd be good at reception, do you?"

"Not offhand, but I'll think about it." I wished her luck and went back to my office, where I sank into my chair and stared blankly at my laptop. So I wouldn't see her here anymore. I frowned. Had she quit early because of me? Was she going to quit watching the girls too? Would she even contact me to let me know?

I went home anxious and frustrated and angry with myself. Of course, I took it out on the kids, snapping at them about homework, barking about chores, and insisting that they eat what I put on the plate in front of them without complaint or I was going to lose my fucking mind. I made Winnie cry, I sent Millie to her room, and I ignored Felicity when she asked me why I was acting like a grumpy old man.

I also put a *lot* of money in the swear jar.

The next day, I apologized and tried to make it up to them by taking them out for tacos after therapy. When we got home, I went into my room and called Frannie. She didn't answer, and I left her a message.

"Hey, it's me. I'm just wondering if you're still coming to watch the girls this week. Let me know." Then I paused, battling the urge to say more, to say I missed her, to say I was sorry, to say I loved her too, but it was too fucking much to handle. "I hope you're okay."

I hung up and threw my phone down on the bed, fisting

my hands in my hair. *Of course she isn't okay, you fuckwit. Are you okay?*

I wasn't. Especially not when her text came about an hour later, which said,

I will be there.

That's it. Four words.

I typed a reply, deleted it, typed another, and deleted that too.

Just leave her alone, MacAllister. It's what she wants. You can give her that much.

On Thursday, I drove home from work with white knuckles. I'd never been so nervous to walk into my own house.

Frannie was at the counter with Felicity, and they both looked up when I entered the kitchen. Neither of them looked particularly happy to see me.

"Hey," I said, testing my voice.

"Hi, Daddy. We're doing my spelling words."

"Good."

Frannie slid off her chair. "Millie is at ballet. I think Winnie's in the bathroom upstairs."

"Okay." I stuck my hands in my pockets.

"Bye, Felicity. See you tomorrow." Eyes averted, Frannie moved past me into the back hall, and I followed her.

"How'd everything go at the new job?" I asked.

"Fine." She tugged on her boots and put on her coat.

"Are you liking it?"

"Mmhm." She freed her hair from the back of her coat and zipped it up. "See you tomorrow."

"Frannie, wait."

She froze with her back to me, one hand on the door.

"I hate this," I said quietly.

"Me too. If you want to hire someone else to watch the girls, I'll understand."

I swallowed hard. "They'd miss you."

"I'll miss them too."

"To be honest, I wasn't even sure you'd show up today."

"It was hard, but …" She glanced back at me. "I came for them."

I nodded slowly. "Can you come one more time? Tomorrow? I'll start looking for a replacement for next week."

"Of course." She paused. "I can tell them it's because of my new job at the coffee shop. That way they aren't confused or … hurt."

She was still putting them first. It gutted me. "I'll handle it. You don't have to tell them anything."

She left without saying goodbye.

That evening was a repeat performance of Tuesday, except I made Millie cry, I sent Felicity to her room, and Winnie didn't even want me to kiss Ned the Hammerhead from Shedd goodnight.

"He doesn't like it when you yell," she told me, hugging the animal protectively.

"Tell him I'm sorry." I brushed her damp hair back from her head. "I had a bad day."

"Do you need a hug?" she asked. "Frannie says a hug makes a bad day better."

I nodded, my throat aching. "Yeah. I think I do."

She sat up and wrapped her arms around my neck. I held her little body close to mine, breathing in her baby shampoo scent and choking back tears. I just wanted to do right by her, by all of them.

But how were you supposed to know for sure what the right thing was? What felt right to me wasn't necessarily what was best for them.

Why did everything have to be so complicated?

Friday afternoon, I was sitting at my desk, my laptop open in front of me, but my eyes weren't on the screen. I was staring at the photo on my desk that Frannie had taken last summer at the Cloverleigh picnic. Winifred was on my shoulders, her tiny hands in mine, and the other two monkeys were hanging off my upper arms, their feet dangling. I remembered that day so vividly because it was the first day since Carla had left that all three kids seemed entirely happy—no tears, no asking for her, no whining of any kind. For the first time, I saw the possibility that we could be okay. There were still good times to be had.

That day, most of the good times were because of Frannie. She'd thought ahead and had plenty of activities she knew the kids would get excited about—games and crafts and time with the animals. She'd occupied them almost the entire picnic, which had afforded me the opportunity to relax with co-workers and friends. Actually, Cloverleigh had always felt more like a family to me, and Frannie had been a part of that.

Now she was gone, and I missed her terribly. It would get even worse when I hired a new nanny to replace her. I wouldn't see her at work, I wouldn't see her at home. The void in my life gnawed at me, a huge, gaping hole—and *I'd* dug it.

I dropped my forehead onto my fingertips.

"Everything okay?" a deep voice asked.

I looked up and saw John Sawyer in my office doorway. "Oh, hey, John. Come on in."

He ambled into my office, hitching up his jeans. "It's nearly five. Why don't you knock off for the night?"

"I could ask you the same thing." I shut my laptop and gestured to the chairs across from me. "Have a seat."

He lowered himself into one of them and exhaled. "I'm on my way out. My wife made me promise I wouldn't work past five anymore, at least not in the winter."

"Not a bad idea."

"She's got all these ideas about how to spend our winter evenings broadening our horizons and getting healthy. And she's on me about retirement all the time. Wants to travel more." He shook his head, ran a hand through his silvery hair. "She's got Chloe and April on her side now too. They're all teaming up against me. Trying to boot me out."

I laughed. "I don't know about that."

"It's true. You'll see," he grumbled. "Your daughters grow up and turn against you, Mack. They seem so sweet and innocent one day, holding your hand while they cross the street, and then you blink, and they're grown, with their own ideas about how to run things and their opinions on everything you're doing or not doing…" He snapped his fingers. "It happens just like that."

I could already see it happening with my kids, so I knew he was right. "Yeah. Time moves too quickly."

Sawyer sighed again. "It sure as hell does. And I suppose you have to make the most of what time you get here. It's not like you get any kind of guarantee when your number's gonna be up."

I looked at him with concern. "Everything okay with your health?"

He waved a hand dismissively. "Eh, I've got some issues with my blood pressure, and the old ticker is getting a little worn, but it's nothing I can't handle."

"That's good."

He looked around my office, and the silence grew slightly uncomfortable. Did he know about Frannie and me? Did he know it was over? I felt like I owed him an apology, like I'd taken advantage of his trust and generosity. I was trying to think of a way to get it off my chest when he spoke again.

"You know, Mack, you're family to us." He picked up the photo of me and the girls I'd been looking at earlier and took it in his lap.

I felt his kind words like a kick in the gut. "Thank you, sir."

"And I hope you know that you'll always be welcome here."

"Thank you. I'm …" I cleared my throat. "I'm very glad to be a part of this team."

He looked up at me. "It's more than a team."

I nodded. My throat was too dry to speak.

Setting the photo back on the desk, he said, "I never had any sons, and my son-in-law isn't around here very often, so if you'd ever like to go fishing or hunting or anything, you let me know. If I am going to slow down some, I'm gonna have some time on my hands. I'd like to fill it doing things I enjoy, spending time with people I care about."

"Sounds like a plan." I attempted to smile, but I felt like shit. I didn't deserve his kindness after what I'd done to Frannie. I didn't deserve to have him refer to me as family or offer to go fishing with me or think of me as a surrogate son. Had that been his way of telling me he was okay with a relationship between me and his daughter? Dammit, I didn't deserve that either! I almost wished he'd come at me red-faced and angry, railing about how I couldn't treat her like that and get away with it. I wished he'd thrown a punch.

I arrived home on edge, and Frannie barely looked at me before hugging the kids goodbye and disappearing into the back hall to put on her boots and coat. Again, I followed her.

"Did you say anything to them about not coming back?" I asked.

"No." She pulled on her boots. "You told me not to."

"I know. I'll do it tonight. I spoke with an agency today. They said it wouldn't be a problem to find a replacement sitter by next week."

"Good." She zipped up her coat and put her hat on. She wore braids in her hair again today, and for some reason the sight of them made me even sadder. I'd never smell her hair again. Or brush it. Or see it spilling across my pillow, dangling above my chest, cascading down her naked back.

I stuck my hands in my pockets, my heart aching. "I guess I'll see you around then."

She barely looked at me before walking out, closing the door behind her. For a few frantic seconds, I tried to think of some reason—any reason—to run after her, keep her here a little longer. But I couldn't.

Instead I went to the living room, moved the curtain aside, and peeked out the front window, watching as she got into her car. She started the engine, but didn't go anywhere right away. I thought maybe she was on the phone or texting someone, but then she dropped her face into her hands and I realized she was crying.

My chest felt like it was being split in two.

"Daddy, what are you doing?" asked Felicity, coming up behind me.

"Nothing," I said, letting the curtain fall into place again.

"Yes, you are, you're looking at Frannie," she said, jumping onto the couch and pushing the curtain aside again. Then she gasped. "Oh, she's crying!"

"She's crying?" Immediately the other two girls jumped onto the couch and craned their necks for a better view.

I yanked the curtain in front of them. "I don't know."

"She is, I can tell," Millie said. "We should go get her. What if she needs help?"

"No!" I yelled. "Leave her alone!"

All three girls looked at me in surprise.

I ran a hand through my hair and lowered my voice. "Sometimes grownups get sad about things. Frannie is fine."

"How do you know?" Millie persisted. "She didn't say anything to us about being sad."

"Because I know," I snapped. I thought about her gentle, trusting father and his kind words to me this afternoon and felt even worse.

"Did *you* make her sad?" Winnie asked, her tone accusatory. "Did you yell at her? You make me sad when you yell at me."

"Me too," added Felicity. "And you've been yelling a lot this week."

"Why did you yell at Frannie?" Millie crossed her arms over her chest. "We love Frannie. You should apologize. You probably scared her!"

"For fuck's sake, Millie, I didn't yell at Frannie!"

"Now you're yelling at me."

"No, I'm not!" I yelled.

Winnie started to cry and ran up the stairs. Felicity and Millie exchanged a look that said OMG Dad Is Losing It.

"Look," I said, trying to stay calm. "Sometimes dads yell. It doesn't mean they don't love their kids. It just means they're having a bad day."

"Frannie says a hug makes a bad day better," said Felicity, pushing her glasses up her nose. "But I'm sorry, I don't really feel like hugging you right now."

"Me neither." Millie shook her head.

Sighing, I flopped onto the other end of the couch and lay my head back. Closed my eyes. "I'm sorry, girls. It's been a tough week."

They didn't say anything for a few minutes. I thought they might have even gone upstairs, but when I opened my eyes, they were still there looking at me. Then I had an idea.

"Frannie is sad because she can't be your babysitter anymore," I said.

They looked at each other and then back at me, their expressions a mixture of shock and panic. "What?" Felicity cried. "Why?"

"Because she's got a new job at a coffee shop and it's going to be longer hours."

"She doesn't work with you at Cloverleigh anymore?" Millie asked.

I shook my head. "No."

"But we'll never see her again," Felicity said, tears filling her eyes.

"She promised to come to my fashion show," protested Millie, her voice cracking. "It's tomorrow. Is she still coming?"

I exhaled, tipping my head back again. I'd forgotten

about that damn show. "I don't know. Probably not."

Both of them started to cry, which made my temper flare again. I'd lost her too, but you didn't see me crying—although I felt like it. "Stop it, you two," I snapped. "There's nothing to cry about. She's just too busy to come here anymore."

That made them sob harder, and Felicity wiped her nose on her sleeve. "It's not fair," she wept.

"If you're going to cry like that, go up to your rooms," I ordered like the ogre I was. "I don't want to hear it."

They jumped off the couch and ran upstairs, and I heard two doors slam a moment later. From above came the sounds of wailing and despair.

"Great," I muttered. "Fucking Father of the Year."

I sat there for a moment and listened to my children sob, wishing I could cry it out myself. This week had been nothing but misery and stress. A little release would feel pretty damn good right now.

But I couldn't. I owed my children an apology, an ice cream cone, and a hug—if they'd let me give them one.

After sitting there for a while, stewing in my own self-imposed agony, I got to my feet and headed slowly up the stairs, my head pounding, my nerves shot, and my heart in a million little pieces.

Twenty-Nine

Frannie

S ATURDAY MORNING, I SLIPPED INTO THE HIGH SCHOOL CAFE-
teria where the fashion show was taking place, hoping I wasn't too late. It was crowded and all the chairs
were taken, so I stood along the back wall with some other
late-comers.

I'd been working at the bakery that morning and had
lost track of time—baking in the huge, beautiful kitchen at
Coffee Darling had salved my soul this week, especially after
seeing Mack Thursday and Friday. It had been even harder
than I'd expected. It broke my heart even further to think
that I wouldn't see the girls much anymore, but I understood why he wanted to get a new nanny. And I'd go out of
my way to visit them when I knew he wouldn't be there. I
didn't want them to think I didn't care about them anymore
just because I wasn't their nanny now.

The fashion show was in full swing, with mothers
and daughters walking the runway arm in arm wearing
matching outfits they'd created themselves. The theme of
the show was Healing Hunger with Hearts, and all pro-
ceeds were going to an organization fighting hunger. An

announcer introduced each model, and I watched eight mother-daughter pairs proudly stroll to the end of the runway and back, hearts on their shirts and grins on their faces. I hoped I hadn't missed Millie and Mack already. Glancing around at the crowd, I spotted Felicity and Winnie sitting together in the front row.

"Our final duo is a little different," said the announcer, and I immediately focused on the runway again. "It's a father-daughter pair, Millie MacAllister and her dad, Declan!"

The crowd cheered, and Mack and Millie appeared, hand in hand. My breath stopped for a moment. Millie was beaming, absolutely radiant in the white T-shirt covered with pink and red glitter hearts she'd made. Mack looked pretty miserable at first, but as they made their way to the end of the runway, which bisected the cafeteria, Millie looked up at him and he met her eyes. Seeing how happy and proud she was must have buoyed his spirits, because he grinned back at her and seemed to walk a little taller, puffing his glitter-covered chest out. When they reached the end of the runway, Mack turned Millie under his arm as if they were on the dance floor, bowed to her, and kissed her cheek. The crowd went crazy.

My heart was pounding so hard I could barely hear the music, and tears dripped from my eyes, but I couldn't help laughing a little. It was the kind of thing my dad would have done for one of his girls, too—my sweet, gruff, and gentle dad who'd come into the bakery for coffee that morning just to see me, because he missed seeing me at the inn.

I'd filled his cup, introduced him to Natalie and her husband, and showed him around. "I'm proud of you, peanut," he'd said, pulling me into a hug. The nickname made my throat close up.

"Thanks, Daddy."

"Are you happy?"

I'd nodded, my eyes filling. Embarrassed, I wiped at the tears. "Yes."

And it was mostly true—I was happy with my decision to leave the inn, partner up with Natalie, and work at the shop, but I was heartsick about Mack. He'd left a hole in my heart that couldn't be filled with anything else.

Watching him now, I choked back sobs even as I clapped along with everyone else when the announcer said, "Millie convinced the committee to rename the fashion show next year to be more inclusive. We hope more fathers and sons will join us for the Healing Hunger with Hearts *family* fashion show next year." The show concluded with all the models appearing and taking a final bow, and for a moment, Mack caught my eye.

My stomach flipped. My pulse skittered nervously out of control. We stood with our eyes locked for a full ten seconds, neither of us smiling, and for a moment I felt like maybe he'd been as miserable as I'd been this week and was sorry he'd broken things off.

But then he looked away, and my heart sank.

I decided not to wait around to talk to Millie. Seeing Mack was too painful. I didn't trust myself to get close to him without crying. Instead, I slipped out of the cafeteria and hurried through the parking lot to my car, where I sent her a text.

Millie, you looked amazing! I am so proud of you and I hope you had so much fun! Sorry I could not stay to chat, I am working at the new shop and have to get back. I will see you soon, I promise!!

Tears running down my cheeks, I dropped my phone into my bag and drove back to work, wondering how long it took to fall out of love with someone.

I wasn't sure my heart could take it.

Thirty

Mack

"**F**RANNIE CAME!" MILLIE EXCLAIMED FROM THE BACK of the car on the drive home. "She was there!"

"I didn't see her," Felicity whined. "How do you know?"

"She sent me a text." Millie read the text aloud. "Dad, she's working. Can we go see her at the coffee shop?"

"Not today."

All three moaned in grand symphonic fashion and followed it up with more whining.

"Come on, Dad. Please?"

"Why not?

"You never say yes to anything."

"You're no fun this week."

"What else are we going to do today?"

"Finally I don't have ballet on a Saturday and we just have to go home?"

Instead of answering, I put the radio on and turned up the volume.

At home, the three girls gave me pouty faces and dirty looks before trudging upstairs to their bedrooms. I stayed in the kitchen and tried to make a grocery list, but when I saw Frannie's phone number in her handwriting on the notepad, I froze. Stared at it. Remembered the night she'd written it down for me, how much fun I'd had with her. She'd taken a shitty day and made it amazing. She could make all my days amazing if I'd let her … but I couldn't. Look how I'd fucked it up already! My kids were furious with me. Frannie couldn't even look at me. I was probably never going to have sex that good again in my life. And it would serve me right.

I was a United States Marine, goddammit. I should have been stronger. I should have been able to resist her in the first place. I should have known that a woman like her could never be mine.

"Dad."

I turned around and saw all three of my daughters lined up tallest to shortest, arms crossed and defiance in their eyes. "What now?"

Millie was the spokesperson. "We're calling a family meeting."

"You are?"

"Yes. Right now. In the living room."

"Can't it wait? I need to make a grocery list." I had a feeling I didn't want to hear what they had to say.

"No. It can't. We've decided."

"Decided what?"

"That you're being an idiot and you need the hard words."

I blinked at her. "Well, damn."

"Living room, please." She pointed her finger in that direction, and I had no choice but to follow the order.

They trailed me to the couch. "Sit there," Felicity commanded.

I sat and leaned back, knees widespread and arms crossed, scowling like an angry teenager about to get lectured.

They faced me with matching angry expressions and stubborn sets of their jaws. "We have something to say," Millie began.

"I know." I waved a hand toward her. "Get on with it."

"It's about Frannie," said Winnie.

I jerked my chin. "I don't want to talk about Frannie."

"Well, you're going to!" Millie yelled, sounding so much like me it was a little eerie (although I probably would have used the word fuck somewhere in the sentence). "Or you're at least going to listen, because we can't take it anymore."

"Take what?"

"Your terrible mood since you two broke up! We don't understand why you're not in love anymore and we want to know what happened."

My spine snapped straight. "What do you mean? Frannie and I weren't in love!"

My daughters exchanged the mother of all eye rolls. Someone sighed dramatically.

"Dad. Please." Millie held out a palm. "You guys were totally in love."

"It was, like, so obvious," said Felicity.

I looked at Winnie.

"It was, Daddy," she whispered. "I saw you in the closet. 'Member?"

"And I saw you in the kitchen," added Millie.

"And I saw you all the time, everywhere, with your googly eyes." Felicity took off her glasses and held them up. "I didn't even need these!"

I shook my head in disbelief. "Girls, you don't

understand. Even if we did have feelings for each other, we can't be together."

"Why not?" Millie demanded.

"Because I don't have any time for her," I said. "I'm busy with you guys and with work. It's not fair to her."

"She didn't seem to mind." Millie raised her brows and tapped her foot. "And she was here all the time, so it's not like you had to leave us to go see her."

I struggled for words. "Girls, you're too young to understand this, but relationships are a lot of work. You have to invest a lot of time and energy into them, and … I'm no good at that. Look at what happened before. I can't go through it again, and I definitely wouldn't put you through it again. I love you too much."

They exchanged another look. "We get that," Millie said. "But we also know that Frannie is not like Mom at all. She's different. So everything would be different."

I shook my head. "I hear what you're saying, but there are other reasons why it won't work," I told them, feeling like I was breaking hearts two, three, and four within a week.

"Like what?" More toe tapping.

Sighing, I fell back again, exhausted and depleted, and wishing I could crawl into bed and never get out. Her father wasn't an issue. We no longer worked together. The age difference didn't seem that big a deal anymore. And my terrible ex was always going to be my terrible ex, with or without Frannie in our lives. "I don't know."

"Daddy." Dropping the tough guy act, Millie dropped onto the couch next to me. "Do you love her?"

Too miserable to lie, I nodded.

"Then it's like I said—remember? When you love

someone, you want to *be* with them. You agreed with me."

Winnie sat on my other side and put a hand on my leg. "It's like me and Ned the Hammerhead from Shedd. I don't feel right if he's not next to me."

I looked at her and my throat tightened. "It's exactly like that."

"You have to get her back, Dad." Felicity knelt in front of me and set her chin on my knee. "Can you?"

"I don't know," I said. "She's pretty upset with me. I told her we had to end things."

Millie sighed. "That was really stupid."

I gave her a look. "Hey. I thought I was doing the right thing. I thought I was doing it for you. Being your dad is the most important thing in my entire life, and I don't want anything to take away from that."

No one spoke right away. Then Winnie sat up taller. "But Daddy, just because I sleep every night with Ned right by me doesn't mean I don't love *you*. It's a different kind of love."

I looked at her in surprise. "You're right, Winn. It is a different kind of love."

"And you have been in the *worst* mood all week long," Millie said. "We really can't take it anymore."

"We love her too, Daddy." Felicity smiled hopefully, clasping her hands beneath her chin. "Please go get her back."

"What if I try and it doesn't work out?" I asked. "Are you going to hate me?"

"No," Winnie said emphatically. "We'll always love you."

"But if you don't at least try to get her back, we'll be really mad for a *long time*," Millie informed me seriously.

I looked at all three of them and thought my heart was going to burst. Was it possible I could be the dad they needed and the man Frannie deserved all at once? Could I be trusted not to mess up *four* lives? Was it fair to ask Frannie to accept all of us and every ounce of emotional baggage we came with? Could I ever be worth it?

I had no fucking clue, but right then I decided I had to try. "Okay. Will you help me?"

"Of course!" Millie jumped up and clapped her hands.

"Yes!" Winnie bounced excitedly.

Felicity hopped to her feet and reached into her pocket. "But Dad! You better take my lucky stone." She fished it out and handed it to me.

Rising to my feet, I took it from her and closed my hand around it. "Thanks. I'll take all the luck I can get. But you know what, girls? Right now I feel like the luckiest man alive because I get to be your dad."

"I'll give you a hug now," offered Felicity.

I opened my arms and they all swooped in, and I thanked God for all three of my smart, sweet, loving girls.

"Can we go now?" Millie asked.

I took a breath, nervous and slightly sick to my stomach. But the girls were right—I loved her, I was miserable without her, and if she'd promise to forgive me for all the times I was less than she needed me to be, I'd promise to be open to anything in the future.

"Fuck, you guys." I looked at all three of their faces. "I'm scared."

"I know, Dad." Millie took one of my hands. "But you can do this."

Winnie took the other. "We believe in you."

"We won't even make you put a dollar in the swear jar

until we get back," Felicity said as she took off running for the back door. "Come on, let's go!"

It didn't occur to me that I hadn't changed my shirt until I was parking the car across the street from Coffee Darling. I turned off the engine, looked down, and groaned.

"What?" Millie asked from the back seat.

"I should have changed my clothes. I'm wearing …" I pulled the shirt away from my chest. "Pink glitter."

"Zip up your coat all the way," Felicity suggested.

"No!" Millie was adamant. "The shirt is a statement about love and healing hearts. Plus Frannie helped make it. He should show her that he's proud to wear it."

I glanced back at her. "You're pretty smart for eleven."

She smiled. "I'm almost twelve."

I closed my eyes and exhaled. "Don't remind me. Okay, let's do this."

"Daddy, what are you going to say?" Winnie asked, her hand in mine as we crossed the street.

"I have no idea."

"I think you should tell her you're sorry for being a big fat jerk," Felicity offered as we reached the curb.

I gave her a dirty look. "Thanks."

"And maybe you should beg for her forgiveness," Millie suggested. "On your knees or something. That's what they do in the movies."

"I think I'll stay on my feet."

"Tell her she's pretty," Winnie said.

"Tell her she's perfect!" Felicity shouted.

"Tell her you *love* her." Millie grasped the door handle

to Coffee Darling. "That's important. She needs to hear you say that."

I shook my head. "I'm going to die."

Winnie giggled. "Not, you're not."

Millie looked me right in the eye. "You're not going to die. You're going to fix this and get her back—for all of us."

She pulled on the door handle. It didn't open. She yanked again, more vehemently, putting two hands into it. "Daddy, it's locked."

"We're too late," Winnie moaned.

"The hell we are." Seeing someone with a broom moving around inside, I pounded on the glass with my fists.

I wasn't leaving here without making this right.

Thirty-One

Frannie

"**F**RANNIE? THERE'S SOMEONE HERE TO SEE YOU. Several people, actually."

I looked up from my batter to see Natalie's husband Miles in the doorway to the kitchen, broom in his hand and amused expression on his face.

"To see me?"

"That's what they said. A guy and some kids." His mouth hooked up on one side. "And the guy is wearing some kind of sparkly T-shirt. You better come up front."

Sparkly T-shirt? Something jumped around in my stomach. It had to be Mack and the girls. What were they *doing* here?

With my hands over my fluttering belly, I followed Miles out to the shop and stopped behind the counter. Sure enough, Mack and the kids stood on the other side of it talking to Natalie, and Mack's open coat revealed the shirt Millie had made for the fashion show.

"Hi," I said warily.

"Hi." Mack took a step forward, then stopped. Opened his mouth and closed it again. He met my eyes, and I saw in them the apology I wanted. The warmth I craved. The fear that he'd messed this up too much already, and it was too late to get me back.

But I wasn't going to save him. He had to go after what he wanted. He had to save himself.

Seconds ticked by.

Miles stood off to one side with his hands atop the broom handle and his chin on his hands, watching the drama unfold. As the tension grew thicker, Natalie looked from Mack to me and back again—I'd confided in her enough this week that she had to know what was going on.

"Dad," muttered Millie under her breath from behind him. "Say something."

"I'm trying." Mack cleared his throat. "This isn't easy. Give me a second."

"Take your time," Miles said.

"Miles, maybe we should give them some privacy?" Natalie gave her husband a look and jerked her head toward the kitchen.

"But Nat, something good is about to happen," said Miles. "I can tell. A dude doesn't wear a glittery T-shirt for nothing. This is big."

Mack looked down at his shirt and winced. "Um."

"*Dad.*" Felicity moved forward and gave Mack a push in my direction. "Come on, already."

"Okay." Mack recovered his balance and stood with his feet apart, hands fisted at his sides, chest forward. He took a breath. "Frannie, I came here today to tell you something— well several things. First, that I'm sorry. I know I hurt you, and I'm so sorry. This is all my fault."

Miles nodded appreciatively. "Taking all the blame. Nice move."

"Miles!" Natalie hissed from across the room.

"What? He needs encouragement," Miles said. He looked at Mack. "Go on, man. You're doing fine."

Mack nodded. "Thanks," he said, tentatively moving a little closer to me. "Not only did I hurt you, but you were right: I did it for a stupid reason—I was afraid." He shook his head. "Fuck, I'm still afraid. I feel like there's no way I can do this, be the best father possible and be the guy you want. There's only one of me, and half the time, I have no fucking idea what I'm doing."

"I hear *that*, brother." Miles nodded. "Being a dad is the hardest thing I've ever done. I can't imagine what it would be like facing that job alone."

"But you don't have to face it alone." Finally speaking up, I came around the counter and stood in front of him. "That's the thing, Mack. I don't expect you to divide your time, to try to be all things to all people at once."

"I know you don't," he said, taking my hands. "Just like I know I'm going to fail you sometimes, and the kids sometimes, and myself sometimes. I've never been a perfect man, but I felt like I had to be the perfect father, to make up for what they lost. And I thought that meant I had to put my own needs aside." His eyes shone. "But I can't."

"You don't have to." I squeezed his hands. "We can make it work, Mack. I know you're not perfect, and I know being a good dad is your most important priority, but *you* deserve to be happy, too." I looked over at the girls. "Right girls?"

"Right," they said.

"And he wasn't happy at all this week," Millie went on.

"He was grouchy," said Winnie.

"And mean," added Felicity.

"Come on, give him a break, girls." Miles gestured

toward Mack. "He was lonely. He'd walked away from Frannie because he thought he was doing the right thing, and he had to spend some time being miserable to realize what an idiot he'd been." He looked at Mack. "Am I right?"

Mack nodded. "Yeah. And it didn't take long." He met my eyes again. "I don't know where we end up. I don't know how all these pieces of my life are going to fit together. I don't know how you're going to put up with all my shit."

"Do you have a swear jar?" I heard Millie whisper to Natalie.

"But I do know," Mack went on, his expression confident for the first time, "that my life is much better with you in it, and if you're willing to take this crazy journey with me—the back seat already full—I'm willing to see where this road leads."

My eyes filled with tears. "Do you mean it?"

"Yes."

"Because he loves you!" Winnie cried out. "He told us!"

"Winnie!" her older sisters admonished, Felicity hitting her on the shoulder.

"What? He *diiiid*." Winnie rubbed her arm. "He should tell her."

"It's okay," I said, embarrassed for Mack to have this moment take place in front of a crowd. "This is more than—"

"She's right." Mack stood taller, his broad chest straining against his glittery shirt. He looked me right in the eye. "I told them, and I'll tell you. I love you, Frannie. I don't know if I'm any good at it. God knows I failed in the past. But I love you. And when you love someone ..." He glanced over at the girls and gave them a wink before meeting my eyes again. "You want to *be* with them. I want to be with you."

"Aw, dude." Miles clutched his heart. "You're killing me."

"Kiss her!" Winnie shouted, clapping her hands. "And not in the closet this time!"

With a smile tugging at his lips, Mack leaned forward and kissed me, softly but not quickly. Someone—maybe Natalie?—sighed.

"Okay, that's enough," Millie said. "Don't get gross."

Laughing, we broke apart and I opened my arms. "Come here, girls. Group hug."

They came running toward us, Mack scooped Winnie up, and we all wrapped our arms around each other. "Thank you, girls," I told them, choking over the words. "This means everything to me. I want to be with your dad, but I want to be with you, too. I want us all to be together."

"*We* love you too, Frannie," Millie said. "You're part of our family."

Miles began slow clapping as he made his way over to us. "That was fucking beautiful," he said.

"Miles! Watch your language!" his wife shouted.

"Oh, that's okay," said Felicity with a grin. "We're used to it."

Mack and the girls went home, and I promised to come by after work. I had orders for six dozen macarons that I had to get over to Cloverleigh for an event later tonight, but after that, I was free.

Miles left shortly after Mack did—the two had hit it off

and promised to get together for beers soon—but Natalie stuck around to chat while I finished filling and boxing the pastries.

"I can't believe he came here that way," she said, shaking her head. "Are you totally in shock?"

"Pretty much. When I left his house yesterday, I was fairly certain things were done. He seemed unhappy but unwilling to budge."

"Thank goodness for those girls, huh? What smart kids." She laughed. "Every time I think about that little one yelling, 'Because he loves you! He told us!' I crack up."

I smiled and placed a pale green cookie on top of the pistachio filling. "Winnie. She's such a doll."

"So you get along with them all?"

"A hundred percent. I know I can't replace their mom, and there will probably come a day when I'll side with their dad on something and they'll hate me for it, but—"

"Welcome to being a parent," she said. "Speaking of which." She put both hands on her belly. "This one is all kinds of crazy this afternoon."

I laughed. "It's been that kind of day."

Since I was nearly finished, I told her to go home and put her feet up, and volunteered to make sure everything was locked up tight for the night. As I loaded the boxes of macarons in my car and closed up the shop, I felt the most incredible sense of accomplishment. I had done this—gone after something I wanted for myself and made it happen.

And now I had Mack and the girls too. Was the road always going to be this smooth? No way. We'd probably never feel like we got enough time together. And there would be times, I was sure, that it would be *me* apologizing for letting *him* down. But we were in this together, and we were in love.

It was enough.

After dropping off the macarons, I ran up to my apartment and took a quick shower before heading over to Mack's house. When I arrived, they were unpacking bags of Chinese takeout.

We ate sitting around the dining room table, each of us taking turns at the end of the meal reading our fortune cookies.

"Find beauty in ordinary things," read Millie.

"You will live a happy life," said Felicity.

"You will be hungry again in one hour," said Mack.

As we laughed, Winnie handed me hers. "Can you read mine?"

"Sure," I said. "It says, 'When one door closes, another opens.'"

"What does that mean?" she asked.

"Well, I think it means that you shouldn't dwell on the bad stuff in life, because something good is about to come along." I ruffled her hair.

"What does yours say, Frannie?" Felicity asked.

"Beware of single dads who can't cook?" suggested Mack.

Millie snorted. "For real."

I cracked mine open and read it aloud. "Nothing is impossible to a willing heart."

"I like that," said Winnie. "But what's a willing heart?"

"A heart that's open to anything," I said as something occurred to me. "And guess what? When I was young, I had *three* open-heart surgeries. So I think mine is open for sure." I winked at the little girl.

"So nothing is impossible for you," Felicity said eagerly.

I shook my head and smiled. "Nope. Nothing."

Later, after we'd watched a movie with the kids and put them to bed, Mack and I turned off the lights in the living room and snuck in a little time alone together.

"Are you sure this is okay?" I asked as he stretched out on the couch and pulled me on top of him.

"Positive." He wrapped his arms around me and I lay with my body along the length of his, my head on his chest.

"This is nice," I murmured, loving the sound of his heart against my ear.

"It is." He kissed the top of my head. "Although I wish you were naked."

I laughed. "Not with the kids in the house."

"I know. But I'm going to get impatient with this high school stuff pretty soon."

"We have time." I picked up my head and looked at him in the dark. "I'm not going anywhere."

He tucked my hair behind my ear. "I'm not either. Doesn't mean I don't want to rip your clothes off and fuck you senseless right now."

"You're so romantic."

Laughing, he pulled me up his body and kissed my lips. "Sorry. But beneath my pink glittery heart T-shirt is an animal with a hairy chest and a hard-on."

"Oh yeah?" Shifting to one side of him, I ran my hand down the front of his jeans. "What do you know? You're right."

He groaned as I rubbed the thickening bulge through the denim. "Are you sure we can't sneak into my bedroom for a few minutes?"

I hesitated, and he sensed his opening.

"Won't that feel so good inside you?" He grabbed my

wrist and held my hand over his cock, pushing it against my palm. He kissed me, his tongue stroking my lips. "Don't you want my mouth on you? We can be *so quiet*," he coaxed, his voice low and tempting. "Come on. Let me make you feel good."

"You're terrible," I whispered as his mouth moved down my throat and his hand snuck between my legs.

"I know. But I love you."

My entire body hummed, and I closed my eyes. "I love you too."

"So come to bed with me. I've missed you so much. And I promise I won't always be so terrible—we'll behave tomorrow night. Tonight, let's give in."

Of course I gave in.

And of course, he didn't keep his promise, and we didn't behave the next night either.

Or the night after that.

In fact, there were very few nights over the next several months when we were able to resist one another, and eventually, he started asking me to sleep over. We tried to hide it at first, sneaking me out before the girls got up, and we thought we were doing a pretty decent job until one Saturday night at the dinner table Winnie said, "Frannie should just move in here. Then she wouldn't have to leave so early in the morning and she could make breakfast sometimes."

"Totally," Millie agreed.

I nearly choked, and Mack turned a shade of red I'd never seen before, but later we discussed it and realized they were right. We wanted to be together all the time, and it would make life easier if I lived at the house. I made sure that Mack talked it over with the girls when I wasn't around, and he assured me that they were completely enthusiastic about the idea. "Not only are you a much better cook than me, but you know how to do all kinds of braids, you smell better, and you're much more patient."

"And you're sure it's what you want?" I asked, standing beside him as we loaded the dishwasher after dinner one Friday night. In the living room, we could hear the kids arguing about whose turn it was to choose the movie. It was our typical weekend evening, and maybe some girls my age would have found it boring, but I'd never been happier. Our relationship wasn't perfect—we had misunderstandings like any other couple, times where we took one another for granted, times when dealing with his ex or our work schedules or bickering kids made us short with one another—but we were always quick to apologize, and every time we kissed and made up, we felt closer than before. Life wasn't easy, but it was beautiful.

"Are you kidding?" Wiping his wet hands on a towel, he turned to me and took me in his arms. "Of course it's what I want. This house wouldn't even feel like home without you anymore. You belong here."

I smiled up at him. "I used to dream of hearing you say that to me."

"Then tell me you'll stay."

Twining my arms around his waist, I pressed my cheek to his chest, feeling like his embrace was the only home I'd ever need. "I'll stay."

Epilogue

FOR MY BIRTHDAY THAT SUMMER, HE TOOK ME TO PARIS.
He arranged everything—brought his parents in to stay with the kids for a week, talked to April and Natalie to make sure I could get the time off, told me to pack my bags for a week away—and promised to tell me where we were going when we got to the airport.

"What? How am I supposed to pack?" I shrieked.

He had no sympathy. "Pack for an elegant destination. Not the beach. Not the mountains. Not the desert. That's all I'm saying."

The girls, who knew where we were going but were sworn to secrecy, came into the bedroom to watch me pack, giggling and shushing each other.

My only clue came when we hugged and kissed them goodbye, and Felicity shouted, "Bon voyage!" and Millie elbowed her.

"Don't ruin it!"

"I didn't! That's what you say when someone goes on a trip, even if they're not going to France!"

On the way to the airport, he finally told me we were

flying to Paris, and I flipped out. "Oh my God! Do you have my passport?"

"Of course I do."

I touched the corners of my eyes and fanned my face. "This is too much. It's just a birthday."

"It's not. It's a chance for me to do something for you and show you how much I appreciate all you do for me. And it was time for you to get a stamp in that passport already."

I laughed. "I can't believe this. Pinch me!"

"I'd be happy to, but you're not going to wake up." He took my hand and kissed the back of it. "This is real life."

It might have been, but not a moment passed that it didn't seem like a dream. We stayed at a cozy little place on the Left Bank, wandered cobblestone streets hand in hand, drank coffee and ate pastries every morning in a different café, hit all the touristy spots and took a million pictures to send to the kids. We lingered over bottles of wine at dinner every evening, and spent all night long in each other's arms without worrying about how loud we were, how naked we were, or how many people were sleeping above us. It was heaven.

Then one morning, Mack told me to pack my bags because the last couple nights of the trip would be spent somewhere else. Excited and intrigued, I did what he said. A few hours later, we emerged from a train in Tours and rented a car. As soon as I saw the signs for the Loire, I knew where we were heading.

"Mack." I grabbed his arm. "No way. You didn't."

He just laughed and kept driving, and in less than an hour, I saw it come into view—Le Château d'Ussé, looking every bit as magical as the fairy tale castle I'd imagined as a girl.

I felt like I was walking on a cloud all day long.

We toured the castle and grounds from one end to the other—the dungeons, the salons, the grand halls, the spiral staircases, the stables, the chapel. We learned about the medieval kings and queens who'd walked the stone floors, the Renaissance works of art on the walls, and of course, the inspiration of Perrault's *Sleeping Beauty*. We walked to a nearby café for lunch and returned to the château to stroll along gravel paths in the gardens and kiss beneath the shade of cedar trees.

It was while we were in the gardens that Mack turned to me and took my hands. "So? Is it everything you expected?"

I nodded happily. "More. I'm only sorry the kids aren't here. They'd love this!"

"We'll bring them back someday. How about that?"

"Do you think we'll come back?" I asked wistfully, glancing at the château behind us, looking even more beautiful and enchanting in the fading sunlight.

"Of course I do. We'll want to show them exactly where we were when I asked you to marry me."

I stared at him. "What?"

He smiled, reaching into his pocket and pulling out a ring. "The box wouldn't fit in my pocket," he said sheepishly. "I didn't plan that part very well. Which brings me to my next point." He took a breath. "I'm no prince, Frannie. I'm stubborn, I'm impatient, I have a foul mouth and a lot of fucking baggage. And I come attached to three small humans who run me ragged every day. But I love you more than I've ever loved anyone."

"I love you, too." I'd started to cry, and he gently brushed tears from beneath my eyes with one thumb before taking my left hand and sliding the ring, a simple diamond solitaire on a delicate platinum band, onto my fourth finger.

"Then I have a question for you." He got down on one knee, keeping my hand in his. "I can't promise to build you a castle like this, or take you to Paris every year, or even clean up my mouth. But I can promise to spend every day of my life, and every night, treating you like a fucking queen—I'm sorry." He looked nervous. "A regular queen. Jesus Christ, I can't even *propose* without cursing."

I laughed, sniffling through my tears. "It's okay. I know exactly who you are, and I wouldn't change you for anything."

"Does that mean you'll marry me?"

I nodded, fresh tears cascading down my cheeks. "Yes. I'll marry you."

He stood up and we threw our arms around each other, and the ground fell away beneath my feet. "God, I'm so glad that's done," he admitted.

"Why? Did you think I'd say no?"

"Not really, I was just afraid I'd fuck it up somehow. Lose the ring, forget what I wanted to say, screw up the directions to get here. There was a lot depending on my ability to get things right, and I don't always trust myself."

"Well, you should. You did it perfectly." My toes touched the ground, but I hardly felt it. "I couldn't be happier."

"Good." He kissed my lips. "Now we should call home, because I told the girls they could stay up until you said yes."

I squealed. "They knew?"

"Only after we left. I didn't trust them to keep the secret, so I called them while you were in the shower yesterday and told them it was happening. But they've known for a while I wanted to ask. And Millie helped me choose the ring."

"She did?" I felt choked up all over again.

"Mmhm. Millie and April."

I sighed. "We're so lucky to have family like we do."

"We are. And maybe we can even add to it."

Leaning back, I looked at him in surprise. "Did I hear that right?"

He shrugged. "I figure I'm not that old. Might be fun to give the girls a little brother."

"Or sister."

He paused. "Um … a house with *four girls* in it?"

Giggling, I kissed his lips. "Five. Don't forget your wife."

He sighed. "We're going to need more space. And I'm going to need a bigger swear jar."

"Relax, babe. It's gonna be okay. I've got you."

"We've got each other." He pulled me close again, burying his face in my hair. "And it's only going to get better."

The End

Also by

Melanie Harlow

THE FRENCHED SERIES
Frenched
Yanked
Forked
Floored

THE HAPPY CRAZY LOVE SERIES
Some Sort of Happy
Some Sort of Crazy
Some Sort of Love

THE AFTER WE FALL SERIES
Man Candy
After We Fall
If You Were Mine
From This Moment

THE ONE AND ONLY SERIES
Only You
Only Him
Only Love

Hold You Close (Co-written with Corinne Michaels)

Strong Enough
(A M/M romance co-written with David Romanov)

The Speak Easy Duet

The Tango Lesson (A Standalone Novella)

Never miss a Melanie Harlow thing!

Want new release alerts, access to bonus materials and exclusive giveaways, and all my announcements first? Subscribe to my once or twice monthly newsletter! harlow.pub / mh-news

Want to stay up to date on all things Harlow day to day, get exclusive access to ARCs and giveaways, and be part of a fun, positive, sexy and drama-free zone? Become a Harlot! harlow.pub / harlots

Want a chance to become a Top Fan and win exclusive prizes? Check out my Facebook page! harlow.pub / ap

Want to be notified about freebies and sales? Try Bookbub! harlow.pub / bb

Interested in excerpts and little bites of my romances so you can read more before buying or borrowing? Try Book + Main! bookandmainbites.com / melanieharlow

Acknowledgments

Much love and gratitude to the following people!

Melissa Gaston, Brandi Zelenka, Jenn Watson, Hang Le, Kayti McGee, Laurelin Paige, Sierra Simone, Lauren Blakely, Corinne Michaels, Sarah Ferguson, Hilary Suppes and the entire Social Butterfly dream team, Gel Ytayz, Rebecca Friedman, Flavia Viotti, Nancy Smay, Janice Owen and Michele Ficht, Stacey at Champagne Book Design, Andi Arndt at Lyric, narrators Teddy Hamilton and Savannah Peachwood, the Shop Talkers, the Harlots and the Harlot ARC Team, bloggers and event organizers, my Queens, my betas, my proofers, my readers all over the world … and especially my family. I love you.

About the Author

Melanie Harlow likes her heels high, her martini dry, and her history with the naughty bits left in. In addition to IRRESISTIBLE, she's the author of the One and Only Series, the After We Fall Series, the Happy Crazy Love Series, the Frenched Series, HOLD YOU CLOSE, (co-authored with Corinne Michaels), STRONG ENOUGH (a M/M romance co-authored with David Romanov), and The Speak Easy Duet (a historical romance set in the 1920s). She writes from her home outside of Detroit, where she lives with her husband and two daughters. When she's not writing, she's probably got a cocktail in hand. And sometimes when she is.

Find her at www.melanieharlow.com.

Printed in Poland
by Amazon Fulfillment
Poland Sp. z o.o., Wrocław